DARK TOWN REDEMPTION

GARY HARDWICK

HARDBOOKS
PUBLISHING

FEB
20

DARK TOWN REDEMPTION
COPYRIGHT 2010 © GARY HARDWICK
ALL RIGHTS RESERVED.

ISBN Number 0972480412

HardBooks Publishing
www.garyhardwick.com

First Edition

Cover Design: Gary Hardwick

FEB - 2011

ALSO BY GARY HARDWICK

COLD MEDINA

DOUBLE DEAD

SUPREME JUSTICE

COLOR OF JUSTICE

THE EXECUTIONERS' GAME

SEXLIFE

SLAM THE TRICK

For my late brother,
Steve Brent Hardwick.

Redemption, too soon.

AUTHOR'S NOTE

The two protagonists in this novel, Robert Jackson and Thomas Riley and their families, are fictional. I also imagined The Vanguard, a violent Black militant group. Additionally, I created the events that befall Marcus Jackson after the Detroit Riots and the aftermath that affects the Riley and Jackson clans.

What is true is that in 1967, the summer of love, there was a riot in Detroit, Michigan that resulted in the deaths of 43 people.

Also true is that in the next year, Dr. Martin Luther King Jr. and Robert F. Kennedy were both assassinated, two devastating losses that tested the will of America.

The Vietnam War really happened and many veterans, Black and White came home to protest and hostility.

And of course the music of Motown is real and is still as wonderful, rhythmic and influential as it was some fifty years ago.

My story is set against the backdrop of these real events and I have sought to capture some of their power, beauty and magic to help make sense of the times.

The 1960's were the defining years of pre-millennium America. The sins of the young nation tested its resolve and character. Kings and princes fell to murderous intent and old ideas were burned to ashes in the all too real fires of change.

The final true thing in my story is that during this chaos, there was baseball, swinging at the speed of history and humanity.

This book's title speaks of a deliverance from the destructive notions that bound generations in fear and ignorance. It is a redemption that changed a city, which changed a nation-- that changed the world.

gh (2010)

"For in the final analysis, our most basic
common link is that we all inhabit this small
planet, we all breathe the same air, we all cherish
our children's futures and we are all mortal."

- John F. Kennedy

"Our objective is complete freedom, justice
and equality by any means necessary."

- Malcolm X

"Baseball is the resplendent metaphor for life."

- Joe Black

PROLOGUE

June 21, 1943.

The two men ran down the block away from the car that had given out on them. They could hear the mob behind them as they rounded a corner close to Hastings Street.

It was late evening and the summer sun was falling in the west. Night was coming and that was not good.

They were in Paradise Valley but it seemed like anything but that this day. There was trouble in Detroit, bad trouble that had even chased the news of the war from the headlines.

People were dying.

"Keep up!" said the older of the two. "If they catch us...."

"Don't worry about me," said the smaller man, just a teenager, really. "I'm too fast for them."

They rounded another corner and the big man stopped short. He looked in the distance and saw roving mobs of men holding clubs and pipes.

"More of 'em," he said, his Irish accent was pronounced. He grabbed the smaller man by the shoulder and pulled him into an alley.

The evening light dimmed further as they enter the narrow passage. It stank of urine and garbage. There were two big wooden racks of garbage cans on the back of a tenement house.

The two men slipped behind the racks and crouched down. It was a tight fit but they could not be seen from the street.

Suddenly, they heard the sounds of the men who were chasing them. It grew louder as they approached, filled with chatter, curses and laughter, which nonetheless felt evil.

"Quiet," said the big man.

Shadows crept up the dimming light from the street as the pursuing men stopped nearby. Someone called out, asking if anyone had seen two men run by.

"No way they went through there," said a voice.

"They had to," said another man. "If they'da doubled back, we'da seen 'em.

"I told you they ran up Church and went around us, man," said yet another man with a raspy voice. The he added: "dammit."

Suddenly, footsteps entered the dark alley and the two hiding men tensed. The big one searched for a weapon but saw nothing he could use. Soon, several men were in the alley looking around, muttering.

Then the crouching men heard the unmistakable sound of zippers, then men urinating in the alley. The piss ran in their direction and pooled around their shoes.

"Hey! They saying army soldiers is comin' this way!" yelled a man from the street. "We gotta get outta here!"

The men in the alley zipped their pants and moved away quickly. Distantly, the crouching men could hear even more men running away.

They waited for what seemed an eternity. The big man shifted then peeked around the wooden rack and saw nothing but dimming light and darkness.

He stood and came out. He sighed in relief. "Come on, he said. Let's go."

"Back to the car?" asked the smaller man.

"No, the other said. "They've taken it by now or set it on fire."

Without warning, something flew from the darkness in the area beyond their hiding place. The smaller man felt it zip by his face a slight wind trailing its heft.

The object landed flush on the side of the big man's head, tearing the side of his face and toppling him over. Blood sprayed into the air as he hit the ground with a thud.

Two men emerged from the shadows carrying baseball bats. The one who had thrown the brick was smiling.

"Knew they was close," said one of the men.

"Run," said the big man to the other. "Run!"

The smaller man took off as the big man got up and rammed himself into the men with the baseball bats.

The smaller man ran from the dark alley into the coming night hearing the sound of his friend being beaten behind him.

He stopped and turned and saw one of the men smash his friend in the side of the head. He teetered for a moment and then fell to the ground. The attackers kept hitting him.

The small man screamed something and then felt his body moving back toward the alley and certain death.

"Halt!" said a voice from a loudspeaker. "U.S. Army, stand down!"

Coming down the street, the small man saw an army jeep speeding his way.

"Here!" he said waving his hands. "We're here!" He turned to go back and help his friend and saw the two men running off carrying their now bloodstained weapons.

The small man ran back to his friend and stopped short. He fell to his knees next to the lifeless corpse, blood staining his pants.

Light flooded the area as the Army jeep roared up behind him, casting long shadows against the old buildings.

PART ONE

WAR'S REDEMPTION

April 1967 – December 1967

"Our country is challenged at home
and abroad... it is our will that is
being tried and not our strength."

- Lyndon B. Johnson

1

HAIPHONG

Sergeant Robert Jackson crouched a little as he waited for it to happen. They were winning this one but they had to hold on or else they'd all be dead.

The jungle wind in this part of Vietnam was unseasonably warm on his face and the sky was the pale blue of a very sick man. It was also a little hotter and stickier than usual and the smells of the bush, animal shit and rotting carcasses pricked at the inside of his nostrils.

The ground seemed to swell beneath his combat boots as he shifted his footing so as not to become too stiff while waiting. He tried to ignore his senses as he kept his mind on defense. Death was never far away in war and that could be a distraction from his current job.

Robert waved to Private Foster who gave him the okay sign. Just a nod really, but filled with confidence. Robert needed that right now. Robert nodded back in kind and he could feel the connection between him and the other man. They were set.

Foster wound up and pitched an arcing curveball to the batter. He swung and hit a screaming line drive over the head of the third baseman. Robert quickly sprang into action. He raced to meet the ball and realized at the last moment that he might overrun it. He slowed his progress and timed it just right. He barely had to leap as the ball slammed into his glove, making that wonderful smacking noise.

"You're out!" Someone said.

There were cheers as Robert pulled out the ball and threw it back into the infield. The two base runners on second and third went back to their bases in respect of Robert's arm. He had thrown a man out at second trying to stretch a single into a double. No one wanted the embarrassment of being tagged out by a long-distance throw.

There were now two out, with two on base and Robert's team was leading four runs to two.

"One more, baby!" Robert said to Foster who was smiling broadly. Foster had pitched the whole game and wanted desperately to go the distance. Robert hoped it would not be at the expense of winning the game.

They were a few clicks outside of Haiphong, a nasty little city that one soldier dubbed "Hell's Waiting Room." They'd been between assignments for two weeks and since the Hanoi bombing was going well, Robert didn't expect a mission anytime soon. So they camped out here and soon the days turned to pleasant distraction.

Robert, as leader of the platoon, decided to let off some steam and he knew no way better than baseball to put a soldier at ease.

There were forty-two men in the platoon, which was a part of the Marine Corps Combined Action Program or CAP. The CAP program strategically placed Marines in villages all over South Vietnam for offensive and defensive measures.

Robert's squad was unofficially called The Cleaners, a platoon that was given the most dangerous missions that came up. They secured red villages, exterminating hostiles; they did recon for major assaults and his absolute favorite, mine detection.

Sergeant Robert Jackson was the leader of The Cleaners, one of the few Negroes given a multi-racial command. He knew that it was a dubious honor but he took it very seriously. He'd been in charge for almost a year and had not lost a single man. He was proud of that.

What he did not like was the Army's tolerance of prejudice and outright bigotry. Many Black soldiers had to leave platoons because the White soldiers, who outnumbered them, brought American racism to Vietnam along with their M-16's and shaving kits. Robert had heard horror stories of the hazing of Black soldiers and rumors that some may have been killed on the battlefield.

The White soldiers were not safe either. Some Black soldiers saw the war as a chance for retribution for the injustices committed back home. Several mysterious deaths had been recorded and there were stories of White soldiers who'd gone into the jungle with their Black brothers and never returned.

Robert had been promoted after his old outfit fought a terrible battle at Cu Chi. Cu Chi with its vast network of tunnels, was a sniper's dream. Enemy soldiers could be picked off strategically while the killer, hidden in a tunnel, was invisible to his prey, like a murderous ghost.

But they had driven the Cong out eventually. Toward the end of it, a group of enemy soldiers were retreating with a box filled with explosives. They had a good head start and were running hard.

Soldiers were taking shots at the fleeing men when Robert pulled a grenade and threw it about a hundred and fifty feet. It exploded just in front of the running soldiers. They dropped the box and it ignited. The red-yellow explosion swelled into a fireball that shot into the pale sky and dug a massive crater into the ground. The bodies of the men holding the crate were ripped into tiny pieces.

Robert would think later that the throw was about the distance from shallow left field to home plate at Tiger Stadium.

"Look alive!" Robert yelled as Percy Turner, a huge Black soldier from Texas, came up to bat. Percy was a natural athlete and Robert had wanted him on his team, but it didn't seem fair, as he and Percy were the two best players in the platoon.

Percy had already tagged Foster for a home run earlier in the game. If he did it now, they would lose by a run.

"He ain't nobody!" said Robert.

But that wasn't true. Several pro teams were scouting Percy before he went off to war. Robert's hometown team, the Detroit Tigers, had scouted Robert in high school. Robert had a good tryout but didn't make the cut. With life in the streets looming before him, the Army had seemed like a better choice.

Foster wound up and pitched a perfect strike to Percy. They cheered but Percy never swung at the first pitch. Percy liked to assess the pitcher's speed and attitude and feel out his current weakness. Percy smiled a little satisfied smile and then dug his feet into the batter's box.

Foster pitched him a crappy breaking ball and Percy hammered it into right field. It would have surely been a home run had the ball not been already hooking away from the plate when it was hit. Percy smacked it foul and Robert breathed easier.

Foster seemed to be relieved as well as the ball was thrown back to him. Robert gave Foster a reassuring smile and moved his arm in a slow circular motion, signaling to Foster to throw him an off-speed pitch. Foster nodded.

This was the moment that Robert savored, the time when fate came into power. The game was life and life was the game, he thought. Would Percy or Foster be the hero? Would his team live or die? Only God knew.

Foster settled in and then delivered the pitch. Percy took a mighty swing but hit nothing but the dank jungle air.

"Out!" yelled someone, and Robert broke into a broad grin. Robert ran in as the other members of the team congratulated Foster. Robert hugged the gangly White kid. The losing team all filed out and they all shook hands and talked trash in the spirit of sportsmanship.

Robert glanced at Percy who had just stood at the plate for a moment not believing he'd struck out. Then Percy, good-natured soul that he was, smiled and walked over to congratulate Foster.

"Good game, man," he said in his Texas drawl. "You got me good that time."

Robert watched as his men bonded through the game. The platoon was about fifty/fifty Black and White with two men claiming Puerto Rican heritage. There was some friction in the beginning but it soon went away when they realized that any man could be called upon to save his brother's life. No perception of color could change that. Death was the fairest man in the world. He did not discriminate.

Robert Jackson did not have much love for White men. But he saw military service as a calling that was higher than petty feelings like prejudice. In Vietnam, there were only the living and the dead and any man who dealt in bias during war was a fool who endangered his life and the lives of his brothers.

Robert looked away from the field and saw one such fool. Peter Cole was a racist. He casually used racial slurs and was bounced from one platoon to another until he landed in The Cleaners. Cole was a soldier from the outskirts of Florida. He was a tough, mean little bastard who had once killed a Vietnamese villager because he "looked at him funny."

Cole didn't like having "a Colored commander" as Cole had once called Robert, but the man was so close to a dishonorable discharge that Cole had kept his mouth shut for the most part.

The Marine Corps didn't discourage racism but they hated insubordination and losing battles, so Robert was stuck with Cole and his attitude.

But the worst thing about Cole was that he was not a baseball player. Didn't like the game, he'd said. It was a queer's game. Football was a man's game, he'd say to anyone who cared to listen.

Robert would have rather been called a nigger. Any man who didn't like baseball was evil and deserving of contempt, he thought.

The platoon broke for mess, which was a sorry collection of leftover food from the past few days. They had not had a supply delivery in a while and it was making Robert and his men restless and irritated.

Robert tried to enjoy his rations by thinking of his mother's fried chicken, hot-water cornbread, yams and black-eye peas. He could almost smell the aromas wafting from the kitchen to the bedroom he shared with his brother Marcus in their Detroit home.

Robert remembered once when he was particularly hungry and sneaked into the kitchen and relieved the planned meal of one of its fried chicken drumsticks. He wolfed down the leg and then deposited the licked-clean bone under his brother's side of the bed.

Of course, his brother got whipped for his sin, but in the end, his father had found out the truth and Robert had gotten his father's best. Robert smiled a little. Only in Vietnam would the memory of an ass whipping be a relief.

Robert pulled up his dog tags. Next to the stamped metal was a picture of his wife, Denise. The only thing he missed more than home cooking was her. He looked at her soft brown eyes and the curve of her hips and before he could stop himself, he was thinking of being naked and between her legs in their bed. Marvin Gaye was on the radio and he was rolling in the slippery ecstasy of their union.

Robert had partaken of the whores on R&R when he felt it was safe. Once, he screwed a young girl wearing two rubbers. It was like making love to a catcher's mitt. Finally, he had given up and had her manually bring him to release.

Over his three years in Vietnam he had had sex a total of three times. That wasn't human, he thought. War really was hell. Robert put the picture away and the memory faded.

Foster came over and sat next to him. Robert smiled at the thin White man. He and Foster had become fast friends. Foster was a volunteer like Robert and had come from a dirt-poor family in Alabama.

Foster admitted that members of his family were racists from long back, including an uncle who was a leader in the KKK. None of that hatred had infected Foster, somehow. Foster had an easy way and lazy smile that made him look like innocence itself. Foster sat next to Robert; his meager rations were hardly touched.

"Got ol' big Percy with that screwgee, didn't I?" Foster said, using the player's term for a screwball. His voice rolled out the words slowly with its southern accent.

"Yeah, you did," said Robert. "You should think about trying out for the pros when you get back."

"I just might," said Foster. "Shit, I know I ain't goin' back to Bama. What team you think I should go out for?"

"I'm a Tiger fan myself," said Robert, smiling.

"Shit, everybody in Vietnam knows that. That's all you talk about. How about the Yankees? That'd really piss off my daddy."

"The Yankees are good but everybody wants to go there. Try a southern team, like the Cards."

Foster nodded in his laconic way, and then tried to eat some of the food.

Robert took in a deep breath and smelled the jungle again and the stink of war just underneath, sulfurous and bitter.

He understood how unlikely his friendship with Foster was. Robert didn't have any White friends back in Detroit and despite his parents' pious teachings; he had not trusted White men very much. But Vietnam was a different story. The two men sat in the middle of the jungle, the human distance between them obliterated by the inhumane.

"Supply jeep!" shouted Foster suddenly.

Robert jumped to his feet. The sentries had already raised their weapons. Just because a vehicle appeared to be American didn't mean it actually was. But as the jeep got closer, ripping dust into the air, Robert looked through binoculars and saw two very American soldiers in the vehicle. The driver was Black and about twenty or so. He looked so much like Robert's brother that it alarmed him a little. The other man was White and a Lieutenant by his insignia. But what made him smile was the back of the jeep. It was filled with supplies.

Robert signaled his sentries to stand down as the jeep approached the camp. The Lieutenant's vehicle pulled in and stopped. Robert went to the jeep and snapped a salute.

"Sir," said Robert.

"Sergeant Jackson?"

"Yes, sir," said Robert.

"I'm Lieutenant Ferguson and this is Private Taylor. I'm new in charge of this sector's HQ."

"What happened to Captain Reed?" Robert asked with a little concern in his voice.

Ferguson's change of expression said it all before the words came out of his mouth. There was a way you knew death had visited. It lived just behind everyone's eyes and words.

"Killed in a fire fight," said Ferguson. "Well, first things first. We brought fresh supplies."

"Thank you, sir!" smiled Robert. "This stuff we're eating is giving us the shits and—- sorry, sir."

"No problem, Sergeant" said Ferguson and Robert could see Private Taylor suppress a smile. "I even got some fresh meat for you but you'll have to cook it soon."

Robert signaled to Cole and some other men to begin unloading the back of the jeep. The other men moved. Cole didn't.

"Did you hear me, private?" Robert intoned louder.

Cole grunted something but went off to help. Robert liked giving Cole manual labor because he saw the insult in Cole's eyes just before he began to follow the order.

"Problem?" asked Ferguson.

"Man don't like Negroes, sir," said Robert.

"You want me to speak with him?"

"No, sir. That would only make him happy if you know what I mean."

"Yes, I see," said Ferguson nodding a little.

Robert told Foster and some others to fire up the meat. And then he turned back to Ferguson. He liked this man, Robert thought. There was little of the arrogance he felt from most officers. Ferguson seemed to know he was in charge by rank, which made Robert an inferior soldier, but Ferguson didn't seem to treat Robert like an inferior person.

"As to your other supplies," said Ferguson. "There are five med kits in there, six new launchers and ten cases of ammo."

Robert regarded the superior officer and knew what this meant. "I guess we got new orders," he said.

"Yes," said Ferguson. "I need your platoon to secure a patch of road in Sector Twenty-Three." Ferguson pulled out a set of papers and a map. He spread it on the hood of the jeep.

The mention of the area made Robert's heart race. Sector Twenty-Three was as bad a place as any in the war. The enemy's strong hold was not far away and they had continually killed anything breathing on its roads. Robert had been there once when he'd first gotten to Vietnam and he'd barely made it out alive.

"We're planning on taking that sector for good," Ferguson continued. "We need a big supply convoy to pass. You're going to get air support as well as ground from the infantry. We'll need that road safe for passage a day from now."

Robert had never maintained any illusions about the possibility of dying in this far off land. There were only two reasons a man even went to war. He was drafted or he had a death wish. Robert had volunteered so the former reason did not apply. Death was waiting for him back home on the streets in some form, so Robert had decided to take his chances doing something worthwhile. He didn't even know why America was fighting the war but it didn't matter, really. Sooner or later every man had to fight.

In basic training, Robert discovered something that pleased and frightened him. He was meant to be a soldier. He was tough, mean and savvy when it came to violence. He was a natural leader and possessed a fearlessness about

him that other men recognized and respected. These things
raced quickly through his mind before he said:

"It will be, sir."

Ferguson smiled a little, impressed by Robert's can-do
attitude. Robert moved to the hood of the jeep, so he could
see the map better. Behind him, he smelled the meat being
roasted. It was like heaven and thoughts of Saturday
barbecues, mini skirts and summertime fun floated through
his head.

"So how are things going back home?" asked Robert.

"Difficult," said the Lieutenant. "People are actually
protesting the war, if you can believe it, cursing soldiers after
they come back home." Ferguson looked away for a
moment, as if searching for the answer to some secret he
contemplated. "The protected never understand their
protectors," he said finally.

"And baseball, sir?" said Robert. "How are my Tigers
doing?"

"Don't know," said Ferguson smiling. "I'm a Red Sox
man myself."

Robert spent the next hour working through the plan with
Ferguson. It would be a tough outing and the prospect of
finally losing a man occurred to him with grimness.

The Lieutenant joined them for dinner. He sat with the
enlisted men and shared laughs and stories with them.

Robert enjoyed the moment but could not help but think
that the officer, though a very fine man, had brought The
Cleaners their last meal.

2

FAMILY PORTRAIT

Thomas Riley tried to keep still as he listened to the Police Chief's closing remarks. The man had been speaking for close to an hour and he sounded like he was winding up.

Thomas was tingling all over his twenty-two year old body. This was it, he thought. The moment he'd toiled for and dreamed about over the last year. In a few minutes, he would become a newly minted officer of the Detroit Police Department.

The ceremony was being held outside on the Academy's grounds. It was a beautiful spring day in the city. The sun was mild and pleasing and though he didn't know it, the cloudless sky was a deeper blue than the one in Vietnam a world away.

Vietnam was a big issue at home these days but that trouble seemed distant to the young cadet. A sweet aroma, probably apple blossom was in the air. War, death and Sector 23's did not exist.

The graduating class was small this year. The war had taken away many good men and others who resisted the draft were in prison or had fled the country. And even if those men were still in the U.S., they would certainly not be considered DPD material.

Thomas was in an excellent position. He had not qualified for military service and so he quickly stepped into the family business. His father, Frank, was a retired officer, a thirty year man who had never made it beyond street duty.

His deceased brother Shaun was also an officer when he died in the Korean War.

His grandfather, Cahan, had been a cop at the turn of the century. Cahan had similarly retired in a uniform. He'd told Thomas once that he would never trade being a cop for a detective's gold shield.

Once the war was over, the city would be overrun with soldiers wanting to become police officers. Since Thomas was going in now, he'd have seniority when that day came. Yes, this was a great day, he mused. The kind you'd never forget.

"... and so as our nation continues the war and we face challenges at home," said the Chief. "It is up to you, the domestic soldiers, to maintain the peace and freedom of this great country in this time of need. God bless you, God bless America and congratulations to you all."

The class broke out in lively applause as the Chief smiled and sat down. The Academy's Dean stood. He was a big man, thick in the middle with piercing blue eyes. He went to the podium as an officer brought out the diplomas. The cadets stood and formed a line to accept their commissions.

Thomas felt a surge of energy race through him as he stood. He was like a kid and now the dream melted into stark reality. Since he was a child, his family had filled him with the dream of wearing a uniform and carrying a gun.

While his classmates in high school talked about college, parties and changing the world, Thomas had only been interested in police work.

"Eric Adams," began the Dean and the first cadet crossed the stage.

Thomas lingered near the end of the line, anxiously awaiting his name. He looked out over the gathering. There were about two hundred spectators. He smiled at his father and his mother, Esther, sitting near the front in the middle of a row. He could see his mother wiping away tears and his father beaming with pride.

His kid sister, Katie, was to their left and next to her was Sarah Nelson, his fiancée. Sarah caught his eyes and smiled sweetly. She was petite and blonde with dazzling green eyes. Thomas regarded Sarah and wondered, as he often did, why she'd gone for him when she could have claimed any man she wanted.

"Carl Henderson," said the Dean.

Sarah and Thomas had met while he was working as security for Wayne State University. Thomas was waiting for his assignment to basic training in the Army and wanted to keep busy until then. Even though as a last son, he could have been exempted, he wanted to serve. This made his father proud. Frank made Thomas promise to join the DPD as soon as he returned stateside.

Thomas had struck up a conversation with Sarah in front of some other students. The men in the group had laughed at his attempt to snag a date with the prettiest girl on campus.

Their laughter was soon turned to shock when Sarah asked him out right in front of them all. Thomas understood then that Sarah was different from the other girls with their mildly phony innocence and shy behavior.

What Thomas didn't realize was that he was a good-looking man himself. In Thomas' world, men didn't think of themselves as handsome. If you did, other men might think that you were queer. And that was not something any man wanted in the minds of other people.

What Sarah saw was a tall, young man in a security guard's uniform that stretched from his wide shoulders. She saw dark blue eyes, thick dark hair and a face of pure innocence.

"Byron Peterson," said the Dean.

Thomas gave Sarah a little wave and she returned it with the peace sign. He laughed a little at this. Sarah was what they called an intellectual radical and a hippie. She was active in the anti-war movement, which he also found interesting and strangely attractive. He just wished his father did.

Sara's politics caused animosity with Frank Riley who was a war hawk and conservative Democrat. But Thomas didn't care. Sarah was his girl and that was all that mattered. By the time it was decided that he wasn't going to war, he and Sarah were engaged.

Thomas perked up as he heard the name of Randall Richardson being called. He was next. Thomas took a breath and put one singular thought in his head. "Don't trip walking to the stage."

He felt a little better about this fear as Randall stumbled on his way up the stairs and caught himself just before his body was about to crash into the stage floor. Now that it was done, Thomas had no fear.

"Thomas Riley," said the Dean.

Thomas walked onto the stage and accepted his commission. He crossed the stage to applause and went down the other side. He stepped off the platform onto the hard ground. Thomas took his seat as the last cadets were called. They remained seated as the Dean took the podium again.

"Congratulations, officers, and welcome to the Detroit Police Department!"

The cadets broke into thunderous applause and tossed their cadet hats into the air. The audience stood and cheered.

Thomas turned and searched for his family but they were already making their way to him. The smile on his face was so wide that it hurt a little. He was hugged, shook and slapped on the back by his fellow rookies even as he moved to meet his family.

"Well, you did it!" exclaimed Frank, patting his son hard on the shoulders. There was still a bit of Irish lilt in Frank's voice. His brother Shaun also had the lilt though Thomas always felt that Shaun was just doing an imitation. Thomas had no hint of Irish in his tones and sometimes he wondered if this meant he was devoid of some deep family power.

"Thanks," said Thomas gleefully.

Frank Riley was what Thomas called a Real Man. A Real Man was a man that played sports in high school, didn't go to college but went to war for his country to kill America's enemies. He drank hard, played harder and he voted Democratic but wasn't a liberal pacifist. And he did something with his hands for a living, something that made him proud.

Shaun was a Real Man. He was a high school baseball and football player, a cop and a Korean War vet. So was his grandfather, Cahan who was a carpenter, a cop and a sergeant in World War I. Thomas had most of the Real Man qualifications but he did not wear them as a badge of honor.

"How do you find your hat?" asked Katie looking at the hats littered across the lawn.

"My name is in it," said Thomas absently. "Mom, are you still crying?"

"Can't help it," said Esther dabbing her flushed face with a handkerchief. "You know what ceremonies do to me."

Thomas couldn't contain himself any longer. He stepped over to Sarah and kissed her.

"Wow, we *are* excited," said Sarah.

"Right out in public," sighed Frank, embarrassed by the display. Katie just giggled.

"Sorry," said Thomas, although he didn't mean it.

A cadet walked over and handed Thomas his hat. Thomas thanked him and put it on his head.

"Well, the Riley tradition continues," said Frank. "And the city is safe for another twenty years." Esther repeated the last part with him and Frank scoffed. "Now all we have to do is get a grandson and——"

"Maybe we'll have a girl and she'll join the police force," said Sarah with a touch of defiance.

"Righteous," said Katie. It was an expression that was relatively new and to Frank; it was Negro talk. Frank cut Katie a cautionary look that silenced her.

"It *would* be righteous," said Thomas not wanting his kid sister to feel bad.

Frank said nothing although he was already on record as saying that women should not be allowed to be cops. He had all the usual reasons for having this opinion but Frank's favorite was the science of aggressiveness. Females were just not mean enough to be police. That was another Real Man sentiment. Thomas wondered if his father felt he was wrong about this when his mother was mad at him and gave him that glare that could wither a rock.

"There's a reception," said Thomas. "We'd better get to it."

"Class photo first," Frank reminded him.

"Right," said Thomas.

The Dean called the cadets together and they all moved away from the parade grounds and into a reception area just adjacent.

The reception room was a big square room that could be filled with whatever the cops wanted. It had flat white walls and a high ceiling. Today, those walls were covered with cadet blue decorations and various police insignia.

A huge Detroit Police Seal dominated one corner with its "Protect and Serve" motto underneath. In the opposite corner was a big RCA phonograph with two bulky, state-of-the-art hi-fi speakers. Thomas called such machines record players while Frank every once in a while still referred to them as Victrolas.

The room was filled with the sounds of Sinatra as the party got underway. Berry Gordy's Motown had taken the nation by storm, but there was still resistance to the "Negro music" and this place was one of them.

Thomas and Sarah stepped lightly on the dance floor while Frank and Esther spun with reckless abandon just a few feet away. Thomas rarely saw his father smile and so he was elated to see the old man so happy. Thomas smiled broadly as his parents swirled by in a flash of cotton clothes and leather shoes.

"What's gotten into him?" asked Sarah.

"He's just happy for me," said Thomas.

"For you or himself?" asked Sarah with a tinge of contempt.

"A little of both, I guess," said Thomas, ignoring the obvious bait.

When Frank saw Sarah for the first time, he was filled with delight. She was the daughter that every father wanted, blonde, beautiful and sparkling with energy, an American beauty. But when Sarah started to talk, it had all gone away. To Frank, she was a radical, a follower of the newest trend in society, hating your country.

Sarah had come to the Riley house in a lovely print dress, her hair beautifully straight and styled conservatively. This she had done because she loved Thomas and wanted to impress his mother. Although Sarah was a modern woman, she still had what was called "home training" and sought to make a good impression.

When the evening moved to the inevitable social conversation, Thomas grew nervous. He dreaded the moment when everyone would know Sarah's beliefs. He fantasized that his father would find her interesting, a challenge to his very pro-American views.

"That's silly," his father would say. "But I respect that. You should know that I..." and so forth.

Sarah would laugh at Frank's old-fashioned ways and the perfect love-hate-respect relationship would be born. Frank would see in her what Thomas saw.

But it had not happened that way. When Frank brought up politics, Sarah had attacked him with the savagery of a tiger. She ripped and pulled at the meat of his logic and challenged him until Frank had lost his composure and called her a "silly girl."

That was a declaration of war to Sarah who was about to go for the jugular when she noticed the alarm on the face of Esther, Thomas' mother. In the end, Sarah had remembered her home training and apologized.

There was a happy ending that day, but afterwards, the two made sure to keep a civil distance between each other. Frank was sure that he had his son's respect and love and Sarah was sure that those things belonged to her. Thomas stood in the middle of the battle, constantly looking in either direction.

"I think he'd rather I be in Vietnam," said Thomas unafraid to keep the conversation away from such things on this day.

"I'm sure," said Sarah. "We need more men to kill those innocent people over there, more boys to die for nothing."

Thomas loved the way her brow furrowed and her nose crinkled when she got angry. It made her look like a kid who just got a toy taken away from her. Except for her eyes. There was green fire behind them in these times and that always unnerved him a little.

"I'm not going to argue with you, Sarah," said Thomas. "Not today."

"You never argue," said Sarah, "with me or with your father. I keep hoping you'll take a side, any side."

"Why?" asked Thomas, smiling handsomely at her.

Sarah sighed and laughed a little in that way a woman does when she's frustrated by the things about her man that she still hopes to change. "Forget it," she said.

Like most men, Thomas didn't know what his woman saw in him. Men, Real or not could never fathom the minds of women. He thought himself lucky to have Sarah's favor and didn't question the motivation.

But Sarah's attraction to him was not a deep mystery. It was not borne from the things he was, but rather those that he could become. To the girl with the green eyes, Thomas Riley was much like America, teetering on the edge of its great potential. And so she fought to change him as she did her country-- for love of both.

Thomas and Sarah took a break from dan
made their way to the food table, where Kati
bored.

Thomas was slapped on the back by a grad
his hand shook by another. Sarah smiled duti
ignored the flirtatious looks from some of the o

Thomas never said anything about how othe ......ooked
at Sarah. Thomas was sure of their relationship and so he
displayed confidence when around other men. This was a
trait Sarah found attractive. After many jealous boyfriends
and a few fights due to it; she warmed to a confident man.

"What's wrong, Katie?" asked Thomas.

"Nothing," she said in that way that lets you know
something was wrong. How did all women know how to do
that, thought Thomas.

"I think she's not having fun," said Sarah. She sat next to
Katie and hugged her with big-sisterly familiarity.

"You said it," said Katie, confessing under Sarah's
protection.

"I'm sorry my life is boring to you," said Thomas. "Too
bad." His face had the mean big brother look on it, the cat
chomping on a pretty yellow bird.

"Thomas," said Sarah and immediately Thomas lost the
edge in his voice.

"Sorry," he said.

If there was going to be any friction, it was cut off when
Frank came up and said, "Time for family history." He was
holding two framed pictures.

Esther was standing next to him smoking a cigarette, a
habit that Thomas hated after being educated by his fiancée.
The true evil of cigarettes was another ten years off, but it
was simple logic to Sarah. How could inhaling smoke from
burning leaves be good for you?

Thomas often asked his mother. "If the house was on fire
would you run or would you stand there and suck in the
smoke?" Esther's answer was glib. "Depends on if the house
was menthol."

"Right, history," said Thomas looking at his father.

"Katie's a little bored," said Sarah.

"She'll get over it," said Frank. "Thomas, let's go and——"

"Maybe we should go to a restaurant or something,"
Sarah interrupted.

as could feel it coming before it happened. One you never did to a Real Man was tried to exert control er what was his. Katie was still a kid and she still belonged to her father.

"Katie, stay here until we come back," said Frank and he glanced at Sarah to let her know there would be no discussion.

There were many things Sarah could have done in this moment. She could have spit venom back at Frank. She could have fell silent and just let the moment pass. She could have deflected the statement with a humorous line like "Hey, I am pregnant—- just kidding!" But what she did was worse than all these things.

She looked at Thomas.

The look asked him to stand up to his father, to back him away from the woman he loved with his own Real Maleness, to declare himself in the world that was different from his father's and all of his beliefs.

Thomas' reaction to this awful gesture was even worse. He looked away. And not with a "you're right look" or even an "I'm afraid of him" look. He turned with the dutifulness of a son who also still belonged to his father.

"Be right back," he said to Sarah. She looked shocked and then sighed as if exhausted.

Frank and Thomas walked off to the corner where the DPD seal was. It was big and noble against the wall with soft light reflecting off its accents.

The two men were both in great shape and looked heroic against the seal and for a moment Thomas felt a surge of positive energy. This was good, he thought. Being a cop was going to be good.

Frank held a black and white photo of his father who smiled in his dress uniform from the 1940's. Thomas held a color picture of his brother, Shaun in his police uniform.

Without thinking, Frank switched pictures with Thomas almost whispering, "Here, you hold your grandfather."

Thomas gave up the picture of his brother without protest. In truth, he felt the whole thing was a little morbid but it was a tradition and what was family without that?

He glanced at the picture of his grandfather. He stood tall and handsome in his uniform, like a great soldier protecting the innocent. A lot to live up to, he thought.

Thomas smiled as a photographer took the picture. He knew they were celebrating the beginning of a career and yet he felt something had ended here in this room with all of its ceremony and good cheer.

Thomas smiled as his father clapped him on the shoulders again. As they walked back, Thomas tried not to look at the green fire in Sarah's eyes as she looked on.

3

SECTOR 23

Rain fell in swirling sheets on Robert and The Cleaners. The drops seemed impossibly large and slammed into everything around them like tiny bombs.

The sound of the rain would have been disturbing were it not for the mortar shell explosions and local gunfire around them.

The roasted pork and chicken, which Robert and The Cleaners had consumed the day before, was a distant memory as bombs thundered and bullets whizzed over their heads.

Robert was crouched behind a barricade and fired randomly at the enemy hoping to hit anything.

The Cleaners had secured the road for the convoy. The supply trucks had rumbled by, taking what seemed an eternity to pass. But moments later, they were cut off from both sides by the enemy who had conceded the convoy but decided that as a consolation prize, they would kill the soldiers who had kept them at bay.

Bullets zipped through the falling water. It doesn't sound the way it did in the movies, Robert thought absently. It's not a low whistle. It's a sharp, ripping sound, like God splitting the air.

The rain only made the fighting harder. There were no light rains or drizzles in Vietnam, Robert mused. Either it was clear or pouring like hell. It seemed that there were no subtleties in the country's politics, its people or its weather.

A bullet ripped the air just over Robert's head as he popped up to take a shot.

"Shit!" said Robert ducking back down.

The other men in the platoon were all in the same pickle. So far, they'd only lost one man. The dead soldier was Wilson Saunders, a kid from a well-to-do family in upstate

New York. He'd defied his family by joining the Army, shunning a college deferment.

Wilson was lobbing some of the new bombs they'd been given when they discovered that the enemy had sent part of its platoon to hit them from another position.

Wilson was shot in the neck by a sniper and the look on his face was one of pure surprise, like he'd been struck out on a sucker's pitch.

Robert grabbed his field radio again. He turned it on and waited to get a connection. When it crackled, he heard the voice of Lieutenant Ferguson, the man who had sent them into hell.

"Sergeant?"

"Sir," said Robert. "We're still in deep shit out here!"

"We lost contact with your air cover," said Ferguson, "but they've got to be close.

A bomb exploded near Robert and he missed the last part of this statement. When he asked again and heard it, he cursed openly in front of his superior officer and did not apologize for it.

Ferguson told them to hold on.

"Yes, sir," said Robert out of instinct.

"I'll see you soon, soldier," said Ferguson confidently but Robert heard the concern under the officer's coolness.

Robert ended the call hoping the air cover commander would come and lay waste to these gooks. Robert had heard and used the words gook, dink and slope many times but had never thought of their relation to the word nigger or the irony of him using it.

He heard the air rip again then the sick sound of a man groaning. Robert looked around and saw Foster lying prone near an open area.

Robert's heart leapt. A commander was not supposed to let his personal feelings interfere with his job but he had to confess that he liked the kid and now he was hit.

Robert crawled quickly over to Foster and half way there, he saw Foster move. Foster began to crawl in the same direction Robert was going.

"Foster!" Robert yelled.

Foster stopped and looked over his hindquarters to Robert. His eyes were clear and he looked scared but uninjured.

"Cole's hit!" Foster said.

Robert sighed a little. It was Cole who had issued the groan. Foster, his friend, was okay.

Robert looked beyond Foster's prone body and saw Peter Cole, lying out in the open. Robert crawled over to Foster and pulled him back.

"Get back!" he said to him.

Foster moved backwards and Robert looked at the body lying in the middle of the gunfight, unmoving. Chances are he was dead already, he told himself.

Robert pulled his rifle aside, getting ready to make a run to the wounded man. Then from the recesses of his mind, from his inner Wartime Fool, he heard the words he felt in his heart.

Leave him.

Letting Cole die would be a boon to mankind, Robert thought. One less racist to worry about said the Fool. Cole had this coming. God let him get hit so he could die here surrounded by the people he despised.

The idea was so attractive. Let fate take care of Cole. Let the inhumanity that is war do some good by wiping Cole from the ass of life. But then another voice piped up. The soldier, the patriot spoke.

Robert pushed the Fool back into his filthy hole and raced out to Cole. God ripped the air around him as he grabbed the fallen man. Cole groaned as Robert pulled the dead weight behind the barricade toward safety. The whole thing took about ten seconds but it had seemed much longer.

Without warning, the enemy sent a mortar towards them. It missed but something shot up from the broken earth and Robert was hit.

His helmet rang, his head rang and then the whole world rang. The ground rushed up, slamming into the side of his face.

Robert lay there next to the life he had saved and stared up into the falling rain. God cut the wind and the enemy exploded the earth beyond him.

Then inside his ringing head, he heard a sound; a sweet, thin melody and it rose, pushing aside the pain and the sound of death and battle. It was an old Temptations song, smooth, calming and beautiful. Just as quickly, the magic words faded and distantly, Robert heard a rumble. He looked up and through hazy vision; he saw dark angels coming over the battle. They moved like huge birds above the falling rain and cut through the air, just like God.

"Coming to get me," Robert thought thickly.

As the first Bell UH-1 helicopter swung low for a strafing run, the darkness took him.

"Sarge?" said Foster as Robert opened his eyes. His lashes stuck together for a moment and then separated with a tiny sound that only he could hear.

Robert was in a warm bed in an army hospital that had been set up near Sector 23. He looked up into the face of Foster and Percy. They smiled like kids at him. His head felt okay, better than okay. He was feeling good. Then he thought: morphine. Morphine had done it. Morphine was good.

You got hit by a rock," said Foster.

"Bet it felt like a grenade," said Percy.

"Cole," said Robert. And he heard the scratchy sound of his own voice.

"That asshole's still in a coma," said Percy. "But he's gonna be okay, I guess."

"You saved him, Sarge," said Foster. "It was a beautiful thing."

Robert sat up in his bed and now he felt something bad. His head pounded dully and his neck was stiff.

"It's my job to save his ass," said Robert. "Even if he don't deserve it."

The army hospital was better looking than it should have been. It had walls and a ceiling. It was probably being held together by string but it seemed like heaven to Robert right now, swathed in white and soft light.

"They got food here?" asked Robert.

"They did but we got hungry waiting for you to wake up," said Percy.

"I ate the Jell-O," said Foster. "Good."

Robert laughed and felt sharper pangs in his head. Maybe he would ask for another meal only this time laced with morphine.

"I think you're up for a medal or something," said Foster. "The Lieutenant's been hanging around all day."

"Shit on a medal," said Robert. "I'd kill for a hamburger and a cold beer."

Percy and Foster shared a look. "We saw some beer when we got here," said Percy. "It was marked for officers."

"Don't even think about it," said Robert. "You go to the stockade for stealing a brew and I'll shoot you myself."

They laughed again as Robert spotted Lieutenant Ferguson walking in. Foster and Percy snapped salutes and waved goodbye to Robert as Ferguson sidled up to the bed.

"Sir," said Robert, saluting.

"At ease, Sergeant," said Ferguson. "Good job out there. Sector 23 is now ours, such as it is."

"Thank you, sir," said Robert.

"As soon as you're up and about I have new orders for you."

Robert heard himself say, "Yes sir." But in his head, he cursed Ferguson. Can I take a piss before you send me out to be killed again, he thought.

"I have them right here," said Ferguson. He handed Robert a letter in an envelope.

Robert read the letter and suddenly, he didn't need any morphine. It was a DD-214, a discharge letter. Robert looked at Ferguson with his mouth agape. He tried to speak but couldn't.

"Congratulations, soldier," Ferguson smiled. "There's a note in there from the Commander. Unusual, but he is a General."

Dear Sergeant Jackson,
Thank you for your service to your country.
God bless you and God bless America.

Sincerely,
General Wilford J. Gill

Robert folded the paper and brought it to his forehead. He fought tears and he thought of Detroit. Home. Denise, sex, life and home cooking. He pulled the paper down and heard himself saying some kind of thanks to God.

"Thank you, sir," he said to Ferguson.

"You deserve it, Sergeant," said Ferguson. "Hold on to that DD-214. Oh, by the way, your Tigers are doing just fine back home. You'll probably be able to catch a few games."

"Looking forward to it," said Robert and now he felt the smile spreading across his face. "Sir, what's going to happen to my platoon?"

"They'll be broken up, sent to other squads. It's looking ugly in the Central Highlands. We expect heavy fighting there."

Robert's look of sadness was obvious to Ferguson. A leader can't be happy unless he knows all of his men are safe.

"Don't worry. This thing's going to be over by the end of the year. At least that's what the Generals are saying.

"Yes, sir," said Robert but with little joy.

Ferguson saluted and left the room. Robert pulled the discharge letter to his chest and sunk back into bed. A minute later, Foster and Percy came back in with wide grins on their faces.

"You sonofabitch!" said Foster.

"Goin' home!" said Percy. "We heard some of the officers talking about it."

"Yeah, how about that?" said Robert.

They hugged Robert and he didn't mind the pain that was creeping back into his body.

"Send me some fried chicken, a case of Jack Daniels and three women with big, juicy asses," said Percy, laughing.

"Big tits on mine," said Foster, "the women I mean," and he laughed as well.

Robert looked at the two men, their faces beaming with true happiness, the kind of happiness that can overcome the worse of memories and deed.

For a second, he didn't want to leave. He wanted to stay in Vietnam and go to whatever destiny the War Gods had in mind for him. Surely, War Gods didn't let anyone go home. But he quickly came to his senses. Going home only meant that he had beaten the War Gods at their crazy game.

Robert wanted to leave Foster and Percy with some words of wisdom, some magical talisman that would protect them and some day find them going home as well.

"Thanks fellas," was all he managed to say.

Percy and Foster shared another look and then Foster pulled up three no-name beers from his jacket. They opened them and toasted Robert's freedom and their fallen comrades.

Robert tipped the dark brown bottle and felt the liquid slide down his throat. It was warm but it tasted great.

He sighed and fought back the tears.

4

<u>ROOKIE</u>

Thomas could not stop the birds flying around in his stomach. It was his first night patrol and even though he had lived in Detroit his whole life, he was worried.

The streets now looked different to him, like a battleground. Stores where he once bought food now looked like innocent victims and the men who had once passed by his vision without thought now looked like the enemy. Also, night calls were often about Negroes and anything could happen when they were involved.

"Hit 'em hard and often," is what his grandfather Cahan used to say about the Coloreds as he called them. Sometimes he called them "Nigras" coconuts, spooks, splibs, darkies and such.

When Thomas was a boy, he wondered why the Colored people had so many different names. He never asked, so no one ever told him and so he used the names like everyone else he knew.

Now he knew that those words could hurt and get you into a lot of trouble if you used them unwisely. And among some in his generation, they were outright taboo.

And now the Colored people called themselves Black with a capital "B." He didn't much like that name either. There was something about it that intimidated him. Black was a color and it invoked images of fear and mystery. Darkness. Why would anyone want to be Black, he thought.

Sarah had made him pay for taking his father's side at the graduation reception. She gave him the cold shoulder and cut him off in bed. For all her progressiveness, Sarah acted like any pretty girl when she was mad. "You don't get to have me" was his punishment. But they had made up with a three-hour session that would go down in his personal history book. He smiled a little at the thought.

Thomas drove the police cruiser down Woodward Avenue and turned onto Grand Boulevard. He passed Hitsville and saw several well-dressed Negroes talking near the entrance. That was where they made much of the music he loved. That place was Motown.

What he didn't know is that one of those Negroes was a man named Marvin who was having his first thoughts about doing a political rhythm and blues album that would change the musical landscape forever.

They soon neared Tiger Stadium. Thomas smiled. So many good memories were in that place, he thought.

"Who do you like, Lolich or McClain?" asked Ned Young. Ned was a vet of more than ten years. He had been Shaun's partner before he went off to war.

"I like them both," said Thomas.

"Pick one," said Ned in that juvenile way a true baseball fan has.

"Why not ask me if Batman can kick Superman's ass," said Thomas.

"Batman?" said Ned. "Who the hell is that?"

Thomas laughed a little as he turned the cruiser back toward Woodward. "Well, Lolich is a hard worker. McClain is a pretty boy. So, I'll go with Mickey."

"Surprised to hear that. I thought you Mc's all stuck together."

"Only when we're drinking," said Thomas and they both laughed.

Ned had volunteered to ride with Thomas after his last partner started riding as one of the Big Four, a TAC squad consisting of two uniformed officers and two detectives. Their main purpose was to keep the peace in designated high-crime areas.

The department always wanted rookies to be partnered with a vet to bring them in slowly. There were no less than three cops who wanted to ride with Thomas. His brother Shaun was missed, and his father was still popular in the precinct house. His grandfather was a legend. It was nice to have an easy transition into the brotherhood, Thomas thought, but it was tough living in the shadow of greatness, especially his grandfather, whose name Cahan was Celtic for warrior.

"Not so fast," said Ned. "We need to observe what's going on. When the people see us moving slow they know they're being watched."

"Swing right up here and let's cruise black bottom," said Ned. "See what we can rustle up there."

The majority of Detroit's Blacks were locked into neighborhoods on the city's eastside. Many of these areas were what people called ghettoes but generally speaking they were working class neighborhoods.

Ned's designation of black bottom referred to the city's old Paradise Valley area where the Blacks settled after the turn of the century.

Thomas headed for the east side in the shadow of downtown. As he did, his stomached turned as well. "Rustle up something" was code for offensive policing which was in itself a euphemism for busting Negro heads.
The cruiser rolled south then Thomas turned east toward their destination.

Frank Riley was not present at the birth of his second son, Thomas James Riley in 1942. He was in Europe defeating Adolf Hitler or at least that's the way Thomas would hear about it when he got older. His older brother, Shaun, the apple of his father's eye, was a freckled faced twelve-year old at the time.

Frank Riley returned home the next year in time to see his newest son walking and to rejoin the Detroit Police Force with his father, a big, strapping giant of a man named Cahan.

Frank came home in January of that year and later witnessed Detroit's first major race riot. It was a bloody affair that arose from the mistreatment of Blacks who were all forced to live in startlingly inhuman conditions. The forced integration of black and white workers at the auto plants to help the war effort also fueled the fire.

Frank worked side by side with Cahan during the riot of '43. On the second night, the family got bad news. Their cousin Dennis and his nephew James had been chased by

Negroes and trapped in an alley. Dennis had been killed, beaten with baseball bats by two men.

Cahan had called for blood but the men were never found. And from that day on, Thomas was often reminded that Black men had killed one of their own.

Young Shaun and later Thomas would look at their father and grandfather with the love and admiration you feel for someone who clothes and feeds you. In the eyes of the young boys, their fathers were men who were strong and spoke with conviction and so their words and sentiments were gospel.

On August 6, 1945, two years after the riots, President Truman gave the order to drop an atomic bomb on the city of Hiroshima, Japan and ended the war.

Two months later, the Detroit Tigers won the World Series against the Chicago Cubs at Wrigley Field. Thomas was three years old and would never remember that he had sat on the lap of his grandpa as they listened to the game on the radio.

With the world at peace and the Tigers the champions of the world, Detroit and the country moved into an economic boom, which benefited both Blacks and Whites, and for a while, the simmering feud between the races fell into the shadow of prosperity.

Thomas was a typical teenager among his peers. He was handsome but didn't know it and was deathly afraid of girls. He was never as popular as Shaun who was an all-state athlete and a notorious ladies' man.

Shaun, the first born, was his father's favorite, but Cahan favored the young Thomas who was named after Cahan's father, Thomas Casey Riley, a steel worker and leader of a street gang in old New York.

Frank saw in his firstborn, Shaun all the things he felt in himself. Shaun had spirit. He was smart, strong and could hold his drink. Thomas was thin, often sick and was a light drinker. Shaun got into fights and often won. Thomas avoided violence and liked to read. But Shaun loved his little brother and protected him from all dangers in and out of the house. And so over the years, a gulf developed between Thomas and Frank that was bridged by Shaun.

Shaun got married to one of his many girlfriends and joined the police department, continuing the family tradition.

He was tall and handsome in his uniform and the department had even used him in a recruiting poster once.

Cahan was retired but was as proud as a man could be at Shaun's graduation. Thomas would never forget the three of them standing together in their uniforms taking a photograph. It was like he was watching a movie of someone else's life. The men seemed foreign, like John Wayne or Gary Cooper, Real Men who fought and protected the weak and innocent. Thomas was only eight but he remembered thinking that he'd wanted to be in the picture with the men he saw before him.

Shaun went off to Korea soon thereafter. He was there less than a year when he was killed in fighting near Pusan. The Army sent what was left of him home in a bag nestled in a coffin with an American flag on it.

The funeral was the saddest day of Thomas' life. It was filled with crying and screaming, drinking and singing. The entire police force seemed to come out for the burial.

Thomas stood next to Cahan, who was holding his hand and watched Frank try to keep his composure. When they lowered Shaun into the ground, Thomas felt that a part of his father went into the cold earth with his brother.

Cahan died a year later and that left Frank as the leader of the clan. Cahan's funeral was in a word, grand. Men came from all over the country to send him off. An Army General even attended. It was quite a blow to the family so soon after the loss of young Shaun but like any family, they held fast to each other and tried to move on.

Frank and Esther immediately tried to have another child, a feat that took them four years to accomplish. When Katherine Abigail was born, Thomas could see the disappointment in his father's eyes. He wanted another boy but God had said no.

Thomas didn't know whether to be happy or sad about this. His father had never favored him and perhaps another Shaun was what he needed. On the other hand, Thomas didn't like the idea of being replaced.

When Katie was born a girl and Esther knew she couldn't have any more children, Frank finally turned his attentions to young Thomas. He set about the task of making the young boy a man. And he set about it in the old school way, with toughness and self-righteous paternal anger.

Thomas soon overcame his shyness with girls and started dating around the neighborhood. Unlike Shaun, he preferred to have one girl at a time; still he was on the list of every young lady in his neighborhood.

Frank took Thomas downtown on a Saturday afternoon once. Thomas and Frank were in Hudson's department store. Hudson's was a pricey joint and they were there trying to find a present for Esther's birthday.

Thomas saw a particularly pretty girl and lingered on her as she passed by. She had hazel eyes and long black hair that cascaded down her back like a river or curls. She smiled at him and Thomas felt a heat in his belly that he had never experienced. It was sharp and a little painful but it felt good, too.

The smack to the side of his head was like a bullet as his father hit him. Thomas looked up, surprised, the pain already building in his eyes. Frank's face was a visage of anger and shame.

"Don't you know a darkie when you see one?" he asked the stunned boy.

"Huh?"

"She's mud," said Frank.

Thomas looked back at the young girl and only then did he see that the woman holding her hand was as dark as a Hershey Bar.

"Some White man has been with that woman and now she's parading that fact all over town," said Frank with anger in his voice.

"I didn't... she looks White," said Thomas.

"Come on," said Frank and he stomped away.

Thomas followed but not before taking a last look at the girl, who despite his father's anger and his stinging head still seemed like an angel.

As little Katie grew up, she turned into a bundle of energy and brought some joy back into the beleaguered Riley house. She was clearly the smartest of all the kids and made straight A's in school.

Frank didn't know what good a smart girl was. She'd only get married and have babies, he'd often mumble.

But Thomas secretly encouraged her to excel. He loved his little sister and tried to be the knight and protector Shaun had been for him.

Thomas graduated from high school and took a job as security at the local college while waiting for the Police Academy to accept him. This was a mere matter of time, he knew, because no one would dare turn down a Riley.

But Thomas was not really waiting for the academy as he told his father. He had decided that he didn't want to be a police officer. He wanted to go to college and maybe open a business or something. He knew this would break Frank's heart but he had a plan. He'd join the Army first.

After President Kennedy was killed, President Johnson, the Texan had escalated the military offensive in Vietnam.

Frank disliked the term military offensive, it was a war and one they needed to fight. Frank had never heard of Vietnam, but people like them had killed Shaun and so any excuse to go there and lay waste was okay with him.

Thomas understood more about the war than his father. He at least knew that the Russians and the threat of Communism were behind the war effort. And he knew war suited his purpose right now.

As the last son in the family, Thomas could have gotten out of the draft, but this was the perfect way to change his life. He would serve a tour, come home and then go to college. His father's macho legacy would be appeased and Thomas could finally own his destiny.

The brighter days that Thomas saw as he went into basic training soon turned to sorrow. A boy's idea of the military was a fantasy forged by books, movies and noble heroism, but the reality of the soldier, the Marines in particular, was man as killing machine.

Thomas was subjected to rigorous training. The philosophy of killing, the necessity of it, was embedded into him each day.

"What are you?" was the daily question.

"I'm a killer, sir!" was the only correct response.

The only thing he looked forward to were the nights and sleep. He'd lay his aching body on the hard cot and let the blackness of slumber seep over him like thick water.

As the days progressed, his sleep was invaded. The corpse of his dead brother would stroll into the barracks, his bloody, torn-apart body hanging on to itself by sinewy flesh. Shaun crawled across Thomas' mind like a demon, whittling away at his resolve and sanity.

Soon the specter didn't end with the rising sun. Thomas saw flashes of the dead man behind trees and barracks, in the shadows and on the makeshift battlefields.

Thomas told no one about his apparitions. His hands shook when he assembled his rifle and the other men kidded him about yelling in his sleep.

The days passed and Thomas sensed the walls of his mind weaken. He saw failure and humiliation waiting like ravenous predators and he fought their existence. And then it all stopped. He no longer felt limits to the functioning of his mind and the tug of reason's gravity.

So when he saw his brother on the rifle range, cadet Thomas Riley ran onto the course to save his brother Shaun from an assault. He galloped toward the ghost as bullets zipped around him and his instructor screamed and cursed to high heaven.

"All men have pain and mental weakness," the Army shrink would tell Thomas later. "Most of us believe we build barriers over these frailties. The truth is strength is built from weakness," he would say to Thomas as he was being processed for discharge. "As you face fear, you use the confrontation to create a new sense of reality and strength," the doctor would say.

According to the Army psychologist, Thomas' loss of his brother and beloved grandfather and the void they left with a father who did not love him were his weaknesses. He never acknowledged this fact and when tested, the weak crumbled, taking the strong with it.

Thomas spent a week in a hospital saying that he was okay. But the commanders didn't buy it. An unhinged Marine was too dangerous a thing to just cut loose.

Frank was called in and after some private meetings, Thomas was let go for having a hearing problem that made him unfit for combat.

Father and son never spoke of it, but Thomas knew how heartbroken Frank was.

Thomas stayed close to home after that. He talked to a priest and kept to himself until the images in his head and the pain in his heart started to subside.

And then, the silence.

Thomas and Frank stopped talking to each other. They were often in the same room but never engaged each other directly. Thomas' mother, Esther noticed this but she was too smart to say anything about it. You had to leave men to be men.

But men have a way of burying problems and letting them decay. The secrets and pain turn to vile soil from which grows the cruelty of family.

Thomas accepted his place as the failed son and Frank took his role as a father crushed by that failure and other acts of God.

Now Thomas was searching for something. He didn't know what it was but somewhere in his life there was a path that led away from the past and the certainty that he'd never be happy.

He just had to find it.

"Twelve-eight!" said the female voice on their radio. "Disturbance on East Adams near John R. Suspect drunk and disorderly." There was just a second of silence and then she said, "NS."

"Roger," said Ned.

Thomas was bolted back from his thoughts. He saw his hand reach for the siren and he stepped on the accelerator. The car shot off down the street. "NS" meant Negro Suspect.

Ned smiled. He was going to get the action he wanted.

The police had many such codes for crimes or disturbances that involved Blacks. There was NWAG, which stood for Nigger With A Gun, CFOD, Car Full Of Darkies and the one that always made Thomas laugh, NOMAD, which stood for Nigger On Mack After Dark. Mack Avenue was a thoroughfare, which led from the black east side of Detroit into the exclusive white enclave of Grosse Pointe.

Thomas and Ned pulled up near the disturbance point. They were first on the scene. Thomas called it in and requested back up. He and Ned moved toward a large figure on the sidewalk. People were scattered around looking on.

As they got closer, Thomas saw that the suspect was indeed a Negro and one of the biggest he'd ever seen. The man stood six five at least and had to have clocked in at two seventy or so.

"Holy shit," said Ned. "It's fucking King Kong."

The big man paced in a little semi circle muttering to himself. Thomas could smell the alcohol emanating from him on the soft wind that blew the twenty yards between them.

Near the man, was another man, Black and smaller. He lay on his face, unconscious. Then Thomas saw the reason for the fallen man. King Kong was holding a long piece of iron pipe.

"Police!" yelled Ned.

The big man turned on thick legs. He leveled his eyes to the cops. His reaction would tell Thomas how bad this was. If the Black man saw the uniforms and showed fear, then Thomas knew he'd go easy. If he didn't, then the suspect was crazy or drunk and they had a situation.

The big man saw them and then straightened his back and growled something under his breath. He turned fully to face them and then raised the pipe and slapped it into his other hand making a thick, thudding sound.

Situation.

"Drop the weapon and get to your knees," said Ned with so much authority that Thomas felt the man would obey immediately.

The big man made no move. He circled the fallen man a few steps then said, "Fug you," in a thick voice.

Ned cursed and pulled the strap off his service revolver. Thomas did the same. Ned moved in and Thomas circled to the other side of the big man.

The big man looked at them both trying to choose which one he'd concentrate on. He picked Ned.

"Come on," said the big man. He flipped the pipe in his hands.

Ten feet away now, thought Thomas. Striking distance.

Then the big man dropped the pipe. It clattered to the ground and rolled. Ned took the opportunity and moved in closer and before Thomas could yell, the big man had scooped up the pipe and was swinging upwards. Ned moved back just as the pipe whooshed past his chin.

"Fuck!" said Ned and he quickly pulled and cocked his weapon. Thomas was on the big man's side and slightly to his rear.

Thomas pulled his gun.

The big man whipped around when he felt the presence behind him. Thomas was in a shooting crouch. Their eyes met and Thomas could see harmful intent.

"I ain't scared," said the big man. "Not no mo'."

Thomas held his gaze and could see Ned take a step closer. In the old days of Cahan and Frank Riley, this man would already have a bullet in his leg or be on his way to the morgue. Thomas was surprised that the swipe he took at Ned didn't result in just that. But times were different and there were witnesses present.

With his eyes still on the suspect, Thomas said loud enough for the big man to hear: "Do I shoot before or after you, partner?"

This statement did something to the big man. His eyes seemed to pull in light and he straightened his back again. He lowered the pipe and took a half step backwards. Somewhere in the alcohol-addled part of his brain, he regained reason.

"Okay, okay," said the big man and dropped the pipe.

"On your knees!" barked Ned.

The big man got to his knees and held his hands up.

"Hands on your head!" yelled Thomas.

The big man complied. Thomas walked over to him as Ned circled around and handcuffed the man. His wrists were so thick that Ned had some difficulty.

"Hey," said Thomas. "This shit ain't so hard."

Ned laughed as Thomas went over to check on the fallen man. He had not been struck by the lead pipe as Thomas had first thought. But he did have a swollen jaw where he'd been punched. Why such a small man would start trouble with that giant was beyond Thomas.

Back up came with an ambulance and Ned and Thomas took in their prisoner, which Ned would give to Thomas as his first official collar.

When the area was clear, Ned went over to the big man, who sat on the curb. His feet were shackled along with his hands now.

His name was Barney Glover and he was an autoworker for Ford. The man he'd hit had refused to pay on a debt from the previous week.

Thomas was about to suggest that they lead their prisoner into the vehicle when he saw Ned take out his nightstick and swing with both hands into Barney's side. Barney groaned and fell over like a big trash can.

"You ever take a swing at a cop again and I'll kill your black ass dead," hissed Ned.

Barney looked up at Ned, pain and anger in his eyes. But what troubled Thomas the most was what he did not see in the man's eyes. There was no surprise. He had expected to pay this penalty for his actions, written in the unofficial statutes of race relations.

Ned looked over at Thomas and nodded towards Barney who had managed to sit himself back upright. Ned wanted Thomas to strike the man as well.

Thomas was a rookie but he had learned the code of the force from his family. Ned had been violated and so now this man had to pay the price. Had Barney been White, the penalty would be left to the courts. But in this case, justice would be doled out now.

Thomas pulled out his nightstick. Barney turned at that movement. He caught Thomas' eyes and Thomas felt a surge of power. He remembered that Negroes had ruthlessly killed one of his relatives so long ago in this city.

Thomas struck him hard in the back and Barney fell over again. He groaned and spat out blood and saliva.

"Back in the day, we'd disappear your ass," said Ned. "Now, get up."

Barney stumbled as they lifted him into the cruiser.

Thomas felt a little sick as he started the car and drove away. The night seemed to melt around him as he moved along the streets and heard the muffled sounds of the injured man behind him.

It wouldn't be until next year that he was no longer officially a rookie, but the newness of his occupation lifted from him in this moment, like smoke blown away by a strong wind.

Thomas drove back to the precinct and all that night, he kept hearing the words of the Negro.

I ain't scared... not no mo'.

5

SIX MILE

He was taking the long way home but it was worth it. Sergeant Robert Jackson had asked his driver to take Woodward Avenue from downtown. The driver, an amiable white corporal named Davis obliged without complaint.

Davis was also blessedly quiet as he drove, not bothering to ask Robert about his tour or the other stupid questions as to whether he was happy to be back. He just drove and let his passenger take in the sights of home.

Robert let the city and its life pour back into him as they drove along. The sights, sounds, smells and faces of the city energized him. He wanted to be human again and if anything could do that it was Detroit.

They turned on McNichols road and headed east. When they got to Dequindre just past the I-75 freeway, Robert asked Davis to stop the car. He was too close now to keep rolling in the Army vehicle. He wouldn't feel completely home until he set foot on the street.

Robert thanked Davis and offered him some money but Davis refused. The discharge money Robert had gotten was burning a hole in his pockets and he couldn't wait to spend some of it on Denise and his family.

He got out of the car. He grabbed his duffel and headed east on McNichols.

It was spring and the weather was mild. The humid summer was still a few months away and this was really the best time of the year to be in the city.

Robert looked up. The deep blue of the sky helped to confirm that he was no longer in Vietnam with its cruel pale blue.

He thought of Percy and Foster, their smiling faces behind dark bottles of stolen beer and hoped that they'd see the skies of their homes one day. He also thought of Peter Cole, whose life he had saved.

When Cole had come to, Robert was getting ready to go home but there had been plenty of time for Cole to thank him. Cole had not.

Robert told himself that he didn't want Cole's thanks but some small part of him hoped that his heroic act had changed the man. He wanted to get in Cole's face and tell him that he would forever owe his life to a Negro.

Robert walked the cracked pavement of McNichols, which was also called Six Mile, which was, according to city legend, approximately six miles from the heart of downtown on Woodward Avenue.

Robert passed by the Midway Market and remembered going there in the back seat of his father's black Plymouth Fury, anxiously awaiting sweet Faygo pop and salty Better Made potato chips.

Across the street, they were clearing a big lot for a new Farmer Jack's Supermarket. It was the first such market built in the Black neighborhood and it was a sign that things were changing for the better.

Robert drew a lot of attention in his Marine uniform. Some people saluted, others waved and smiled but some gave him disapproving frowns. He nodded and smiled anyway.

He knew the war was unpopular but these people didn't understand how Vietnam would change the perception. People were enlightened now, they had integrated sports and schools and soon everything else would be as well. The war in all its evil would be a boon to Blacks.

Robert Brent Jackson's childhood was filled with trouble almost from the moment it began. His birth had been complicated and for a while, the doctors thought his mother's life would be in jeopardy. In the end the baby came and the mother got a scar that would always remind her of the burden of carrying life.

Robert's parents were both very devout people who were heavily involved in their church. This fact did not stop young Robert from getting into as much mischief as he could.

Robert defied his parent's rules and ran in the streets with a dangerous crowd. They smoked, drank, stole and eventually engaged in premarital sex, a revelation that almost sent his mother, Theresa, to the hospital's emergency room.

Robert had no idea where these impulses to do wrong came from. He liked the thrill of danger and girls seemed to like that about him. He was good-looking and bigger than everyone in his age group. He looked like a man when he was still a young teenager.

Robert commanded respect from his male peers because often they were too afraid to do the things he would do in a heartbeat. This made him feel powerful.

His parents told him he was a bad example to his younger brother, Marcus but Robert didn't believe that. Marcus admired him and even though they had the normal sibling rivalries, they loved each other.

Robert was proud of his little brother who liked to read and never missed school or church. He was proud of Marcus' goodness mostly because it reaffirmed his own power as the tough badass brother.

Robert could never bring himself to admire these same attributes in his father, Abraham. He guessed that brothers don't impose their will on each other. Fathers do.

When he was fifteen, Robert looked so mature that he started a business buying alcohol for underage kids. For this feat, he'd take a small fee. He had a phony ID made and soon he was the go-to man for such endeavors. For girls, he'd do it for free if they were pretty enough and would let him take certain liberties.

And so it was inevitable that Robert fought with his father. Abraham was a big bull of a man like his son but his spirit was as gentle as a kitten. Robert didn't understand why his father was so soft. He could make people do what he wanted and yet he chose to be mild, like his heroes, Martin Luther King and Ralph Abernathy.

Drugs soon became important to Robert's varied enterprises. The police were cracking down on the business but it was too lucrative to pass up.

Soon, Robert had a little crew that specialized in marijuana. He didn't like heroin and pills. Even he could see the danger in that shit. But weed was cool and the White kids loved it, which made it even more profitable.

Abraham threatened to put Robert in a reform school while he was still a teenager. The church had a relationship with a boy's school in Ionia. He showed Robert the application as a threat designed to make him straighten himself out.

Although it was a shame for a man to admit he couldn't control his son, Abraham held no illusions. This was America and if he didn't do something, his son would likely end up dead.

And death did come. Dennis Ballet was one of Robert's best friends. Everyone called him Dennis Bullet. Bullet was a mean, nasty customer who everyone agreed wasn't quite all there in the head. Bullet was from a family of drug addicts and in that nightmarish upbringing had found crime to be his only salvation.

One of Bullet's favorite things to do was dart out into traffic and cause accidents. He'd wait until a particularly nice car was coming and then he'd just time it, jumping into its path.

If Bullet was lucky, the driver would swerve and slam into a pole, hydrant or another car. If he wasn't, the car would just swerve and maybe hit him. Bullet had cause six accidents and was swiped twice but never seriously injured.

Bullet and Robert had taken to each other right away. Robert's boldness and Bullet's fearlessness created an irresistible and unbeatable team.

They were out one night selling their wares when they spotted a rival drug crew. These guys were into every narcotic and for some reason, Bullet hated them.

Robert and Bullet confronted the rival crew and soon a fight broke out. Robert was an excellent fighter and he put two of the three men down.

When he glanced over at Bullet, he was slamming the bloody head of the crew's leader into a brick wall and laughing.

Whatever filament had held Bullet's sanity together had finally snapped. Bullet was still tearing and squeezing at the pulpy flesh of the man's head when the police came to take him away.

The cops saw the madman over his victim and pulled their guns. Bullet always kept a switchblade and Robert prayed that he wouldn't take it out. But Bullet pulled the weapon and was dead before he could get to his feet.

For weeks, Robert sat at home feeling like he didn't want to live. His future wasn't going to be any different from Bullet if he didn't change. Death was a permanent resident in their world and it seemed to be coming for him.

Robert had seen pictures of Death in his schoolbooks. The tall, thin man in the dark hooded robe. But that was a lie. Death was a cop with an attitude and a license to kill, death was the friend that went to jail and came out hard and ruthless. The real Grim Reaper was the people you saw every day.

Abraham and Theresa offered their son the bosom of the church to replace the thrill of the street. They hoped the power of God and promise of His Son could save the troubled young man and lift his soul from depravity.

After Bullet died, Robert vowed to get his life together. He tried to study harder and started dating a pretty girl who was on the cheer team. Denise Barnes was a long, willowy girl with an angelic face and athletic body. She was also on the track team and Robert loved to watch her race around the track in her tight shorts.

He courted Denise but she was as afraid of him as she was intrigued. Soon, they were an item, but try as he might, Robert couldn't get her to have sex with him. Normally, he would have dropped her but he was a different man now and there were always those girls who would do that for you.

He stayed with Denise and her sweetness opened him to feelings that he used to think were for punks and weaker men.

Robert graduated from high school with no academic distinction. He was a baseball jock and set his sights on making it in the major leagues. Baseball had recently begun a full-scale integration. The Detroit Tigers, unfortunately, were among the last teams to integrate and it was his dream to play for them.

Robert tried out for the team but didn't make the cut. He soon drifted back to the only thing he knew and the friction rose between him and Abraham again.

He started a new drug crew. But now things were different. The game had become much more dangerous in just a few years. Everybody carried guns and a rival dealer would kill you rather than fight.

Robert had a hard time keeping this from Denise who had a very keen and intuitive mind. The lies piled up and soon she was distant and cold to him. Denise thought he was seeing other girls along with his criminal activities. She broke up with Robert but did not start dating another man. That gave Robert some comfort.

Robert's choices were limited. He could stay in the street game and fight. He'd either be killed or he'd end up on top, at least for a while. But the game was the game; it always led to the graveyard or the penitentiary.

Somehow the draft had missed Robert. He had always vowed that if it came, that he'd run to Canada or let them send him to jail. He did not want to fight in the White man's war. But now the Army didn't seem like such a bad thing. He looked into it, talked with recruiters and decided to enlist.

Abraham was proud of his son. He beamed and boasted to his friends that his son was going to be a Marine, the elite fighting corps. Abraham had been in the infantry in World War II but had not seen any combat. Vietnam was a whole other story. Black men fought with honor, just like their White comrades.

Denise was happy to know that her man was giving up the street life but was deeply worried about him going off to war. Robert would tell her with confidence that he was coming back alive and whole and she so desperately wanted to believe him. But before he went off to war, he had one more thing to do.

Denise and Robert got married in his father's church on a warm summer day. The wedding was attended by both big clans and was probably the happiest day of Robert's life. They sang, ate, danced and drank with reckless abandon.

Robert took Denise's virginity on their wedding night and he felt a sense of calm. He was a man now and as such he had obligations. The war was his challenge, his way to make up for what he had been and a gateway to what he was yet to become.

Robert left for basic training with a sense of destiny. He was out of the city for only the second time in his life and it felt good. The pull of the street and hopelessness melted away like fragile memory.

Denise followed him to boot camp and lived just off base. She wanted to be with him for as long as possible and hoped to get pregnant before he went off to Vietnam.

Robert arrived at boot camp ready for the worst. He'd heard that the Marines had one objective: to make killers and weed out the weak.

This proved to be true. Robert was trained in hand-to-hand combat, demolition, and of course, marksmanship. He excelled at all of these things. It seemed he'd found his calling; he was a natural born killer.

The Marines ran them, cursed them, beat them and exercised them as if they wanted them all to die. Some days, he felt like he would die but his already fit body became even harder and soon he felt indestructible.

Robert became a favorite of the camp, looked up to by most of his peers and admired by many of the officers.

The notion that Negroes were cowards or incompetent soldiers had been widely held by the military establishment. Many felt that the oppression of Blacks would turn them against their White brothers in combat.

This theory was disproved in World War II and even more so in Korea. And now with Vietnam, America would finally see the whole truth, that Black patriotism was real and the tenets of American Democracy overrode its awful history. They would see that stars and stripes resided in the hearts of Negro men.

But Robert didn't delude himself. It would take time. Things changed slowly in America. He hoped that one day his son would look at pictures of him in his uniform and see the beginning of a better life.

So Robert went off to war, leaving his doubt and fear behind him but also leaving loved ones, which he desperately hoped to see again.

And in Vietnam he had seen another face of Death. The face of tiny men in uniforms that looked like pajamas carrying

swift, silent death, children wired with bombs and leaders
who traded hills and roads for the lives of soldiers.

Robert walked up to his family's home. They could not
see him as he approached the house from the rear. They
were waiting for the Army car to pull up, he thought.

Robert smiled as he got an idea. He went to the house
and up the back stairs. He found the door open and entered.
His mother never locked that backdoor. It was some kind of
silly southern superstition as he recalled.

Robert entered and soon he heard his family in the living
room. He savored the moment as he charted each voice:
Marcus' now bass-laden baritone, his father's voice, a
booming Kentucky-dipped tone, his mother's sing-songy alto
and Denise's sweet, tinny intonations. He smiled picturing
them waiting on him with anticipation. He placed his duffel
on the kitchen floor.

Robert checked his pockets. He felt the money the Army
had given him in small bills. He was ready.

Slowly, he walked further into the kitchen. The smells of
the food hit him like a punch to the gut. Since he'd gotten
back, he had purposely starved himself, eating only bland
food, saving himself for what he now saw and inhaled.

Fried chicken, short ribs, ham, macaroni and cheese in
two big black pans, greens, candied yams, fried tomatoes
and okra, cornbread, cakes, pies and a banana pudding. And
on a counter Robert saw his favorite, his mama's baked
spaghetti, purposely over-cooked and thick with cheddar
cheese.

Robert's stomach made a happy noise so loud that he
thought his family would hear it and discover his surprise.
He tried to ignore the feast as he continued his stealthy
approach.

"Damned Army never could do anything on time," said
Abraham in the living room.

"I'm telling you, we should call," said Marcus. He was
sitting on the arm of the sofa, something his mother would
never allow under normal circumstances

"I'm getting worried," said Theresa. "Maybe there was an accident. Oh Lord, that would just be my luck. Boy gets out of Vietnam alive and gets hurt on the Davison Freeway."

Denise was silent as the other spoke. She just sat breathing in measured rhythms. She had dreamed of this moment and no thoughts of disaster would ruin it for her.

"Take more than an accident to stop me!" said Robert from behind them.

They all turned to see Robert standing near the kitchen in his uniform. He looked tall and noble just like they did in the movies. For a second no one said anything. They just looked at him as if making sure they were not all having some group hallucination.

Then there was a loud, joyous shout from Theresa and they all stampeded toward him. Robert's already big smile was getting broader as they neared. Robert shoved his hands into his pockets, pulled out his Army pay and tossed it into the air.

"I'm home!" he shouted. He stomped the floor and threw open his arms.

Theresa got to him first and covered his face with kisses. He felt Marcus and Abraham grab pieces of his arms and shoulders and squeeze. They were all talking, saying beautiful things, the wonderful things he'd been dreaming of in the jungles of Vietnam.

But Robert didn't hear them all. His head was filled with light and sound as he took in the picture before him, savoring it and sliding it into his unforgettable memory as the money fell around them like confetti.

Denise clamped her self onto him, crying. Robert embraced her and thought about her beautiful face keeping him company while he was in hell. Later, he would be proud that his first thought of her was not of sex. It was of love.

Robert pulled Denise's face up and they kissed. They lingered, getting into each other's mouths such that Marcus laughed and Theresa blushed.

"Come on now," said Abraham. "Plenty of time for that later."

Robert and Denise kept up the little kisses as they separated. The heat between then was rising like bad thoughts and Theresa blushed again.

"You hungry?" asked Theresa.

"Hell yeah!" said Robert reluctantly breaking his connection to Denise.

Marcus was picking up the money Robert had tossed and smiling like a kid. "How much of this is mine?" he asked.

"Shoot, you can have it all," said Robert.

"Come on and get a plate," said Theresa. "The party don't start until later."

They all went into the kitchen and Robert made himself a huge plate of the food. His father brought him a cold Pabst Blue Ribbon Beer. They all watched him eat as he told stories of jungles, friends and death.

Marcus' smile had faded somewhat and Robert had no idea why. He supposed the kid was just afraid. He'd be eligible for the draft soon and Marcus had never been a fighter.

When Robert was done eating, he groaned and loosened his pants. They all laughed, happy that he was happy.

Robert and Denise glanced at each other with obvious intent. Abraham made an excuse about needing something for the party. He stood up announcing his departure and asking for Theresa and Marcus to go with him.

The sound of the closing door was still in the air when Robert started ripping at Denise's clothes. He was surprised to find that she was tugging at his belt and panting. He knew women liked it, but he'd never seen Denise like this.

"I just... wanna see it," she said.

"Damn," said Robert laughing.

Denise freed his penis and slipped him into her mouth, moaning something he didn't understand. Robert grew light-headed from the contact and felt his knees wobble. Denise had always been hesitant about this particular activity but now she hungrily swallowed him, licking wetly and making sexy noises.

Robert pulled her head away because he could feel his orgasm rising inside of him. He tried to pull her to her feet but she pulled him down to the floor with her instead.

Denise took her blouse off and jammed Robert's face to her chest. She gasped loudly as his mouth made contact with one brown nipple. She gasped again as his fingers found her panties and pulled them aside. The same fingers slipped inside her seconds later. Denise shuddered and threw her head back holding on to Robert's shoulders.

"Damn!" Robert said again.

Denise stood and pulled off her panties as Robert dropped his pants and they made love on the kitchen floor. It didn't last very long for Robert, this first time but it was like he had never had sex before.

As he felt his climax come, Robert envisioned his own life force filling him up, chasing out the anti-life that was war.

Robert rolled to his side, breaking the connection. He held Denise close and could feel her heat.

He closed his eyes and for a second, he thought that when he opened them again he'd and find himself on the moist ground in Vietnam, walking a step ahead of death.

But when he opened his eyes, he was still on his mother's kitchen floor; sinfully half naked with the woman he loved.

6

THE STACKED SUPREMES

Sarah put on a stack of 45's on the little record player. The phonograph's small speaker soon blared out Diana Ross' seductively pleading voice. Sarah turned and began to dance around the foot of the bed.

Thomas liked the new Negro music that was coming out of Detroit. It was different enough to intrigue and yet it had a familiarity to it. Some of the other Negro music was too much for him. It was like a language that he didn't understand, but Motown was fun and made him feel like he was cool for liking it.

When Sarah danced it usually meant sex. Thomas hummed along with the tune but wasn't completely in the mood. The Black man he'd beaten was still in his head, blocking the process.

He could still feel the strain as he leaned into the swing of the nightstick and the sick thud of the wood against the man's thick muscles.

"I ain't scared... not no mo'."

Sarah pulled up the t-shirt she wore as she moved closer to him. She let it get up to just where he caught a glimpse of her panties underneath. Suddenly, Barney the Black man was gone from his head.

Sarah took off the t-shirt and flung it at him in the bed. It landed on his chest and he smiled. She gyrated in her bra and panties and Diana Ross wailed her love.

The bra and underwear were soon shed and Sarah straddled him. Thomas was still in his underwear but that did not deter her. She licked and bit and played with him and then he swelled beneath her.

Sarah pulled him out of his briefs and inserted him inside her. She uttered a high note that matched the ones coming from the record player. The warm flesh of her wrapped around Thomas tightly and he lifted his hips, raising her off the bed.

Sarah ground herself onto him and pumped in a steady rhythm. Soon, she was lost in her desire, calling out his name, uttering random curses and the name of God.

When it was done, Thomas broke their connection and rolled behind Sarah and embraced her. She was still making pleasant sounds as she clasped his hands over her flat belly.

"Is it my dancing?" she asked. "Is that why it's so good?"

"It's everything," said Thomas. "Everything."

"You can be so sweet."

Thomas smiled but his brain immediately registered the qualifier "can be." Sarah had many qualifiers when it came to him. It always reminded him of their basic ideological differences and the fact that she had taken it upon herself to change him. Always with her he was a work in progress.

"Can be?"

"Yes," she said. "Sometimes you are and other times...."

"What?"

"You're not."

This was the place where he usually stopped talking. Sarah had a way of allowing you a way out of an argument, like a ramp on the freeway.

"Guess I'll have to work harder," he said.

Sarah laughed and he felt her stomach flex. "That's even sweeter," she said.

"Why do you like me?" he asked.

"Not that again," said Sarah. "I keep telling you these things aren't science."

"You mean like opposites attract?"

"I don't believe in that. Opposites fight like hell."

"We fight like hell," said Thomas with quiet authority.

Suddenly, she turned to face him. "What's this about?" She asked with concern in her voice.

"Just talking," he said. But truly he wanted to know.

She turned back away from him. "I like to think, Thomas that some people were meant to be together, you know like they say in the eastern religions; it's kismet, fate."

"I like the sound of that," he said.

She adjusted herself and he did as well, holding her tighter to him. He thought of God moving lives together, sealing fate with His will. And then he saw the face of the big Negro again, filled with anger and eyes that looked into him.

"So, you coming with me to McGinty's this week?" asked Thomas driving the man out of his head again.

"McGinty's." said Sarah grimly. "No thanks."

Thomas was cool but he desperately wanted Sarah to come with him. The cops met regularly at a local bar and it was an important social event. Not only was it a time for bonding, but careers were advanced there as well. Once the Mayor and the Chief both came by unannounced.

All of the single men brought their girls to show them off. If he kept showing up without her, they'd know she had a problem with cops and as soon as that fact had been accepted, they'd think Thomas was weak.

"It would mean a lot to me," he said.

Sarah said nothing and for a second Thomas felt that he would lose this one and have to show up without her and answer the "where's that pretty little thing of yours?" question all night.

"I know it is," said Sarah finally.

"I mean, I know it's not as important as the peace rallies and stuff we go to, but it's all I got, you know."

He hoped that she would find his comment sincere and not sarcastic. He was trying to let her know that he did a lot of things with her that he didn't like but he did them anyway out of love.

"Okay," said Sarah still facing away from him. "And don't think you're fooling me. You're always a good sport about the peace movement. I know you only go to please me."

She got up and headed for the bathroom. Thomas watched her walk away and savored the jiggle of her ass. She was a difficult woman, so unlike his mother who seemed to blow whichever way his father breathed.

Still Sarah made him feel great about himself and you couldn't put a qualifier on that.

Another record dropped and Diana sang about love again. Most of the Motown songs were about love, he thought. He could hear Sarah singing along in the other room and he smiled.

His life was not perfect but this part of it had moments. He had become wedded to the idea that he would build a life with Sarah. Life without her was an unpleasant thought, one that left emptiness in its passing.

But this was a bad dream that need not live in happy hearts, he thought. He thought only of The Supremes and love as Sarah emerged from the bathroom and danced her way back to him.

7

MARCUS

Levi Stubbs's voice thundered off the walls of the little house. The place smelled of food, beer and the sweat of dancing people. It was one of those cozy events that reminded Robert of the old quarter parties, warm summer night affairs given in someone's cool basement where you spent the night grinding on your favorite girl.

After making love to Denise three times, he had gone out with her to look at his old neighborhood. He'd been worried about coming back to a place that he didn't recognize. Three years in the service seemed like ten. He was pleased to find things still in pretty good condition.

He looked around the party and saw familiar faces from the neighborhood. There was Tyrone Griffin, T-Griff, his old high school baseball teammate and his older brother, Monkey Griff, who had gotten his name because of his long arms.

He smiled at Miss Stevens, a fifty-year-old widow, whose husband had died in a plane crash. She'd gotten a lot of money and spent her days going to church and taking care of her kids and grandchildren. She was on the dance floor moving like a woman half her age.

There was John Wesley, his summer league coach and Gwen Reed, a girl he'd dated before Denise who had remained his friend.

Robert felt warmth in his heart and the last vestige of this all being a dream were swept away by the happy faces in his home.

The Four Tops sang "Sugar Pie Honey Bunch" as the room rocked and the floor creaked with dancing.

Robert sang badly to Denise while holding a beer. She laughed and sang back to him just as badly. Robert looked over and saw his mother and father doing the same.

"Go on, daddy!" said Robert.

Abraham smiled at this and spun around eliciting cheers from the onlookers. Robert took another swig of beer and saw Marcus holding up a wall tapping a foot.

Robert broke away from Denise and grabbed Marcus and pulled him out to the dance floor.

"No, you know I can't—-" Marcus began.

"Everybody can dance tonight," said Robert.

Robert placed Marcus between Denise and Abraham and the family all danced together.

Marcus smiled and for the first time Robert realized that his brother had not smiled much since he'd gotten home. Marcus was pleasant but he had not been as elated as the rest of the family. Distantly, Robert's keen sense of his family sent off a soft alarm.

The group dance ended with the Four Tops song and Robert kissed Denise.

"I'ma get another beer," Robert said.

"I can get it honey," said Denise.

"No, you don't have to wait on me. I got it," said Robert and then a little belch escaped him. "Excuse me."

Robert walked off as Smokey Robinson's floating tenor sounded. He ambled into the kitchen past Monkey Griff who was eating a plate of food and talking to a girl.

"Monkey Griff!" yelled Robert. "What it be like?"

"It be like you tonight, Bobby," said Monkey Griff in a voice so deep that it seemed to slow his words.

Robert entered the kitchen, saw the Pabst Blue Ribbon piled into a bucket of ice and grabbed one. He opened it and took a drink. He'd had three beers already and each one tasted like the first. He remembered drinking the warm, no-name beer with Foster and Percy and a smile danced across his face.

Marcus entered the kitchen and Robert saw the flat, serious face of his brother had returned. What was it, he thought, that could have clouded Marcus' happiness on this day?

"Want a beer?" Robert asked.

"No, thanks," said Marcus. "Alcohol is part of the White man's plan to keep us weak."

Marcus had always been the family scholar and militant. It seemed that the last few years had only deepened his beliefs.

"Yeah, I heard that." Robert took a deep drink of his beer and laughed. "Man, when I was your age, I was drinkin', smokin' and everything."

"I know. I heard the arguments," said Marcus

"Yeah, I was a handful," said Robert in that way that difficult people have when they are impressed by their own sins. "But the service saved me, you know. I learned discipline, leadership. No tellin' where I'd be without it. Probably the graveyard-- or prison."

"The White man's Army saved you?" asked Marcus. "You saved yourself, Bobby. The man just used you to do his thing."

The militant was back, thought Robert through the haze the beer had put on his brain.

"What's wrong with you?" asked Robert. "Ain't you happy I'm home?"

"Yeah man," said Marcus, his face showing how suddenly guilty he felt for dampening his brother's return. "I am, but you know, this Vietnam thing and how they treat us back here—-"

"I know how people feel about the war, but you'll see when it's over, everything's gonna change."

"For who?" said Marcus with the same tone as before. "Not Black folk. Hell, even White people are against the war. Dig it, do you know who Shaun Thomas is?"

"That actor from TV, right?" said Robert a little drunkenly.

"No," said Marcus with some irritation, "This Shaun Thomas was a soldier like you, Black like you and he was killed last month by some White men for nothing. And the police and the newspapers tried to cover it up. But the Black paper, *The Chronicle*, did a big story on it." Marcus sounded like a schoolteacher lecturing a wayward student.

"Yeah, I remember. Mama told me about it. I know it was bad but so what?"

"After that, some pigs shot a Black prostitute and tried to blame it on a Black man, just gunned her down like a dog." Marcus' voice had grown louder now.

"For what?" asked Robert sobering a little at this revelation.

"Because they could," said Marcus urgently. "No matter what else she was; she was a person and a sister. The Big

Four are out busting heads every night, like them secret
police in Germany. The brothers are living in the worst
neighborhoods, no money for our schools, second-rate city
services and treated like we're still on a plantation. We're
tired of it, Bobby. This city's like a bomb waiting to go off.
Open your eyes."

And now Robert knew what had stolen his brother's
happiness. The Movement.

The Civil Rights Movement was a set of two separate
agendas. Martin Luther King led the non-violent movement.
Then there was the radical movement, advocated by the likes
of Malcolm X and the Black Panthers. They believed only
confrontation could free Black people. It was obvious that
Marcus was of the latter mentality.

"Look, little brother," said Robert. "We can talk about
this some other day. Today, I am celebrating and you know
why?"

Robert reached into his pocket and pulled out a buck
knife. It was a specially crafted blade that he'd bought from
a trader in Vietnam. It was steel with a black handle and
brass accents. He used it for utility but once had cut a Viet
Cong in a fight with it.

"This here is my reserve fighting blade," he said to
Marcus. "I ain't got no need for weapons no more. I feel like
I gotta get rid of all the war in me, you know. I know you
really can't do that but it's, what you call it?"

"Symbolic," said Marcus.

"Yeah. That there is the old me," he pointed to the knife.
"No more hurtin' my fellow man," said Robert and handed
the knife to Marcus. He did it slowly like he was exorcising a
demon from deep within himself.

"I know the man has a ways to go," Robert continued,
"but so do we."

Marcus took the knife, and Robert could tell that he didn't
want it but he accepted it, not wanting to hurt his brother's
feelings.

"Thanks," Marcus said without much feeling. "I know
you went through a lot over there. I want you to be at peace
about it, you know."

"I knew you'd understand it, Marcus," said Robert. "I can
always count on my baby bro."

"Hey, you know you can get into college easier now being a vet and all," Marcus changed the subject. "We need to learn all we can if we're going to change this country."

"Naw, I ain't no book guy. That's yo' thang. I'ma get a job at the plant or something, get me a little place with Denise; work on some little ones. Have a life, you know? I got a line on a job as a driver at the Faygo Plant."

They stood in silence for a moment, Robert finishing his beer and Marcus watching him. The sound of the party was cheerful but Robert could feel the unease in his brother.

"So, you got yourself a girl, yet?" asked Robert. "I know you shy." Women were always something two men could talk about freely.

Marcus blushed visibly. He was indeed shy when it came to girls. Once he had climbed a tree in order to see a girl he liked. He fell out of it and almost broke his arm.

"Yeah, yeah I got a girl," Marcus said smiling.

"What's she like? She's a fox, I know."

"You know she is."

"That's my little brother," Robert and Marcus slapped five on it. "On the black hand side," said Robert, then he and Marcus flipped their hands over and slid them across each other.

"I meet a lot of girls in The Van... guard," said Marcus and the last word slipped out in two distinct syllables as if he had not meant to say it at all.

"Van what?" Robert was a little drunk.

Marcus took a moment, his face showing that this might be a touchy subject with his big brother. "Vanguard. It's a political group."

"Political how? Marches? Rallies and shit?"

Marcus took a moment, then: "No. We don't believe in non-violence."

Robert's face clouded. That was the first time Marcus saw the soldier look, the hard, flat emotionless face of a killer. He felt himself recoil from the dark intent in his brother's eyes.

"You with them dudes who bomb shit and start fires?"

"It's called civil unrest, Bobby."

"It's called a damned felony in Detroit. How we gonna change things if we tearin' them down, burnin' them up? This is why Negroes can't get nowhere."

"I ain't no Negro. I'm Black," said Marcus.

"You're foolish. That's what you are," said Robert.

Marcus faced the larger man and tried to twist his face into the angry snarl that matched his brother's but to no avail. Whatever produced that look was not in Marcus.

"You go risk your life and kill some poor Vietnamese guy who lives in a hut because some White man says jump. Who's the fool?"

"The protected never understand their protectors," said Robert remembering the words of Lieutenant Ferguson. "You think I'm crazy because I served my country?"

"No, you're crazy if you think this *is* your country. I hear that mess all the time from daddy. I'm not buying it."

Robert took a step toward the smaller man, and then stopped. He had just given up his anger and now here he was about to hurt his own blood. He moved back a step and then the soldier face disappeared. He was just a man again.

"Look, we ain't gonna solve no problems in this old kitchen. Go on back to the party. I'll rap with you later."

Robert hugged his brother and Marcus didn't fight it. Marcus walked out of the kitchen carrying the knife, the symbol of his brother's former life.

Nothing was easy in life, Robert thought. Marcus was a kid when he'd left home. He was still a baby with baby ideas and a baby's love of his big brother. Now he was a man and his big brother had been replaced with ideas and hope. How could any man compete with those formidable giants?

The American people sent him and his comrades off to war. These same people who enjoyed the peace and freedom of this country didn't seem to understand it was purchased with death and blood. And so now they turned their safe, well-fed faces toward him with evil, judging eyes.

He'd marched into hell for an ideal and saw that ugliness become fodder for dignified speeches and self-righteousness. That's what it meant to be a soldier, a patriot, he thought, understanding that all great civilizations are built upon the most uncivilized of behavior.

Robert finished the beer, then grabbed another. He looked at the bottle for what seemed a long time and then put it back in the bucket. Enough drinking for tonight, he thought.

Robert walked back into his party but it had been drained of some of its joy.

8

<u>MCGINTY'S</u>

There was no alarm on McGinty's bar. No bars on the windows, even in the back facing a dark alley. The owner, Brian, was the fourth McGinty to run the place and he felt no need to even lock the door sometimes.

There was good reason for this lack of security. McGinty's was what the locals called a blue bar or cop bar. This meant that at any time of the day, there was likely to be several armed, off-duty policemen in the place.

Ian McGinty, a thin, snaky man, had opened the place in 1878 while still a cop on the police force. His son and grandson had kept the tradition.

If you were stupid enough to steal from McGinty's, you would be swiftly tracked down and dealt with. And it wouldn't be on the job. The cops would do it off the books as it were, and they'd administer their own brand of justice.

McGinty's was filled to the brim this night as Sinatra crooned in the background from a jukebox. The juke boasted one hundred and fifty songs. None of the artists were Black.

The place was done in a green that had faded from its glory days. There were Leprechauns, shillelaghs, four-leafed clovers and the like. It wasn't the most inventive décor, but no one came to McGinty's for the ambience. They came for the drinking, for the love and for the Irish, the love of drinking.

Thomas and Sarah hugged near the bar as Ned Young regaled a small crowd with his story. Thomas smiled dutifully and tried not to interrupt. Ned loved to tell stories and he was good at it. He embellished sometimes but that was part of being a good storyteller.

"... so this nigger, black as night and big as an elephant, is drunk and disorderly," Ned continued.

Thomas blushed at the use of the word nigger and he felt Sarah stiffen beside him. She made a disgusted noise but fortunately, no one else heard it.

"He's got a lead pipe big as a car in his hands," said Ned. "I'm looking at him thinking, goddamned spook's holding a Buick in his paw." There was more laughter and another louder sound from Sarah.

"People are running, women screaming," Ned continued. "I mean this big bastard's scaring the bejesus out of everyone within a mile. So we get up to him and I tell you, this guy's the size of a train."

Ned looked to Thomas who smiled and nodded like a good partner.

"So, we announce our arrival," said Ned. "But the nigger, he don't blink, this one. So, we move in and this sonofabitch is still not flinching. I get close and the bastard takes a swing at my head with the Buick!"

The officers laughed and chuckled and some of their dates gasped. Thomas felt like he was hugging a statue now. Sarah was pissed and he knew if he looked at her, he'd see her eyes ablaze.

"So now I'm mad, right?" Ned went on, happy to have control of the crowd. "So, I pull my weapon and the rookie here follows suit. I figure we'll just blast this darkie back to the jungle. We start in and still the guy's not flinching. I don't know what's gonna happen. Then the rookie asks me? 'Hey, do I shoot before or after you?'"

The group of officers exploded in laughter and applause. The crowd broke into random commentary and then Ned settled them.

"Well, the sonofabitch is thinking about it now. He looks at the rookie then at me then back to the rookie and drops the Buick and lays down all nice like."

More applause and someone slapped Thomas on the shoulder. He felt the statue he was hugging stiffen even more.

"So we cuff him and the damned things barely fit over his thick wrists," said Ned. "Then I hear the rookie say:" Ned turned to Thomas to finish the story.

"This shit ain't so hard," said Thomas to more laughter and applause.

"Then we——" Ned stopped. Thomas knew he was not about to talk about the beating they'd given the Black man. Ned was a little drunk but not so far gone as to admit to a felony to a room full of people. "We took the asshole in," he finished.

"Shit, they're making rookies smarter now," said Donald Brady, a tall, dark-haired cop that Thomas had seen around the precinct.

"He's a lot smarter than you were, Ned," added Matt Reid, Brady's partner. Shorter and much better looking, Matt Reid favored a young Gregory Peck.

"Up yours," said Ned.

"Buy you a beer?" said Reid smiling.

"I take it back," said Ned and the cops all laughed again.

Thomas laughed as well and turned to Sarah and saw her angry face.

"What's wrong?" he asked knowing full well what was bothering her.

"I'm going out back to smoke," Sarah said and without another word, she disengaged his hug and walked off.

"Where's she going?" asked Brady walking over with Reid.

"Ladies room, I guess," Thomas lied.

The small crowd was breaking into smaller conversations. Brady and Reid stood on either side of Thomas and for some reason, he felt uncomfortable. He knew their reputations as tough cops and no friend to Blacks.

Reid had been the subject of several brutality complaints and Brady had put a Black man in the hospital and had barely gotten a slap on the wrist.

Brady also had a cartoon on his locker that depicted a Black man hanging from a tree while several Klansmen watched. The caption read: "Another happy night in Alabama."

"Listen, even though you're a rookie," said Brady. "My partner and me want to invite you to the weekly poker game."

"You got grandfathered in—- literally," laughed Reid referring to Thomas' police pedigree.

"Thanks, but I'm not too good at cards," said Thomas.

"All the better," said Reid. "It's small stakes, no big deal."

"All right," said Thomas finishing his beer. "The game's at Bunson's place, right?"

Brady and Reid shared a look, just a glance, really. Thomas could tell it was partner telepathy, the way two cops who rode together had of knowing what the other is thinking.

"No, that's the *other* game," said Brady. "The company's better at our game. They let anybody in at the Brunson game. We're exclusive, elite."

"Come on, partner, don't shit the kid," said Reid. "There are no darkies at our game, Riley, just regular cops."

Thomas was glad Sarah was gone at this moment. She would have glared at him and dared him to accept the invitation or worse she would have unloaded on both men.

"Sure, I'm in," said Thomas.

"Good man," said Reid. "Wednesdays, nine sharp."

"Hey, look who's checking you out Riley," said Brady. He nodded his head in the direction of a woman with red hair who was keeping company with three men at a table across the room.

The men were all talking but the red head was looking at Thomas. She smiled and raised her glass a little. Thomas instinctively waived to her.

"'Ol Bedtime Barb," said Reid laughing.

"Who?" asked Thomas.

"You don't want to know," said Reid. "Shit, with that nice little thing you got, you don't need to know." And then the two cops laughed again.

Thomas looked at the two smiling faces on either side of him. It was as if they were forcing him to join some covert group. Race had become a divisive issue within the force over the last few years. Black cops had been added over the objections of veteran officers. Some White cops even refused to serve and had quit or retired. Thomas' father had been one of the resisters. He'd said many times that you could not trust a Negro with a gun.

Many of the new Black cops had been harassed and threatened; one was even shot at on duty under suspicious circumstances.

Another happy night in Alabama.

But in the end, integration had come in small numbers and old thinkers had moved on. But a cold war had started in the department and there was no end in sight.

"I'd better see where my girl has gone," said Thomas and he excused himself, feeling a small wave of relief as he slipped from between the two men. They were scary those two, especially Reid, with his stark blue eyes and square jaw. Something about the handsomeness of his face belied the malevolence Thomas felt from him, which made Reid seem even more evil.

Thomas entered the dark alley and found Sarah standing in the shadows smoking a joint. It was one of the few things he did not like about her.

Marijuana was the current way to give your country the finger. Sarah had asked him to try some but he had resisted. He hated the smell of it as much as he hated his mother's Winstons.

"Sarah, why do you... there's a bar full of cops in there," he said grabbing the joint from her fingers.

"Hey!"

Thomas dropped the vile thing on the alley floor and stomped on it. Sarah cursed and picked it up, putting the extinguished roach in her purse.

"Lighten up," she said. "I bet all of them have tried it."

"That's beside the point," said Thomas. "They don't do it in public at a cop bar."

"I can't believe I stayed in there as long as I did," she said. "Those fucking racists are the reason why things are so bad."

"They're good guys," said Thomas.

"I don't know if you ever heard this, but Black people don't like being called niggers."

"But there are no Negroes in there, Sarah."

"I'm sorry, that makes it okay." She said sarcastically, shaking her head. "They're worthless, all of them."

Thomas didn't like the way she shook her head at him all the time, like a mother whose kid has put his hand where it didn't belong. He was a little tired of it and prize or no, she needed to understand.

"Sarah, my father and grandfather were men just like the ones in that bar, he began.

"Yeah, I know," she cut him off which is why I work so hard with you—"

"Can you ever let me finish a sentence?" he asked with mild anger. Sarah stopped, looking a little guilty. "Sure, the men in my family weren't the smartest men on the block," Thomas continued. "But they kept me in clothes and they kept food on the table. They protected me and taught me right from wrong. I told you I was willing to work on changing how I think about things, but you're gonna have to excuse me if it takes a while for me to condemn everybody I love."

Sarah looked at him and might have had more argument in her but Thomas saw that logic had taken hold. She had a bad temper but she was always a woman of reason.

"But you're trying, right?" she asked almost like a little girl.

"For you, yes, I am. Every day."

"Good because our parents can't continue to control our future," she said. "We have to reject all their ideas in society and rebuild a new one."

"When did freedom and nobility go out of style?"

"When we denied them to other people," said Sarah flatly.

Thomas embraced her. "I love it when you talk like a commie. Makes me horny."

Thomas kissed her, cutting off her laugh. He grabbed her ass. He felt her fumbling at his zipper and his eyes widened.

"Here?" he asked in a low voice.

"Yes," she said smiling. "It'll be fun."

They moved further into the shadows, preparing to complete the sinful deed in their heads.

Thomas grabbed at her chest through her blouse and he felt his penis pushing against his zipper. He felt her hand pull down the zipper and make contact. He reached for her pants.

Before he met Sarah, he would have never dreamed of having sex in public like this. She was changing everything about him, he thought, and some of it felt real good.

Suddenly, there was a loud commotion from the bar. Sarah heard it too. She stopped and turned toward the back door.

They quickly began to put their clothing back in order. Sarah might smoke a joint in an alley but she didn't want to get caught doing this.

Ned burst into the alley. It took him a second to find the couple and his face never registered the compromising position they were in. Ned looked troubled and Thomas saw something else in his eyes: fear.

"Partner, we got trouble! All shifts are called in," said Ned.

"All shifts-- what is it?" Thomas asked walking back into the light holding Sarah's hand.

"The niggers," said Ned. "They're burning Detroit to the ground."

9

THE OLD BLOOD

There was fire....

Flame consumed wood and fabric, reducing them to carbon and dotting the landscape with evil, twinkling eyes.

Shocked and teary-eyed citizens watched as their homes and businesses died like men ravaged by disease.

Smoke plumes lurched toward heaven and without a summer wind to move them; they hung in the sky, evidence of cruel intent.

The long-suffering Blacks rampaged, burning, looting and menacing anyone with white skin.

Whites were moved to violence, some in defense of home and livelihood and others because the riot offered the chance to vent long-held hatred of the dark people.

The simmering pot of race relations in Detroit had boiled over again after a party at a blind pig, gloriously named The United Community League For Civic Action, was raided by police.

The city fathers knew the Negroes were on edge and angry. But hell, they were always angry, always complaining about something.

What they didn't understand was that the death of Shaun Thomas and the anonymous hooker had pushed nature beyond civilized boundary.

Within the Negro community, these killings were the latest un-avenged murders; slaughters by a White master whose viciousness had created centuries-old injustice.

And somewhere between the perceptions of Black and White, was the reality of man and his worst capacities. The connection to his savage evolutionary past overran the logic of civilized restraint.

The riot reminded many that whenever one man acted from the old blood; it awakened the same viciousness in the victim, and then comes death.

Krikor Messerlian, was sixty-eight years old the night the riots came. The genial man, whom everyone called George was driven into the street by the coming violence and looters at his beloved shop.
He fought to defend his little piece of America, using an old ceremonial saber. He wounded one of the looters but soon George fell to the assault and later died. He was the first person killed in the riot.

Robert Jackson watched the news of the death of the old man on television and knew things would get worse. The first body was always the worst, he mused. It confirmed reality.

He watched the flickering black and white images with shock and anger. The violence agonized faces and the uniformed men arresting civilians struck an ugly and familiar cord deep inside him. He had left the war but it had come home right behind him, like a rotting corpse rising from the grave.

Robert sat that first night wanting to go out and do something. He did not want to loot or do violence. But neither did he want to persuade people to stop. He knew all too well why his people were angry. There was too much violence in their history, too much pain. Too much blood. Like overripe fruit hung too long in a tree, the city had fallen to earth and burst open.

Marcus tried to leave the house, to go out and join what he called the revolution but Robert and Abraham had physically restrained him.

"Let me go!" said Marcus. "Our people need me out there!"

"We need you alive," said Abraham.

"Slow down little bro," said Robert struggling to hold him.

"How could you?" Marcus said to Robert. "You *know*! How could you?"

The tears in his brother's eyes made Robert understand why Marcus got involved in the Movement. They were only a few years apart in age, but those few years had seen a new attitude in Black America.

Robert in turn was different from his father. Abraham believed in religious-inspired non-violence. Marcus did not and Robert was in the middle. And so he stood facing the violent crisis and he was paralyzed, Jesus in one hand and a gun in the other.

Detroit burned all that night. During the day, the wounds of the assault were revealed in the light and the world was horrified. News services swarmed to Detroit, chronicling every bit of history they could.

Robert went to work that day. Many businesses had shut down but not his. His bosses were hard asses and did not want the "trouble" as they called it to stop their cash flow.

Robert had not received a call to stay home and so he'd gotten up and taken the bus in. Also, if he didn't come in, his bosses might think he was involved in the trouble and take it out on him.

Robert had gotten the job driving a truck for the Faygo soda pop company. Faygo was a hometown favorite. They made lots of flavors in wonderful bright colors. When you shopped for it, it was like picking Crayolas to consume.

Robert walked toward the gate to the facility and saw the frightened look in the eyes of his foreman, a Polish guy in his forties who had an unpronounceable name. And Robert saw something else. Guns. The security guards held shotguns and the foreman had a bulge in his jacket that had to be a pistol. But Robert had seen plenty of guns in his day. He never broke stride as he walked up to the gate.

"We got no work today, Jackson," said the foreman.

"What about pay?" asked Robert a little too quickly.

The foreman seemed to be insulted by this. "Since you showed, you'll get credit for the day," said the foreman. "Now go home to your family." Robert walked off, not looking back.

On the trip back home, Robert saw the destruction that had been wrought. Someone had knifed his beloved city and left it to die.

Robert got home well before nightfall. Marcus was safely home and still upset but not as much as the previous day. Robert regarded this with some suspicion but said nothing.

Instead, he joined the family who was glued to the TV for the rest of the evening.

As the sun slipped from the sky, Robert felt the dread rise from Detroit's still smoldering bones. Light faded and it looked like life itself leaving the body of man. Still, as the sun fell, Robert hoped the worse was over.

It was not.

The deaths continued. People were shot in acts of random violence or gunned down for looting by police. Even a firefighter, and a Black cop in uniform were killed in the chaos.

Robert realized the source of his suspicions about Marcus in the days to come. His brother was sneaking out in the wee hours to join in the rioting.

Robert decided not to challenge him, to let Marcus find whatever he was looking for. When he was Marcus' age, there was nothing that could keep him from street life. It was part of becoming a man, he reasoned.

What Marcus did out in the streets, Robert would never know, but each time Marcus went out, Robert prayed that his brother would return with the dawn.

Marcus bonded with his brethren devoted to the cause of destruction. If there was no freedom, then no one would have the city, they would burn it all down.

They were near Woodward Avenue on the third night of the riots, watching a real estate office. Although there was no evidence to support it, they all agreed that whoever owned it was not Black and was probably discriminating against Blacks.

Marcus and his cohorts moved toward the building, hiding in the shadows and looking for an opportunity to cross the large expanse of Woodward.

Suddenly, they heard vehicles coming. They ducked back into darkness. The vehicles came close and soon it was clear that it was not the police.

Marcus' eyes widened as he saw military men, not national guardsmen who were already in the city but infantrymen from the U.S. Army roll by.

"Muthafucka," said one man.

"They gonna kill us all," said another.

And now Marcus, for all of his anger, was afraid. Did they really want to die in a revolution? How could they resist tanks, rifles and trained soldiers? For the first time, the futility of the movement occurred to him.

But every revolution had heroic casualties, men and women who gave their lives for the cause to rally others around them. It was time for Black people to awaken and take their share of America and if it meant he had to die, then so be it.

Marcus and his crew moved away from the real estate office. The soldiers had spooked them too badly. They went back into the neighborhoods and turned their attentions to helping anyone who might be in danger.

On a street not far away, in the middle of chaos, a man tried to disperse an angry mob. But not just any man, this one wore a baseball uniform.

Willie Horton, one of the first Blacks on the Detroit Tigers' baseball team, stood astride a decimated car and yelled at the rioting crowd.

"Damn, it's really him," said someone.

"He's a fool," said Marcus. "Gonna get himself killed."

Marcus stared at the tall, muscular Detroit native as he pleaded with the people to stop what they were doing, telling them that they were only burning and stealing their own lives.

Marcus moved away from the famous athlete and turned his eyes back to the night.

Officer Thomas Riley stood on aching feet. He had been on those feet for more than twenty-four hours. As far as he knew, every cop and reserve in the city was patrolling somewhere.

Thomas, Ned and about ten other officers had suppressed a large group of Blacks near downtown. They made over thirty arrests. There were so many people and so few resources that many of the arrestees were hauled away on a flatbed truck.

Thomas had fought with a Black man who'd reached for his service revolver. Thomas hit the man in the face with his nightstick, breaking his nose. He could still hear the wet crack of it in his head. The image of Barney, the giant soon followed.

What bothered Thomas was not the violence he'd done but how easy it had been to do it.

As he watched the city burn and people steal the lives of others from their homes and stores, he heard the voices of his father and grandfather and how they felt about the dark people. And against his promise to Sarah, he believed every word, believed that they were as wretched as they'd said.

Ned sweated in his uniform as he hustled men into a truck. Ned was usually happy when he hassled prisoners but not this night. He looked tired and a little afraid. There were many more Blacks than cops and only guns and badges separated them.

"Heard a mixed unit had an incident at a hotel," said Ned. A mixed unit was National Guard and local cops.

"How bad?" asked Thomas, as he watched the last of the arrestees get onboard.

"A massacre is what I heard," said Ned. "Some niggers in a hotel with some White girls. Probably kidnapped and raped them, I imagine. Anyways, they're all dead."

"All of them?" Thomas' voice rose. "The women, too?"

"Didn't hear nothing about that. Just that the men bought it." Ned took off his hat and wiped his brow.

Ned's eyes darted off and Thomas, ever the alert partner, turned to see what had grabbed his attention.

Two Black uniformed officers were working the crowd. The department had called in all officers and they made no exceptions. One of the cops was tall and very dark the other was light-skinned and looked almost White.

"Look at that," said Ned. "You think they can be trusted at a time like this?"

"They're cops," said Thomas moving closer to his partner. "They wear the uniform." He heard himself say the words but he didn't know if he really meant them.

"I'd keep 'em all locked up and take their guns," said Ned, putting his hat back on.

The dark Black officer nodded at them. Thomas raised his hand and did a half salute. Ned mumbled a curse.

The truck carrying the prisoners rolled off. The street rumbled beneath their feet as it did. It took Thomas a few seconds to realize that it was not the police truck that made the ground shake but something else.

The cops working the area stood back as a military transport rolled down the street. It was filled with infantrymen in full gear. They carried M-16 rifles and wore camouflage uniforms. One of the men saluted them and Ned snapped one back.

"Oh, it's lights out for darkie now," Ned laughed.

This he said too loud because the light-skinned Black cop turned with an angry look on his face. He took a step in their direction and for a second, Thomas saw himself in the middle of a nasty incident but the other Black cop pulled his partner back and they walked off. Ned never saw this, which was good because he did love a fight.

Thomas and Ned walked back to their cruiser, when a White cop whose name Thomas could never remember approached them.

"Did you hear?" asked the cop who was thin and had brown hair.

"About the hotel thing?" said Ned. "We heard."

"No, worse than that," said the thin cop. "Somebody shot a Black kid, five years old. Killed her."

"A kid?" asked Ned. "How the hell—-"

"Said it was a sniper house," said the cop. "They saw a light and just fired."

Thomas now saw true fear in his partner's eyes. The death of a child was a chilling, heartless thing and for the first time, Thomas suspected that Ned realized that the subtle, often benign prejudices cops carried were just as deadly as the overt ones.

The cop with the red hair moved on telling anyone he could find the news.

Thomas stopped in his tracks by the door of his cruiser. He looked at the burning city and chaos and had a terrible feeling that there was more to come. He took in a sharp breath and then it seemed to burst from his lungs.

"Jesus," Thomas whispered.

"Don't think even he can help us tonight," said Ned.

The fires were extinguished, the wounded tended to, the dead catalogued and the soldiers redeployed.

The curfew was soon to be lifted but the wreckage of the past ten days would be with the little city by the river for decades to come.

Unthinkable acts had touched the lives of average people who'd never dreamed such things were possible in America.

Those old enough to remember the riots of 1943 had lived a nightmarish *déjà vu*.

Not many saw the startling parallels between the two riots. The nation was at war both times. The government turned its attentions toward international crisis and away from domestic concerns. A resentful White majority was left to work with the descendants of slaves who took jobs and opportunity in service of that war. And the Blacks felt justified in this because the government promised freedom and prosperity. But in the end, it never delivered.

Forty-three people officially died during the ten days of the riots, thirty-four of them were Black. Thousands more were injured, over four thousand arrested and millions in property damage was done. It was the worst urban riot in the history of the nation.

In the annals of the world, it was a small tragedy, not comparable to genocide, war, plague and natural disaster. But in those days, in that city, it looked like the end of everything.

The city pushed out the old blood with orgiastic ferocity. It was over, but a terrible levy had been paid and if there was a Devil, he was dancing.

The sun rose on that last day and the summer wind blew dark ash across the sky, like the tears of fallen Angels.

10

<u>REGION</u>

Robert's head was pounding as he awakened. In the dream, he was fighting the Cong, only he was in downtown Detroit and the Cong looked strangely like American soldiers and every man he shot had the sneering face of Peter Cole.

The riot was over, or so they said. The city was still under Marshall Law and the curfew had only just ended. But a city under Marshall Law is not a city, he thought. It was a zone, a sector 23; a place whose meaning was defined only by the destruction men had wrought. Detroit was now just a region.

He felt like a coward for not doing something about the problems he saw. But after being in one war, he knew that he could have gone out into the night to be some kind of a champion and maybe catch a bullet for his trouble.

It seemed as though the police and the soldiers were just shooting any Black person they found in the wrong place at the wrong time. He couldn't believe that grown men went out and risked their lives for a bag of groceries, some cigarettes or a TV set. It wasn't like the war, he thought. It wasn't like they needed the stuff to live.

Marcus had told him that the urge to loot was an act of defiance. The men who did it cheered the apparent fall of a tyrannical order and in the wake of it, everything was for the taking. And that's why the police killed them for it. They were protecting the order.

Robert didn't understand any of the fancy ideas his brother spoke of; all he knew was that it was silly to die for a pack of Camels and a beer.

Robert walked into the kitchen with food on his mind. He found Denise and his mother having breakfast. The bacon and grits were a pleasant diversion from the ache in his head.

Robert and Denise had made love almost every night of the riot and the desperate feelings that drove them to it were never spoken of. He had never had sex like that, borne of a mixture of fear and love. And it wasn't so much good as it was vital.

Abraham came in and Theresa shouted down to Marcus who now slept in the basement. There was no answer. She called again but not a sound emanated from below. Finally, Theresa headed to the basement door, which was just off the kitchen and the pantry.

Something in Robert panicked.

"I'll get him," Robert said. He got up from his seat and went to the door then down the creaky stairs.

The basement was big. Many of the old Detroit houses had large basements for storage. Root cellar, his mother called it. Robert vaguely remembered the coal chute that was now gone, a gas furnace in its place.

Robert got down to the bottom of the stairs and saw immediately that Marcus was not there and from the still immaculate bed had not been there all night. Then he heard a window open on the far side of the big room. Marcus entered, wiggling through backwards.

"Get up boy!" Robert said for the benefit of his mother. The sound startled Marcus who almost fell while sneaking back in.

Marcus turned to face his angry big brother. Robert pointed up to the kitchen. "Lazy ass!" he said again. Marcus nodded and began to undress.

Marcus joined the family feigning sleep and hunger. He had obviously not eaten and hadn't slept so the ruse went over. Robert tried not to look accusingly at him during the meal.

All the breakfast conversation was about the riot, how it was over and what it meant. Marcus said precious little and soon excused himself to go back to his room.

Robert wanted to wait until later to talk to Marcus. Theresa went off to church and Abraham was going to the stadium to work on the field. The riot had chased the team away but now that the worse was over, the Tigers were coming home.

Robert was actually excited about this. The Tigers and the Red Sox were in a two-way race for the pennant. If the Tigers prevailed, they would go to the World Series.

After his parents were gone, Robert found Marcus on the kitchen phone, talking. Marcus stopped talking when Denise and Robert entered. He spoke in vague "Uh huhs" and "Yeahs," then hung up.

Denise could sense a conversation coming, so she went into their bedroom and closed the door.

That Robert had covered for him was not an issue. That's what brothers did for each other. Robert wanted to know why he been made to take the action.

"Where were you?" asked Robert.

"With a girl," said Marcus flatly.

Normally this might have been the end of the conversation. Robert would slap five with his baby brother and do some male bonding. But Marcus' admission was missing something, that sense of lusty satisfaction a man got when he was sneaking.

"Bullshit," said Robert. "You was running with them niggas, The Vanguard.

Marcus looked at Robert with the eyes of a man, a very angry man who was fed up about something.

"Okay, I was. I saw the girl, then I got with the Guard and we did some things."

"What things?" Robert could feel his anger swelling.

"Protecting our people from White killers," Marcus said as if surprised that Robert would not know this mission. "They killed a baby, did you know that? They are shooting Black people on sight. We went around telling people to stay in and discouraging others from looting."

"And y'all didn't set any fires or beat down any White folks?" asked Robert angrily.

"I can't talk about the group's actions," said Marcus. "I'm sworn to secrecy on that kind of thing."

"Secrecy," said Robert derisively.

"At least I'm doing something for my people," said Marcus, the accusation was laden with spite.

Robert didn't know how to respond. He could not deny that things were bad and he had felt the urge to go out and take action but had done nothing. Still, he was the big brother and needed to show Marcus his folly.

"It ain't your job to save stupid folk while this shit's going on."

"Fuck that!" Marcus said. Robert could not remember his brother ever cursing. "This is it, the revolution is here! The chickens have come home to roost."

Robert knew that he could not engage Marcus in a debate. He was not smart enough to win that kind of fight.

"Don't go back out," said Robert with conviction.

"The curfew is over today," said Marcus.

"I don't care. You're still a minor and you can't just do what you want," said Robert surprised of his parental tone.

"I'm not going to stop," said Marcus defiantly. "We have a mission."

"Fuck your mission," said Robert. "You go, I come after you."

Marcus shook his head sadly at his brother. "What the hell did they do to you over there?" asked Marcus. "Aren't you tired of seeing your people get killed, raped and lynched? We got a chance to do something. I'm taking it."

"There ain't no glory in war," said Robert. "It's all death and pain. You and some fools are going to try to take down the government? Be for real."

"That's what they said to Washington and Jefferson and *them* fools. There are plenty of White folks who see things our way, too."

"You're being stupid," said Robert.

"I'm being a man." Marcus set himself straight and looked his brother right in the eyes. "Not like you."

Before Robert knew what had happened he saw his hands around his brother's throat. Marcus hit him hard in the jaw but Robert took the blow like it was nothing. Marcus hit Robert again but this time the blow landed in his flat, hard belly. All the while, precious air was being cut off from Marcus' lungs.

Marcus grabbed Robert's arms and pushed as hard as he could. He thought he dislodged the bigger man but Robert had let go voluntarily.

Robert shot out a hand and slapped Marcus hard across the face. The slap hurt but it was the humiliation of it that stung the most. Women and kids get slapped, not men.

Marcus kicked out and caught Robert in the gut. This time the big man backed up, infuriated by the attack.

The soldier's face appeared.

Robert crouched a little and advanced toward the younger man. He looked at Marcus' eyes, trying to decide which action to take to hurt him. There were several easy ways to do it. He just had to choose....

"What the hell is going on in here?" asked Denise from behind Robert.

The sound of her voice cut through Robert like a bullet. In an instant, he remembered life, home, love and peace. He remembered his renouncement of violence and that he loved his brother.

"Nothing," said Robert coming out of his fighter's crouch. "We're just talking."

"Brothers fighting," said Denise. "It's stupid."

"Ain't no brothers in here," said Marcus grimly. "Not anymore."

Marcus turned and ran out of the kitchen's back door. Robert bolted to stop him but felt Denise's hand on his shoulder. He stopped and turned to her, his face filled with regret.

"What did you do?" she asked.

Robert had no answer. He just looked out at the day which was already half over and knew that the city would soon descend into darkness with his brother in it.

Thomas felt the aspirin he'd taken dissolving his headache. The last ten days had taken a toll on him. He didn't feel like a rookie anymore, although it would be some months before his probation was over.

He'd missed the war over seas, but his trial by fire during the riots made him feel fully battle-tested. He'd never forget the flames licking the sky or the bloodied Black faces being loaded into paddy wagons and trucks. But mostly he'd remember himself, a young man thrust into hell and fighting to make sense of it.

Thomas drove as he and Ned patrolled an affluent part of the west side. After the riot, this was like a vacation. Many officers had taken medical days. They were burned out and living with the memory of what happened and what they'd done to stop it. Any cop who had been involved in a shooting had been told to take time off. Thomas thanked God again that he hadn't had to use his weapon.

It was night, but you could see that the houses were big and the lawns green. It was as though there had been no riot in this part of town. They passed a house with a cherry red Cadillac in the driveway. Thomas loved that car and had always dreamed of owning one.

"They're living pretty good out here," said Thomas.

"Tell me about it," said Ned. "I should be so fuckin' lucky."

"So, I hear the soldiers are going to leave soon," said Thomas.

"Yeah, it's a shame. Don't think we would have survived without 'em."

"Do you remember the forty-three riot?" asked Thomas.

"Do I?" said Ned. "It was a helluva thing. It started with a fistfight on Bell Isle. It was mostly Polish and Black that fought. And you know how tough them Poles are. Well, it escalated and soon, Black and White were roaming the streets just beating the shit out of anybody that came along."

"We lost a cousin in that riot. Dennis. Beaten to death in an alley. What the fuck causes all this?" Thomas wondered aloud.

"Who knows with them people? You saw what happened out there. They're like goddamned animals."

Thomas did not respond. He heard Sarah's voice saying that the real cause was a lack of freedom. But if she could have seen what he'd been through, she might well change her mind, he thought.

He was as open-minded as the next guy but the Blacks he saw were far from peaceful and civilized. They burned and wrecked their own neighborhoods as if they didn't care and braved death for a few trinkets.

"Yeah," he heard himself finally say.

They saw another patrol car pass on the other side of the street. Then they heard the booming voice of Don Brady.

"Wake up you lazy bastards!" he said over the radio.

"*You* wake up," laughed Ned.

"We're assigned the north and southeast section," said Brady.

"And we got the rest," said Ned. "I guess after all this shit; the rich folk wanna feel secure.

"Hol-lee shit," Thomas heard Matt Reid say.

"What?" Asked Ned.

"Some darkie," said Brady. He's headed your way."

"Copy," said Ned. To Thomas, he said. "Look out for him." Then he mumbled. "That's all I need tonight."

"But there's no curfew anymore," said Thomas. "What's he doing in this neighborhood at night, rookie?" asked Ned. "Let's find out."

Marcus hoped the cops who'd just passed hadn't seen him. He moved faster. The blow up with Robert was bad enough but now he'd let the sun set on him.

He'd been assigned by The Vanguard leader to watch one of the other members. It was rumored that the FBI and the local police were trying to plant informants within Black militant groups.

The man Marcus was assigned to watch hadn't done anything suspicious and so he'd gone to see his girl. They had sex and it was good but he'd lost track of time and the night had caught him when it was time to leave. Now he was trying to get back home without being seen. Even though there was no longer a curfew, there was still the unwritten law of being Black in a White neighborhood.

Marcus cut through a backyard. He walked quickly across it, moving around a child's swing. He was about to jump the back fence, when a dog darted out at him barking furiously.

"Shit!" Marcus almost yelled. The dog, an albino German shepherd growled and snapped at him while it strained the chain that was fastened to its collar. Marcus saw lights go on in the house from the corner of his eye and bolted over the back fence.

He darted across an alley and out into the next street. He had to stay on the residential streets because the cops and the National Guardsmen who were still present patrolled many of the main thoroughfares.

The police car's lights almost made Marcus jump out of his skin. The short blast of a siren was like a bolt of lightening. He felt his muscles charge with adrenalin and before his mind could fully register the dilemma, his body had leaned forward into a run.

Thomas saw the Black man come into the street and hit the siren. Then he saw him take off so fast that it was like he was never there.

"We got him!" said Ned into the radio. "He's headed east!"

"Copy," said Brady. "We'll try to cut him off."

"We'll never get him in the car," said Thomas.

"Okay," said Ned. "You go after him. "I'll keep circling so that he won't know you're after him. Brady and Reid will back you up.

Thomas got out of the car and ran after the suspect. He felt the wind curl around his face as he hit his stride. He'd never catch a man as fast as the one he'd just seen fly off. His only chance was to outsmart him.

Thomas cut through the yard he'd seen the Black man go in then headed for the next street.

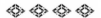

Marcus moved to a house with a big yard but found no place that would hide him. He thought about ducking under a car but that was no good either, too easy to figure out if he just disappeared. Most of the garages were locked and if he broke in, he might be heard.

Marcus stopped in the side doorway of a house whose lights were all turned off and caught his breath. He was in the shadows but only partially hidden. He cursed his bad luck.

Suddenly, his heart leapt into his throat. He saw a man move down the street. He only saw him for a second and ducked back into the doorway. When Marcus looked back out to the street in the other direction, he saw a White uniformed cop.

"Damn," he muttered under his breath.

Marcus backed into the yard of the house and jumped over the fence landing in an alley. At the end of the alley, he saw a patrol car roll by slowly at the cross street.

Panic gripped him and for a second, he was frozen, paralyzed by fear. There were two cops who had split up or worse there were two patrols and they were all after him.

Dread filled him and he had visions of being caught by the officers, beaten, tortured and killed. The fact that they were even after him when he had done nothing told him that it would not be pleasant if he were caught. He vowed that they wouldn't catch him; that the forces of fate would fall to his side of the struggle.

"Move," he said to himself. "Move, dammit."

Thomas had lost the man. He could be hiding in any of these yards, he thought. He suddenly felt that it was not worth it. He was just some guy who went out for liquor and lost track of time.

And then he remembered that there were no liquor stores close by and there had still been incidents of violence against Whites. Okay, he told himself. The man was probably up to no good and so they had to find him.

Thomas got to the corner and moved over to the next block. As he passed by the alley, he saw a figure standing there. It was a man. Thomas only saw him for a second before he ran off, jumping a fence into another yard.

Thomas took off and followed the man's path. He ran down the alley after him. His feet pounded the gravely ground and his vision jumped with each stride. This man was quick and smart but he didn't know this neighborhood. If they didn't get him soon, he'd make it to a main street and once he did, he'd blend in with the other Negroes who were bound to be out.

Then he saw something else move. It looked like another shape following the first one but he couldn't be sure.

Thomas got to the place where the man or men had been and saw a figure running into the next street.

He checked his gun and then went after him.

Matt Reid and his partner got out of their patrol car and ran after the Black man they had seen. He had darted across the street and was moving east as they had been told.

He was fast, they thought. They each pulled their service revolvers and began to search. This man, Reid mused, was the unluckiest man in Detroit.

Marcus was panicked beyond all reason. If he didn't lose them soon, they'd close in on him and there was no telling what might happen after that. He'd heard horror stories of Black men disappearing or being held in secret locations and beaten or worse.

Marcus crouched behind a parked car. He took out the knife Robert had given him. He thought about tossing it away to avoid a weapons charge but what if he needed it? Even though the riot was over, the cops still thought they had license to do whatever they wanted to any Black man caught in a compromising situation and this definitely qualified as one. Marcus put the weapon back into his pocket.

Marcus looked at the next street from behind the automobile. It looked clear. He walked from behind the car and into the street. By his calculations, he was close to safety. All he had to do was avoid them a little longer.

Marcus ran out and up the street. He made it to the corner, which was blessedly dark. He moved into the welcome shadow then stopped short.

Someone was already there.

The gunshot sounded like thunder. Flesh and muscle were torn and shock pushed the eyes of the young boy open. Warm blood flowed from the wound in his neck and he felt the dominion over his body slip away.

He descended.

His body moved backwards the short distance between himself and the sidewalk.

And then he fell again. He fell from his mother and her giant hugs and unconditional love. He fell from his father whose emotion was guarded but always present behind his strength. He fell from friends, love, sex and hope of the future-- and he fell from Robert; his brother who had always been in his life in more than body.

Marcus hit the hard pavement, bounced off the concrete and then crumpled into itself.

And the last picture of his life, the last thing he saw was the blanket of the night sky filled with stars.

11

<u>CAIN'S MOURNING</u>

Robert had seen death. He'd held it and looked it in its eternally pitch eyes. Death could do terrible things and one of its worse acts was to pass you by and take someone you love.

Marcus' murder hit the Jackson family like a stroke from God himself. Theresa had passed out twice, once when the police came to tell them the bad news and again at the wake.

Friends embraced the family in their grief and everyone understood the irony that one son had returned from the war unhurt and the other was killed by an enemy at home.

Denise had cried a river and did not eat for two days. Finally, Robert had to force her to eat for fear she would make herself sick.

The family sat at the gravesite on the day of the funeral. Marcus' coffin was perched on a platform like an unwatchable apparition. Robert could barely look at it. He sat there like a child trying to will it away. This had not happened. No one killed his kid brother, shot him down at seventeen and snatched him from a bright future and the love of his family. No, that thing, that box was empty, a container filled with a bad joke.

The official report said that Marcus was out after dark and had been shot by persons unknown. It was surmised that he'd gotten into a fight with someone using a knife and was shot in the neck, tearing his jugular vein apart. He'd bled to death in a matter of moments.

Three White policemen were at the scene of the death and a fourth had arrived later. None of their weapons were discharged or matched the slug that was taken from Marcus' corpse.

Had there not been a riot, these circumstances would have aroused suspicion and anger. There would have been investigations, accusations, and blustery Black ministers wailing about injustice in that soul-stirring cadence, telling the world that this boy's death was another injustice born of hatred. Marcus' face would be plastered all over the newspapers and TV. He'd be a symbol for lost youth, innocence and tragedy.

But so many were already dead. Many lives had been lost in the days of rage and Marcus' death was not an official riot casualty. So, no one seemed to care. There were no stories, no angry preachers and no murals painted on the walls of vacant buildings. There was nothing but the deep silence of personal anguish.

What people were still angry about was the child that was killed by police and the unarmed men who were shot to death in the Algiers Motel for being with two White women. The latter was the perfect story. It had sex, violence and the taboo of miscegenation.

Abraham had taken the death hard but as usual went through it with quiet resolve. There were times when Robert was amazed at his father's strength. The prejudice Abraham had suffered in the south and then later in Detroit would have broken weaker men. Abraham faced a parent's worst nightmare speaking only of faith and eternal salvation.

"... God practices forgiveness," the Minister said over Marcus' coffin. "In these troubled times, we must remember the lessons of the Son who paid the ultimate price and his Father, our Lord, who sacrificed Him so young men like Marcus Jackson could know the Kingdom of Heaven."

Abraham nodded silently as if the Minister had read from his heart. Theresa was crying and just shaking her head, unable to look at the awful coffin.

Guilt gnawed deeply at Robert. He had given Marcus the knife and he had driven his brother out into the streets, filled with anger.

He felt like Cain after he slew his brother. Robert turned his eyes away from God, not wanting to pray or call on Him for help.

Surely God would ask him where his brother was and unlike Cain, he could not say he was not Marcus' keeper. He'd tried to protect Marcus but had let his anger get the better of him.

There were so many other ways he could have handled
the fight, but hindsight was a cruel companion that never
understood the realities of the heart.

He couldn't remember if the Bible said anything about
Cain's mourning but Robert was sure that Cain did mourn
and that his lament was soiled with self-contempt and
radiated a power that could move Heaven and Earth.

The Minister finished his eulogy and the family stayed
while the coffin was lowered into the ground then covered
with earth.

The small crowd of immediate family that was left broke
up and moved away, leaving the funeral.

Robert noticed a young Black girl wearing a black scarf.
She was looking at the family. Other people milled about
her but she just stood there, staring at them.

The girl was pretty and had big, beautiful eyes that were
moist with tears. They were an unusual shade of light brown
and jumped out from her dark face. She covered them with
a pair of dark sunglasses and walked off.

Robert helped his mother leave. She was still crying and
Denise was starting to cry as well. Abraham took Theresa's
other arm and nodded to Robert to go to his wife. He did
and Denise managed a half smile at his touch.

Robert moved toward the funeral home's car, a black
caddy that gleamed on a hillside near the street. He noticed
the headstones that dotted the area and wondered how
many families had made this walk recently.

And then he saw him.

It was just a moment and Robert was sure that the man
did not know he had been spotted. He was behind a tree on
the hill. The interloper stood out because there had been
none like him at the funeral.

A White man.

He was tall and wore casual clothes. Definitely not
invited, he reasoned. Robert caught his full face as he turned
and walked quickly away.

Robert stopped walking as the image of the White man
kicked his mind into a higher gear. Why was he spying on
the gathering? Did he work at the cemetery? Or was he one
of those weird guys who were fascinated by death?

"Are you okay, baby?" He heard Denise voice rise beside
him.

Robert turned to her and saw the sad and concerned look on her face. He tried to look comforting, as he did not want his wife to hurt anymore than she already did.

"I'm fine," he said and started moving again.

Robert took a few steps and then turned in the direction of the White man he'd seen but the man had moved on. He was far away from them now; a dark shape against the bright morning.

The police ruled Marcus' death an unsolved homicide, a case whose file would eventually be put on a shelf and forgotten.

Robert had made it his business to find out the names of the officers who were at the scene. Officers Donald Brady, Matthew Reid and Thomas Riley. The fourth officer, Ned Young, had reportedly arrived to the scene late.

Robert wanted more information on the cops but he didn't know where to begin. He needed an inside man but he didn't know any cops. But he did know vets, he quickly reasoned.

He went to the VA and set about finding a Black cop who'd been in Vietnam. It didn't take long to find one, a guy his age named Levi Underhill. Levi had been in combat and was lucky enough to get wounded and returned stateside.

They met on the eastside in at a little Polish café near the Martha Washington movie theaters. They were in Hamtramck, a little city within the city of Detroit, an enclave for residents of Polish ancestry.

Levi had heard about Marcus and was more than happy to assist. The Black cops in the department were still treated unfairly and Levi was sure that there had been foul play.

"They ain't never had no heart in this department," Levi said in his smooth voice. He had been a singer once and you could still hear the lilting tenor in his tones. "DPD is getting' better but we still got some bad apples, you know"

"I'm just tryin' to find out who killed my brother," said Robert.

"Well, be careful. They would not blink before killing another brother, you know."

"I ain't that easy to kill."

"So, I heard," said Levi, laughing a little. "I hear you was a real badass in the Corps."

"I got the job done." Robert smiled a little.

It took Levi only a week to come back to Robert with the info he needed on the police officers.

Levi had come to Robert on his day off and they both went downtown together. They waited until the shift change and camped outside headquarters and waited.

One by one they walked up. Brady and Reid came by first together. They looked thick as thieves as they glad-handed people on their way in. They were treated like two minor celebrities, these two.

Robert burned their faces into his memory.

And then he saw Thomas Riley, the same man who had invaded Marcus' funeral.

Something exploded inside of him; an anger and rage that he'd never known. His muscles tightened and his fists curled into hard weapons.

Levi asked him something about being okay but all Robert heard was white noise.

The man was guilty, he thought. So guilty, that he had come to the funeral and risked being seen. So guilty, that he had waited to watch the body lowered into the earth.

He did it, Robert thought. He killed Marcus and couldn't bear the strain of the remorse he felt.

"You okay, man?" asked Levi.

"Huh? Yeah, I'm cool, " said Robert

Robert said nothing to Levi of what he knew. He liked the man and didn't want what he was about to do to involve him.

Robert thanked Levi. He offered him money but Levi seemed to be insulted by the gesture. They shook hands and went their separate ways.

Robert let the anger course through him. It felt good, like redemption. If the war had followed him home, then he would engage it with everything he had.

Robert Jackson walked away from police headquarters, putting his pledge of nonviolence into the grave with his brother.

PART TWO

MAN'S REDEMPTION

January 1968 – May 1968

"A revolution is coming... we can affect its character; we cannot alter its inevitability."

- Robert F. Kennedy

12

THE DEAD CLUB

The gun was slippery with blood in Thomas' hand. It felt heavy and his finger could not settle on the trigger without sliding. He wiped his hand but the blood was constant.

Whose blood stained him he did not know. Either it was someone else's or it was his own blood and he was dying.

He moved along the darkened street, his legs heavy with effort. His footfalls sounded like wet crashes. He saw dim light in the distance but it wasn't real; it was a shimmer, a mocking brightness that suggested hope.

"I am dreaming," he told himself. "This is not real. I've been here before. I need to wake up now. *Now!*"

Another step.

He could sense the room he was in, the bed, the sunlight from the window, Sarah's warm body next to him, still he could not awaken.

He kept moving. He was after something he thought, yes he was chasing something but it was elusive, a notion just outside of his perception.

He tightened his grip on the weapon as he moved faster and somehow he knew there was only one round left in the chamber, one chance to save his life.

Thomas headed toward the scornful light. As he approached, he saw it expand. Voices rose on all sides and he felt the wail of the riot's victims, the roar of fire uncontained, the scream of a woman, the bass grunt of a man struck with a nightstick and the tiny, screech of a child shot by a bullet.

He entered the light and felt his already tired legs begin to buckle as he saw his beloved Cahan lying next to the bloody body of Dennis, the cousin who they'd lost in the '43 riot. His face was a mass of swollen flesh and one eye sat milky and colorless in a socket.

More startling was the gun Cahan held to the head of Shaun. Cahan's face was filled with hatred. Thomas knew he meant to do it, kill Shaun again. And then he saw Shaun's face contort into an angry glare as he raised his hand. In it was another gun and Shaun leveled this at the head of Marcus Jackson whose bloody neck gushed a steady stream of red.

Marcus smiled.

Thomas wanted to run because in that smile was malevolence that struck clear to the bone. But it was too late. He tried to turn but he was in that thick dream haze; that state that froze you until you saw the end of the apparition.

Suddenly, the Black boy's dark hand was near his face and it lifted yet another gun-- and fired.

Thomas pulled himself into consciousness, the threads of the nightmare held him for just a second before they were gone. A dull throb rumbled in his head and his heart thundered.

He'd been having this vision since the funeral of the dead boy. Sometimes it was Shaun who shot him, sometimes Cahan but always, he was killed.

He got out of bed and was hardly aware of his body as he stepped into a warm shower moments later.

Detroit had not healed. A scab had grown over the wounds of the previous year. Winter covered the city's ugly face with ice and snow, making it easier for the mind to forget.

But spring was coming in a few months. Thomas and every cop in Detroit had been told that another evil had seeped into the city after the riot. Militant Negro gangs, communist sympathizers and other "pinko" groups had come into Detroit to exploit its troubles.

Racial animosity still lingered and this was a useful recruiting tool. No pro-Black group could be trusted and the police suspected that many otherwise legitimate organizations, including churches were harboring criminals and supporting violence.

Of less concern to the police were the various "White Power" groups. They were to be watched also but only insofar as they could incite violence with other targeted groups.

Thomas could feel the tension that hung behind the post-riot life. People were less friendly, more suspicious and seemed to move more quickly not wanting to linger when outside.

And you didn't have to look hard to find some of the Black militant groups. Most of the known ones were very vocal. They preached of revolution and freedom in the land of the free.

The Panthers and Black Muslims were seen as viable alternatives to the SCLC, C.O.R.E., the NAACP and other nonviolent groups. Which way would the Negroes go?

But these vocal militants were not the groups the police briefed Thomas on. There were more extreme subversive groups like, Mandingo, Dark War, The Vanguard, Black Cong and others. These were really terrorist organizations. Poverty, anger and resentment were their currency. They descended on the city, spreading the message that violence was the only choice left to the Black man in America.

Thomas and the other officers were given as much info on these groups as the FBI could share without losing its secretive and superior nature. He had even attended a seminar conducted by an FBI special agent on how to infiltrate subversive organizations with street informants.

Thomas finished his shower and dressed. The ghosts that haunted him were gone. He grabbed a cold piece of chicken from the fridge, kissed a still slumbering Sarah on the cheek and left for work.

He drove toward downtown, pass the rubble and burned-out buildings and felt a familiar pain in his heart. Something had died and not just a neighborhood or even a city. Something of America was gone, he thought and he couldn't put his finger on it.

Later, Thomas stood at his locker in the ready room, getting changed for work. The room smelled of man-funk and cleaning solutions. That smell had offended him a year ago but now it was pleasant; it was home.

Many officers wore their uniforms to work but Thomas liked to make a transformation at the precinct. It made him feel like he was a superhero, like Superman going into a phone booth.

He and Sarah had postponed their wedding after the riot. They'd told everyone that it was just school and work that had gotten in the way; the truth was Sarah was getting a bad case of cold feet. Not the kind where she wondered if she was doing the right thing; it was the kind that centered on the man she was supposed to marry.

Thomas had taken the news hard. He was no longer a rookie and looked forward to the rest of his life as a cop. As he took this first confident step, Sarah told him that she didn't see any change in him, that he had not kept his promise to her.

The riot had taken a lot out of Sarah. She had not run away from the ugliness like a lot of White people. She and her protestors had shifted away from the war and joined the civil rights groups in damning the Mayor, Governor and the President.

She was out all day and came back in during curfew. She was on her feet for three days straight during one stretch and nearly passed out from exhaustion.

When it was all over, when she had looked into the heart of America, into her own heart, Sarah considered the man she loved and had doubts.

She had told Thomas that a man was made in childhood. Thomas had two generations of intolerance and ignorance in his home. How could he ever turn his life away from the things that had made him?

Thomas wanted to tell her to go to hell, just dump her and fall into the bosom of the people around him. Sarah thought his friends were racists and bigots but those were just words, perceptions that could be seen different ways by different people. And hadn't he asked her to be patient with him? Why wasn't *that* an issue? How she pushed and prodded him to be what she wanted but had no stomach for her own change?

He could find a girl who didn't judge everything, have some kids and go on to his destiny. There were plenty of them out there. There was one girl who worked for the courts who had big tits and a cute face. She was always flirting with him and her father was a cop.

But when Thomas looked into Sarah's eyes, he saw the truth and the truth was that he was disjointed, out of sync with the changing world and holding on to notions that felt like they were crumbling into dust.

If only he could get his head around it, he thought. He didn't dislike Negroes. Mostly, he didn't think about them. He did think they had some bad habits but he guessed it was just how they were. Hell, the Irish were no goddamned prize either. Just a couple of generations ago, they were the scum of the earth.

But he could not deny that he felt superior to Negroes. Everything he saw told him he was. His people had been immigrants and many of them indentured servants. They were treated like cattle and discriminated against. They'd built America and had not complained about their treatment. And eventually, they claimed a share of the American dream.

Why did the Negroes have to blame everyone for their problems?

Because they were not as good, Cahan had said, not as smart as other races of men. They'd allowed themselves to be enslaved and so they got what they deserved in the dog-eat-dog world of mankind.

Thomas took out his uniform and regarded it. The deepness of the blue always made him feel noble, and then the sharp bolt of guilt hit him again. He was unworthy of what he beheld. He'd gone to that funeral and watched them all cry while they put the young boy into the cold ground.

He saw Marcus Jackson lying in a spreading pool of blood, his eyes open filled with shock and surprise. And then he saw Marcus from the dream, blood staining his evil smile.

"Riley," came the voice from behind him.

Thomas jumped a little as he pulled up his pants and turned at the same time. He kept his balance but barely. When he'd completed the awkward turn, he saw the handsome face of Matt Reid. Next to him, was his ever-present other half, Don Brady. The two cops who were there that night.

"Hey," Thomas said, turning back around.

Thomas had been avoiding the two since the night Marcus Jackson died. He even stopped going to the Whites-only poker game everyone loved so much. He'd tried to keep to himself as much as possible.

"Got a minute?" asked Brady and it wasn't really a request.

"Just getting ready for my shift," said Thomas weakly, still with his back turned.

The couple shifted around Thomas on either side and he got that sense of being ganged up on again.

"Did you hear?" asked Reid.

"Hear what?" asked Thomas.

Brady and Reid shared a look behind Thomas' head, speaking in partner telepathy.

"Some political agitators, and Colored troublemakers are stirring up the pot," said Reid, his handsome face trying to scowl. "They're pushing to open up some of the riot deaths."

Thomas could not stop the alarm that leapt into his heart. This had been one of his silent fears over the last few months.

"And?" said Thomas coolly.

"And there's a rumor that the Jackson kid's death might be part of it, too," said Brady with a little fear in his voice. "Funny thing is, that wasn't a riot death. So, we kinda been wondering why it's on the table."

"My partner has a very bad way of beating around the bush," said Reid. "We wanted to ask you if anyone has been nosing around, asking questions about that night."

"Not to me," said Thomas who was almost fully dressed now.

"You sure?" asked Reid.

"Why wouldn't I be sure?" said Thomas a little forcefully.

"Of course you are," said Reid. "Sorry. But you should know that we've been through these witch-hunts before. Politicians are willing to take down good cops to keep the natives happy, if you know what I mean."

"So, nobody's saying anything about what happened on those nights, understand?" Brady was all aggression now. He was the Bad Cop to Reid's bullshit angel.

Thomas tucked his shirt into his pants and buckled his belt. "You guys want me to swear another oath or something? I swore to the public and now I can swear to you." Sarcasm was not Thomas' strong point but he felt that this statement had just the right amount of sting in it.

"We want you to sign a bluepact with us," said Brady flatly.

Thomas' face clouded. A bluepact was like a blood oath taken by cops whenever they crossed the line and wanted to assure loyalty. Essentially, the cops all admitted guilt in a form that could be used against any of them. All parties to the bluepact were given copies. If anyone broke the oath, endangering the others, that cop's pact would be revealed and he'd go down as well.

Cahan had signed a bluepact but never revealed its contents or its origin. Frank had never been party to one but he knew what it was and had once assured Thomas and Shaun that they were real.

"No," said Thomas.

"Why the hell not?" said Brady who had a look of fear in his eyes.

"It's okay partner," said Reid in his best Good Cop voice. "It is kind of an old school thing. But remember, we're all in this together, Riley." Thomas hated the way his name rolled off Reid's tongue. It sounded like an insult.

"No one tells tales in the brotherhood," said Brady.

Thomas closed his locker with a bang. "I don't need you to tell me the code. I know it."

Thomas walked away from the two and passed Ned who was just coming in. Ned was already in uniform and said hello and they stopped to talk as Brady and Reid walked by, all smiles and slaps on the back.

"What were you guys talking about?" asked Ned.

"They're worried about an investigation," said Thomas. "Wanted me to sign a bluepact."

"Jesus, are you kidding?"

"No."

"You didn't do it did you?" Ned looked shocked.

"No," said Thomas.

"Good," said Ned. "You don't need that. Not after what they did."

Thomas and Ned walked out to the lot. The familiar sights of the job passed by him in blurry shadow. His head was filled with the stark reality of his current situation and most of it did not seem good.

As they got into a police cruiser and pulled out of the lot, Thomas kept hearing Reid's undeniable words and understood their truth. They were indeed all in this together.

13

THE CHAIR

Robert drove the big Ford truck back onto the lot of the Faygo distribution warehouse with a sense of dread. Things were different now after the riot. People still wanted soda pop, but at the warehouse, the men who delivered it had fallen into distinct camps.

The White men huddled together, whispering and turning away from former relationships with Black coworkers.

The Black men, of which there had never been many, did their job but did not associate as they had. They stayed away from each other as though congregating in too many numbers would invite trouble.

Robert ignored them all. He talked to the Whites, forcing them to acknowledge him and he kept close to the Black workers and followed them if they walked away.

The new Robert Jackson was not playing by anyone's rules. The new Robert was defiant.

Robert returned the delivery truck and punched out from work. He collected his paycheck making sure that the missed days were accounted for. They were. His boss was a man of his word, he thought absently.

He took the bus over to Twelfth Street as he had done many days after the riot. He did not know if he was fueling his rage or chasing ghosts of the war, but each time he walked through the riot-torn neighborhood, he felt better for it.

No one at the Jackson house knew that Robert had attended another funeral, presiding over the death of his nonviolent promise, reclaiming the hardened soldier who called places like Sector 23 home. And they didn't know these things because the change was not outward. Robert had simply closed his heart.

What his family did notice was that he was surly, moody and often, just plain evil. This they attributed to grief.

Denise knew it was more. It was guilt that drove her husband. He had not forgiven himself for the fight that drove Marcus into that fateful night.

Abraham was particularly at odds with his remaining son during these days. There was only room for one man in the house and Robert was clearly challenging his father for that position. They had clashed often when Robert was a teenager. The Marines had helped them both make peace. Now the old battle lines were redrawn in a new war.

Robert railed about the White man's evil and such, but saved his most venomous tirades for the police and the city. It was worse than the Kennedy assassination, he'd say. Lies piled upon lies.

Abraham wanted a spiritual solution to the loss. He promoted God and the local church and quoted Dr. King, but Robert would have none of it. He met his father's peaceful assertions with declarations of action.

Many days, Abraham couldn't stand to be in the same room with his son and sometimes left as soon as the younger man came in.

The one thing they still did regularly was attending baseball games, though they often didn't say a word to each other.

Abraham would get a ticket for Robert and they would meet near the dugout and watch from there. It had been a three-man tradition until Marcus was killed.

Robert approached the flashpoint of the riot near Twelfth Street. It looked like a bomb hit it, buildings scarred with darkness, cars turned over exposing their bellies, old furniture scattered about and shells of houses with jagged tops jutting up like broken bones. There was sadness over the place that weighted you down, filling you with its gravity.

Robert heard Jimmy Ruffin asking "What Becomes of the Broken Hearted?" from a parked car as he trudged through the debris on the street. He looked upon the ruins before him and knew the answer to Jimmy's question. They fall to fatal ambition. They maim and kill and lose their souls in hopeless battle. The broken hearted had little brothers who were murdered.

There was a lot of talk about rebuilding the city after the riots and the Mayor, who was a thirty-five year old Irishman;

just a kid really, had sponsored a commission called New Detroit that had Negroes on it. So far, they had done nothing but talk.

Jimmy Ruffin's melancholy plea faded as he approached a group of people standing by the side of a vacant building, pointing and chatting loudly. There was always some kind of rally or protest going on and so Robert approached this one with little curiosity.

"Some fucked up shit, ain't it?" asked a lanky dark man about Robert's age. "I used to live not far from here."

"Yeah, it was bad," said Robert absently.

"JoJo," the man offered and extended his hand. Robert could hear the southern accents in his voice so common to Detroiters. This one was pure Mississippi.

"Robert," and he slapped five with the man.

They moved closer to the commotion and saw three Black kids putting the finishing touches on a mural on the wall of the building. It was a picture of the riots. Noble Black men and women fearlessly battled scared looking White cops. A little girl lay dead in the streets with an angel rising from her corpse.

But it was not these images that got to Robert. It was the words emblazoned at the top of the mural.

DIE FOR FREEDOM
NOT FOR WAR

"See, that's what I'm talkin' 'bout," said JoJo excitedly. "That's it, right there, the whole damned thing." He clapped his hands together loudly.

Robert stared at the wall and felt himself draining of strength. He had been blind, so blind, he thought. He was so wrapped up in his own personal troubles, that he'd never considered the bigger picture of the war and the plight of his people and the lethal irony of it all.

"Whitey sendin' niggas off to die overseas to get more power to kill us at home," said JoJo. "That right there, that's it."

Robert didn't respond. He just walked away from the crowd, a picture burying itself into his mind. He saw himself killing the enemy and the enemy at home killing his brother.

He took the bus the rest of the way, regarding the ravaged streets and the hopeless faces of the dark people in it. Blackness was heavy, he thought, heavier than any White man could know.

The smell of his mother's cooking greeted him as he walked through the front door of the house. He suddenly realized that he had not eaten since lunch. He said hello to Abraham who responded and then ducked back under his newspaper.

Robert found Denise in the kitchen helping out and this brought a smile to his face. There were still some things that settled him, he mused.

"Dear Lord, we thank you for this meal and for family and the grace you have given us. Amen." Abraham intoned an hour later at the dinner table.

Robert barely heard the words his father uttered as he began to eat. He was still seeing the mural condemning his life and not even his mother's smothered pork chops could chase that away.

Since Marcus' death, he had been planning to do something, to strike at the cops who had killed his brother. But so far, all he knew was their faces and a little information about them. He was working, looking after Denise, trying to get her pregnant and watching over his mother who had become more and more depressed. And something else.

He was afraid.

Even though he had braved Vietnam and lived to tell, he did not want to test his luck at home. This was not a real war and if he went after the cops, he might regret it. Absently, he thought his mother could not survive the loss of another son.

The family ate in silence for a while. A chair was at the table but unoccupied. Robert saw his mother glance at it now and then, looking sad.

Robert felt haunted by his brother's passing. To have a life pulled from the course of your own leaves you weak and tentative, afraid and unsure of your next step; it makes foul air and bitter water and mocks happy thought. That was what a real ghost was, he thought, an empty chair.

"The Tigers are looking real good this season," said Abraham breaking the silence. "McClain is throwing like a man possessed. Everyone's healthy, too. After being so close last year, I think we got a shot."

Denise and Theresa smiled and murmured assent although they knew very little about baseball. The comment was really for Robert.

"Did that lawyer say anything about the case being reopened?" asked Robert ignoring the topic.

"Just that they're looking into it with some other cases," said Abraham dimly.

"I know just how much they gonna look into it," said Robert with energy in his voice.

"That's at least something," said Denise innocently.

Robert shot her a nasty look. "They have to do that to make it look good, Denise. They don't want to know who killed him."

"I thought we said we wouldn't talk about this at the dinner table no more," said Abraham.

"Bobby, we tried everything to bring a case and got nothing," said Theresa not hearing her husband. "The police are on this now so——"

"They said Marcus got into a fight with some man with a knife," said Robert. "The man shot him but somehow he got away. Four White cops and none of them did it? Come on, man."

"I don't... can we talk about something else?" asked Theresa her voice breaking a little.

"What else is there?" Robert pointed to the terrible chair. He ain't here and no talk about baseball is gonna change that." He lowered his finger and now the chair seemed even more awful to everyone. "I went over to the riot area over on Twelfth Street."

"Why?" asked Abraham with mild anger. "There's nothing over there for you"

"People are trying to rebuild and I just want to help," said Robert, knowing that this statement had to quiet his father. The relief effort was something Abraham had approved of and he couldn't gainsay that now.

"You know what I saw?" Robert continued. "Some kids were painting this big picture on the wall of a burned-out building. It was a picture of the riot and the movement and it had a message against the war and demanding freedom for our people. And when I saw it, I realized that I've been wrong, thinking this country loves me."

Abraham put down his knife and fork. "Things have always been hard for our people but we're making it like we always do. It just takes time——"

"How much time, daddy?" Robert's voice rose. "You were in World War Two and what did it change? Nothing. They wouldn't even let Black men fight. How many dead brothers before we get our day? Uh huh, no, I ain't waitin' no more."

This last statement brought the silence back. The whole family knew that Robert had a bad temper and wasn't afraid of anything. He was big, strong and had a violent streak.

"Bobby, what... what're you going to do?" asked Theresa.

"Whatever I have to." Robert said without hesitation. "By any means necessary."

"It's not your place to do anything," said Abraham with authority. "There are still laws and where the law fails there is God. He will take care of it."

And now Robert dropped his knife and fork with a clank and looked at his father. Robert's face had an expression as if his father had just put on a ridiculous looking hat.

"Which God is that, daddy? The blue-eyed Jesus over the mantle who looks just like the men who killed my brother? That's not my God."

More silverware fell as Theresa said: "Don't you blaspheme at my table, boy!"

"My god lives in a rice paddy half a world away," Robert said, ignoring his mother. "My god kills the weak and the foolish. So, you wait for your God, the God the enemy of our people forced upon you. You embrace Him and His peaceful ways. I'm going to find Marcus' killer."

Robert got up from the table and marched off. Abraham bolted upright and took a step away from the table to go after the boy. Theresa's hand on his forearm stopped him and he slowly sat back down.

"Excuse me," said Denise and got up and went after her husband, leaving Theresa and Abraham alone with all the empty chairs.

Denise found Robert in the backyard of the house. He stood next to a big apple tree and looked across the street. In the distance, he heard music from Simpson's Record Shop. The Temptations were singing "I Wish It Would Rain."

The sad song stopped Denise for a moment as she looked at her man and felt some of what he was feeling. Suddenly, she saw him as she first had, tall, scraggly Afro and boyish face and those eyes, hard and mischievous. She went to him and hugged him from behind.

"Thought you'd be mad at me," said Robert.

"Not this time," said Denise. "This is all complicated, you know."

"I'm sorry about all that, but daddy just don't get it sometimes."

"They're old, Bobby. "You have to cut them some slack."

"I can't just do nothing. I've been working, trying to get back to life but every time I close my eyes, I see Marcus walking out the door, saying how he ain't got no brother.

Denise just hugged him tighter. "So, you gonna go out and get them? Maybe get killed yourself?"

"No," said Robert. "I thought about that. That ain't the way, but waitin' ain't neither. I'm gonna find them guys Marcus was running with, The Vanguard. Maybe they know something. And I can put some pressure on them cops, well, one of them, at least."

"The one that came to the funeral," said Denise knowingly.

"Yeah," said Robert remembering that he'd told her about Thomas Riley. "That's where I'm gonna start. He was there, so maybe he did it."

They became silent but it was different than the silence they'd just left. It was a purposeful quiet that made Robert feel like he was finally seeing things right.

"You pregnant yet?" he asked.

"Not yet," said Denise. "But it's been fun trying." She laughed.

"Well, we gonna work on that some more tonight." Robert managed a little smile.

"Wanna go back in?"

"Naw, not yet." Robert let his mind drift as Simpson's Record Shop changed to a song by the Marvelettes.

14

THE SILENT NEGROES

Thomas and Sarah shared breakfast. The eggs and sausage were good to him as he thought about starting his day. Sarah was a decent cook, not as good as his mother who made every meal a feast, but decent.

Sarah had an early class and he was back on days. He had not been sleeping well lately and his conversation with Brady and Reid had not helped. They were arrogant cops who thought their badges gave them some kind of super power. And in a way, it did. They were respected and feared in the precinct. Thomas could not get their accusing faces out of his head.

... all in this together, Riley.

The memory of the night the boy was killed made him sick to his stomach but what was done was done and it was too late for any of them to get out of it.

"You can talk to me about it, you know?" he heard Sarah say.

"Huh?" said Thomas, her words bringing him out of his thought.

"You look like the world has fallen on you," said Sarah. "I just wanted you to know that I'm here."

Thomas managed a smile and he knew it wasn't totally sincere. "I'm okay. Just some work stuff."

"Like what?" asked Sarah.

"It's nothing, really," said Thomas and he took another bite of his food.

Sarah stopped eating and just stared at him with those piercing eyes. He could see the anger behind her expression. She knew he was hiding something and she didn't like it. Considering their current cold war over the wedding, he decided to talk.

"Okay," Thomas relented. "The department might be looking into some of the deaths associated with the riot."

"That's great," said Sarah, the angry look fading. "They need to get into some of the injustices, especially the slaughter at the Algiers Motel."

He wanted to tell her that those men were doing drugs with White women at a suspected sniper location during a race riot. But he knew if he said that, she would be all over him about how Negroes had a right to do whatever they wanted with whatever kind of women they wanted in their own space. She'd talk about the Constitution and the Fourth Amendment and all that radical shit.

"My case, the Jackson kid might be one of them," Thomas said calmly.

"But it wasn't a riot case," said Sarah.

"I know. It's just a rumor but it's got me a little worried."

"Why?" she asked and in that instant he knew he had made a mistake.

Sarah had believed him when he gave his account of the shooting. She believed him because she had no reason not to. Ballistics cleared them all of firing a gun and no weapon was found. The Jackson kid had a large knife on him and it was open and near his hand. And even though Brady and Reid had spotty records, they had citations as well and Thomas' record was new and clean.

"I don't know," he said. "I think if it's true, it's just to appease certain people."

"Black people?" and Sarah said it like she was looking for a fight.

"Yes," he said defiantly. "And some of the White ones, too."

Sarah looked pensive for a moment. Thomas wondered if she wanted to question him, ask him if he had told her everything? Or perhaps she was being as careful in the minefield of their relationship as he was.

"Try not to worry," she said finally. "I'm sure it's nothing."

Thomas let the conversation go, afraid that it might take another nasty turn. He finished his meal and they said their goodbyes. He kissed Sarah and he could feel the unasked question still on her lips.

Thomas got to work and made his transformation to officer of the law. He was about to head out knowing that Ned would be late again. He was always the last one in lately. In fact, Ned had been different since the incident with the Jackson kid. He was railing on Brady and Reid and asking Thomas to distance himself from them.

As Thomas headed out, he was approached by Carl Rogers, a Police Commander. Rogers was a very overweight White cop who had been with the department for over thirty years. Rogers was a decent sort and was known as a straight shooter. He was also famous for getting cops out of tight jams. Rogers walked over to Thomas with a flat look on his chubby face.

"Got a minute?" Rogers asked. He was from the east coast, Boston, and still had a bit of the twang in his voice.

"Sure, sir," said Thomas. "What's up?"

"Some people wanna talk to you."

"Who?" asked Thomas feeling himself tighten a little.

"Look," said Rogers. "You don't have to talk to them if you don't want to. It's a committee, some political types." Then he waited a moment and said: "It's about the Jackson kid."

Thomas unconsciously took a half step away from Rogers. He felt a shot of heat streak through his chest.

"What the fuck do they want?" asked Thomas doing his best to sound strong.

"They're looking into cases, you know, and yours came up. They're talking to Ned, Brady and Reid, too."

"What if I don't go?" asked Thomas and he wasn't sure he wanted to ask that question aloud.

"It's informal, so nothing will happen," said Rogers, "but my advice to you is to go."

"Why?" asked Thomas.

"Because the big bosses are behind this. I'm talking about the Mayor and the goddamned Governor. They got Negro activists and lawyers coming out of their asses. And a lot of those guys have the ear of Senators and the President. You don't go and they'll think it's suspicious and push to reopen the matter. You go and they'll probably just ask a few questions and then let it go."

"Did Brady and Reid go?" asked Thomas and even he could hear the tension in his voice.

"Yeah, they're talking to them now," said Rogers. "They laughed when I told them. Nothing scares them two."

"And Ned?"

"He's going in after you," said Rogers. "I ain't worried about him."

Thomas felt unsure of himself. This committee had sprung this on them intentionally, he thought, to make sure that they wouldn't have time to think about their answers or story. What he couldn't believe is that the department was letting them do it like this.

"I know it ain't right but since the riot, a lot of shit ain't right," said Rogers seemingly reading his mind.

"No IAD?" asked Thomas.

"Hell no," said Rogers. Otherwise, I'd tell them to stick it up their asses."

"Okay," said Thomas and it sounded like defeat. "Where are they?"

Rogers led Thomas to a room on the fourth floor of the precinct.

Thomas walked down the hallway, like it was The Last Mile. He was a cop sworn to protect and serve and he felt like a criminal.

When he got to the room, Brady and Reid walked out. They seemed in good spirits. Reid even smiled a little. They gave Thomas the thumbs up sign and walked on.

"Here you go," said Rogers. "Fifteen minutes max is all they got." Rogers looked at him like he was sorry and Thomas got the feeling that there was something going on that he didn't know about.

Thomas walked into the room, which was an old detective's office. There was a wooden table, some chairs and an old desk, which had been shoved into a corner.

At the table were two White men and two Negroes, one male, the other female. Thomas tried not to stare at the two Negroes. They were dressed in nice business suits and didn't seem like they were from Detroit.

"Hi," said one of the White men. "I'm Paul Jones from the Mayor's office. This is Andrew Summer from the Governor's office," he pointed to the other White man. "And these are Dana Von, an attorney for the NAACP and Samuel Johnson from C.O.R.E."

Thomas said hello to them all and noticed that the two Negroes had pleasant looks on their faces. Considering the circumstances, he was surprised that they did not have angry expressions.

"This is an informal committee," said Jones. "We're here to gather information on matters pertaining to the riot last year."

"We're looking into cases where Blacks died during that period," said Andrew Summer. "In this case, one Marcus Jackson."

"That case wasn't technically a riot death," said Summers, "but it occurred in the same time period and so we're just being thorough."

The Negro woman, Dana Von, shuffled some papers. Thomas looked her way out of instinct and he noticed that she was fair-skinned and quite pretty. Her eyes were light brown and they seemed to float in her visage. He remembered the girl from Hudson's who had made his belly flip when she smiled at him.

"So we've all read the reports," said Jones. "And we talked to officers Brady and Reid. Do you have anything to add to what you reported last year?"

"No," said Thomas and he felt that he answered too quickly.

"Can you tell us again what happened that night?" asked Jones.

Thomas took a breath and told the story again. When he was done, the Negroes shared a look then looked over to Jones.

"You and the other officers concluded that the victim, Marcus Jackson was killed by an unknown assailant?" asked Andrew Summer.

"Yes," said Thomas.

The two Negroes again nodded to Jones.

"Okay, officer," said Jones. "That's all."

Thomas sat for just a second then he got up and left. When he got into the hallway, Rogers was gone. For some reason, that troubled him.

He started down the hallway to the elevator and wondered why the two Negroes never asked him a question. It was as if they were there to read his mind and his heart, to run him through some magical filter and sift out the good from the bad. The White men had done all the talking, but the Negroes had said so much more with their silence.

When he got to the lobby he could not find Ned. There were a few cops talking and the usual traffic from the courts and police staff.

Thomas walked into the lobby, saying hello to Sergeant Dennison, a big amiable cop who was riding the front desk. He took a few steps away, when a big Black man approached. He wore a Marine uniform.

"Got a minute, officer?" asked Robert Jackson.

Thomas looked at the man and felt a vague familiarity. But he didn't know many Negroes and certainly he didn't know this one.

"Desk Sergeant Dennison is over there," said Thomas pointing to the big man behind the desk.

"I talked to him already. He let me wait here for you. He's a Marine too," said Robert. "Amazing how the uniform gets you respect, Officer Riley."

Thomas was about to walk away but the sound of his name made him stop. "Do I know you?"

"Oh, I'm just a soldier," said Robert, "a man who went to war and served his country. But then I came back to this city and someone killed my brother, Marcus."

Thomas straightened up his stance at this. He immediately went into a defensive posture, putting a little distance between himself and the bigger man.

"What do you want?" asked Thomas.

"I just need some information," said Robert.

"Is there a problem?" Dennison called from behind Robert.

"No," said Thomas confidently and not turning around. He said it looking right at Robert as if to say there had better not be. "I'm sorry for your loss but the whole thing is a matter of record now."

"I'm not buying that record," said Robert and moved closer. "Not buying it."

Thomas didn't back away and he spoke up loudly and clearly so that there would be no mistakes about his intentions. "Look, you need to consider where you are. You can talk to the other cops on the case but I have nothing to say."

Thomas stepped around Robert, headed for the door. If the man was foolish enough to touch him, he would be taken down in about two seconds.

"I would have, but they didn't come to my brother's funeral, like you did."

Thomas stopped against his own will and turned. "What?" he asked.

I got good eyes, officer," said Robert. "All that training in Vietnam. I saw you at my brother's funeral. The question is why were you there?"

Thomas couldn't manage a word. He wanted to deny it, to lie and say he hadn't been the one but to do that seemed to be beyond him and somehow another indignity to the dead boy.

"You're crazy," he said to Robert.

Dennison and another officer walked up to Robert and Thomas who were now locked in a staring match.

"Everything okay here?" asked Dennison who was a towering presence and his arms looked like they were made of steel.

The other officer was smaller but looked just as tough. Robert quickly sized them up but did not back down from the confrontation. If it got ugly, he'd surprise the big one with an attack and the little one would be so shocked that it would give him an opening.

"Everything's okay, Sarge," said Thomas. "I'm going my way and he's going his." And to Robert, Thomas said "Right?"

"You didn't answer my question," said Robert.

"You can't walk in a police house and get belligerent with a cop," said Thomas. He felt that he had to be assertive now that there was an audience.

Other people were watching the strange scene. Three White cops facing off with a Black man wearing the nation's proud uniform.

"I'm waiting on that answer," said Robert defiantly.

"That's it," said Dennison.

Dennison and the other officer stepped around Thomas and grabbed Robert by either arm. Robert didn't resist. He locked his gaze on Thomas and held it all the way to the door.

They pulled Robert to the front door and gently shoved him out onto the steps.

Thomas watched as they released Robert on the front steps. Dennison pointed a beefy finger at Robert and said something, which elicited no verbal response from Robert. Thomas saw Robert salute and then walk off.

"What the hell was that all about?" asked Dennison when he came back.

"Nothing," said Thomas. "Guy's nuts." He tried desperately to look like he didn't care.

"All us Marines are," Dennison laughed a little.

"You think that kook is a real Marine?" asked the other officer.

"Oh yeah, that uniform was the real deal," said Dennison. "Two Purple Hearts, too."

Dennison and the other officer walked off. Thomas turned to look for his partner. Then he remembered that Ned was being questioned after him.

He was upset but didn't want anyone to see it. Why had the kid's brother been so bold to come into the police station? Did he know something? And if he did, what was it?

These questions troubled Thomas for the rest of the day and he didn't know what was worse, the angry man who had invaded his job and tried to embarrass him or the Negroes who sat on the committee but did not speak.

15

<u>THE GUARD</u>

The Vanguard was one of the more notorious Black militant groups. They had chapters in all the major cities and were known to be linked to White radical groups as well.

The Guard, as they were sometimes called, was implicated in violent protest, including the firebombing of a police station in Baltimore.

For the first time, Robert wondered why they would have taken in a boy so young. Then again, Marcus was exceptionally smart and had a lot of personality.

Robert had gone out in search of The Guard. He was lied to, led on and robbed of his money with false information. But over the days, he gathered enough real facts to lead him where he was going today.

Robert stood in front of a vacant building on Linwood. This was reportedly a Vanguard hideout. But no one had hidden out in this place in along time, he thought. The building teetered on its foundation and looked as though a strong wind could topple it.

It was late afternoon and a wind was indeed blowing from the east. The faint smell of fire was still in the air and although Robert knew it was the wood and debris, it made him feel uneasy.

He thought of Thomas Riley and their altercation at the police station. In retrospect, it seemed foolish and he was lucky he had not been taken into the back and beaten with a rubber hose.

The confrontation had been somewhat satisfying, but in the end it was futile. He had hoped to rattle Riley and send him running to his co-conspirators. But it had not worked. He'd followed Riley that night and all it led him to was a cop bar and Riley's pretty girlfriend.

He knew it would be hard to break the cops, so good detective that he was, he decided to poke in the only other direction left to him on this case.

An old Black man sat across the street from Robert on the stoop of what looked to be an occupied building. The old man was in a lawn chair smoking a cigarette. He was not watching Robert but he wasn't *not watching* him either, Robert thought. The old man just looked up and down the street slowly just puffing then blowing smoke.

Robert walked over to the old man and stood in front of him. The old man looked at the younger man and blew smoke.

"You blocking my sun," he said casually.

"Ain't you dark enough?" asked Robert.

"Cain't never be too Black these days," said the old man.

"Sorry," said Robert and he moved aside letting the sunlight hit the man's dark skin. "I'm looking for something."

"Ain't we all," said the old man.

"Well, I'm looking for some men, a group really," said Robert. "Maybe you heard of them, The Vanguard."

"Don't know no guards," said the old man lighting a cigarette off the last one. "Nothing around here but fools and hos. And if you ask me we got too much of one and not enough of the other." He laughed a little at his own joke.

"Well, if you ever hear of them," said Robert. "Let me know. I hear they contact people here and so I'll be coming back until they do."

"Sure," said the old man.

He and Robert slapped five and Robert walked off. The old man adjusted in his chair and waved the hand with the cigarette into the air.

From down the block, two Black men came out of a doorway and began to follow Robert.

Robert was going to a corner store he'd passed to get a drink and maybe a snack. He was going to come back to the vacant building the next day and every day after that until he saw someone who could lead him to The Vanguard.

Robert was halfway up the block when he felt the presence behind him. He saw the two men in the reflection of a car's windshield. This neighborhood was not known for its safety, so he kept moving, careful not to quicken his pace. If you moved faster, that was a sign that you were afraid.

Robert turned a corner and stopped. He leaned against a building and waited for the men to come around the corner.

When they did, they had moved to the other side of the street.

One of the two men was bald and dark. He was a thick man who looked like an athlete. The other was fair-skinned and had a scraggly beard. The bald man looked over and saw Robert. He said something to the other man and they both crossed the street.

Robert quickly assessed the pair. The bald man was the bigger of the two and so he'd concentrate on him. The other man didn't look as dangerous and so Robert would intimidate that one if he needed to.

The men got to Robert who had his arms folded as if waiting for someone.

"You brothers lost?" asked Robert.

"We ain't the ones lost," said the bald man in a menacing tone. "What you doin' 'round here asking questions, nigga?"

"Look," said Robert to the fair-skinned man. If y'all gonna try something, then get the fuck to it. You can't scare me with this loud talkin'.

Robert took his arms down and crouched a little as if ready for a fight.

Both men were a little shocked. Robert just looked at the bald man then back to the other one as if waiting to see which one he would attack first.

"We can kick yo ass if that's what you want," said the bald man. "All day on that."

"Still with the talk," said Robert. And now he raised his hands in a fighting pose.

The bald man coughed a laugh and raised his fists as well. He waded in to Robert.

The fair-skinned man was about to say something when Robert stepped quickly to him and delivered a kick to his stomach. The fair-skinned man doubled over. Robert quickly moved to the injured man's side, putting the man between himself and the bald man who was swinging wildly. The bald man ran into his partner and missed Robert by a mile.

Robert pivoted and threw a blow that caught the bald man on the jaw. This stunned him and Robert knew he'd only have a second before he recovered.

Robert kicked the bald man hard in the stomach, then straightened up and brought his forearm into the under side of his chin.

The bald man fell backwards. The fair-skinned man was still on the ground holding his stomach. Robert took a step to him and the man held up a hand to say no more.

Robert turned back to the bald man who was groaning and trying to get to his feet.

"I assume you brothers are with The Vanguard," said Robert. If you are, then we got business."

The bald man got to his feet and was ready to charge Robert. It was obvious that he was the local badass and was not used to anyone getting the better of him.

"That's your ass!" screamed the bald man.

"Stop," said the fair-skinned man getting up. "Naw, man. He had a right." He moved between the bald man and Robert.

"You from The Guard or not?" said Robert.

"Supposed we was," said the fair-skinned man.

"Then I want to meet the man."

The bald man laughed. "Nigga, you crazy."

"I'm Marcus Jackson's brother," said Robert.

The two men looked at each other for a second, then back to Robert assessing the resemblance. The bald man pulled the fair skinned man away and they talked in hushed voices. The bald man was obviously upset and wanted to keep fighting and Robert supposed that's what he was talking about. Finally, the fair-skinned man walked back to Robert.

"Okay, but you gotta wear this," said the fair-skinned man. He held out a black blindfold.

Robert nodded then walked with them to a car several blocks away. Robert got in and the bald man sat next to him in the backseat.

Robert put the blindfold on and expected to feel a gun jabbed into his ribs. Then they would beat him and dump his body from the moving vehicle. But all he felt was the rumble of the car's engine as it started and rolled down the street.

Robert's eyes took a moment to adjust to the light as the blindfold was removed a half hour later. He stood in the middle of a big room. It was dimly lit and there were tables and chairs pushed against the walls, which were painted with afrocentric pictures. On the far wall, was a black fist holding America in its grasp.

Standing before Robert was a man about his age. He was tall and rough looking. His skin was dark and scarred near the chin and he stood under a crown of hair styled into an immaculate Afro. Robert thought he looked like a less handsome version of the pro football player, Fred Williamson.

"Why didn't you just say you were Marcus' brother?" asked the man. His voice was flat, nasally and higher than Robert thought it would be.

Robert stood in the middle of a room with the new man and the ones he'd beaten up.

"Didn't have a chance," said Robert. "Your boys came at me hard, so I did what I had to do."

The man with the immaculate Afro laughed showing a row of white teeth. "You must be bad," he said. "Vince and Bohan here are two of my best men. I'm Yusef."

Robert could tell from the way he spoke that Yusef was an educated man. He had no trace of the accents common to most Blacks in the city and his words had no rhythm or melody in them; they were pronounced crisply and cleanly.

Robert walked over to the two men and extended his hand.

"No hard feelings," he said.

Bohan and Vince just looked at Yusef who nodded. They both took turns shaking Robert's hand.

"Bohan," said the bald man.

"Vince," said the fair-skinned man.

"Need you to show me some of them moves," said Bohan but he didn't smile.

"Is this the whole group?" Robert asked Yusef. "I pictured a lot more people."

"There's more," said Yusef. "You don't think I'd let you see their faces before we checked you out."

"Makes sense," said Robert. He moved closer to Yusef. "You know why I'm here. I want in."

Robert heard Vince and Bohan whispering behind him. Yusef only smiled.

"Why?" said Yusef.

Robert looked at the three men and for the first time it occurred to him that he was outnumbered. If they decided not to let him in, what would they do to him? And something else, he felt embarrassed. These men were trying to do something for their people and what was he doing?

"My brother," Robert began. "He was right. He tried to tell me but I wouldn't listen. I can't get my brother back but I can't just stand by and let them do what they're doing to us. If you won't let me in, then I'll do what I can on my own, but either way, something's gonna get done."

Yusef looked at Robert then nodded to Vince who walked to a wall and rapped hard three times. Three doors around the room opened. The doors had been hidden by the pictures on the walls. It was real secret agent shit; Robert thought then again, these people were defying the United States government.

Out of the doors came about thirty Black men and women all in their twenties or thirties. They moved to the center of the room and formed a circle around Robert.

Robert scanned the faces and saw a familiar one, the young girl with the big brown eyes who stared at him at Marcus' funeral.

"These are some of our people," said Yusef. "People," he spoke louder. "This is Marcus' brother, Robert, the one who served in Vietnam. He wants to join our illustrious organization. What do you say?"

"Hell no!" yelled the assemblage in unison. Robert was not fazed. He got the feeling that this was always the first answer to that particular question.

"Yes," said a lone voice. It was the girl again.

"Yes," said Vince.

"Yes," said Bohan and surprised Robert by smiling.

"Don't look good, Brother Robert," said Yusef. "Only Vince, Bohan and Linda here seem to want you. I think you might have to prove yourself."

Robert looked at the girl Yusef had called Linda and smiled a little. Then to Yusef he said: "Whatcha got?"

16

<u>CATCH</u>

The baseball slammed into Thomas' glove and he felt the familiar sting of it. Frank still had a strong right arm and he'd really flung the last one. Thomas nodded his head to his father signaling that he respected his power.

They played catch in Frank's backyard. Thomas was over for dinner but had not brought Sarah along. There was always tension when she came to visit and Thomas didn't need any more stress in his life right now.

When Shaun and Cahan were alive, they'd play four corners catch. He smiled a little at the memory.

When he was a kid, all he wanted was to be grown up and now that it was here, he missed the days when he was carefree. He supposed that you never had a time in life where you were completely satisfied with anything.

Thomas reared back and threw the ball as hard as he could. Frank caught it and tossed it back just as hard.

Thomas suddenly realized that his father was never in the nightmare in which he was always shot. But that made sense, he thought. Frank was still alive. The others were men whose time had come and had gone on to glory. He was aware that it was just the two of them now, the last of the Riley men.

"Dinner," said Katie from the rear door.

Thomas threw the ball back to Frank and they both walked toward the house.

Esther Riley was an excellent cook. In fact, it was well known in the neighborhood that she could cook any kind of food. This night, Esther had prepared Italian, Caesar salad, minestrone soup and a big beautiful beef Lasagna.

Early in the marriage, Frank complained about his wife's eclectic tastes in food. He was an American and he wanted American food. He held this opinion until he tasted Esther's

culinary product. Now he loved her specialties and even
bragged about her prowess to his friends.

"Sarah studying late?" asked Esther lighting up a cigarette
and ignoring Thomas' glare at the act.

Thomas didn't want to say what he said but it was out
before he could stop it. "She's organizing a peace rally."

"Cool," said Katie.

"No, it's not," snapped Frank. "People have no idea what
their country has to do to keep us safe."

"But daddy," said Katie, "they say the war is wrong, that
we—"

"Katie, stay out of adult discussions," said Esther.
"You're still a child."

Frank turned to Thomas with a serious look on his face.
Thomas knew what was coming before he said it.

"Tommy, are you sure about this girl?"

"Dad, we've been over this. I love her," said Thomas.

"Ouuu luuuvvv," said Katie and she made kissing noises.
Frank cut this off with a stern look.

"Katie, excuse yourself," said Frank.

"But I—-"

Another look from Frank stopped this statement by Katie
as well.

"I'm done anyway," said Katie. "Excuse me." Katie got
up and left taking her plate.

Thomas had hoped to come home to avoid conversations
about life. He and Sarah were barely speaking and now he
had to trudge through the "Why are you marrying a radical
female" minefield again.

"You need to think seriously about this girl, Thomas,"
said Frank. "With all the political bullshit going on, there's
no telling what she's into. It could blemish your standing as
an officer. So it's a good thing she stalled the wedding. It's a
sign."

"I'm not talking about it," said Thomas defiantly. He
ignored his father's gaze and looked into his plate, which
was almost empty.

"No one thought I should marry you, Frank," said Esther
with a sly smile.

"Yeah, but your parents are crazy," said Frank.

"That's what they said about me when I told them," said Esther. "You follow your heart, Tommy. It's the only way to go."

Esther got up and left still smoking her cigarette. Frank scoffed even as she kissed his forehead.

Frank grabbed his beer from the table and went into the living room. He turned on the TV and settled into his chair.

Thomas entered after a while and sat next to him. Thomas' desire for peace had only been the first reason he came home. He wanted to talk to his father about something but given the already strained talk about Sarah, he wondered if he should just leave.

"I'm right about that girl," Frank said. "I know how you feel about her, but a man is only as good as the woman behind him. She's not behind you. She's behind herself. And that ain't right."

It was more Real Man philosophy in all its one-syllable power.

"Seems like all the women my age are like that," said Thomas.

"Not Alice Parker," said Frank. "She's pretty, she goes to church, a good girl."

"You and Mr. Parker plotting something?" Thomas said with a knowing look.

"Of course we are," said Frank. "Alice is getting courted by long-haired draft dodgers and hippies. Dutch told me he saw a nigger looking at her one day. Of course, that's all they ever think about, those ones."

Thomas heard the forbidden word and just as quickly he envisioned his father, wrestling with him and Shaun in their old house. His father coming home covered in snow with food and his father showing up at his school in uniform smiling like a hero right out of the movies.

"So, I wanted to tell you..." Thomas began haltingly and he wanted to take it back but it was too late. "The brass... they're opening some of the riot cases— the deaths."

Frank reacted casually to this, drinking from his beer. "That's what brass does. How they call themselves cops, I don't know."

"One of them is the Jackson kid, the one I was involved in."

"Yeah. So?"

"I'm worried about it, I guess, what they could ask me," said Thomas. "You know how political things are getting downtown."

"Your partner will support you," said Frank. "That's what partners are for."

"Ned and I got separated while we pursued the suspect, remember? So I was the only one of us there when we found the kid."

"So Ned should just say he was there," said Frank.

"He didn't," said Thomas. "I don't know why but he didn't in the official report."

"Jesus, what kinda fuckin' partner did you pick?" said Frank with disgust. "Well, then the other two cops will tow the line. That's how it goes." Frank sighed heavily as if trying to expel something from his body.

Thomas gathered his resolve. He knew he was walking onto dangerous ground now. "My watch commander asked me to talk to some people on a committee from the Mayor's office and the Governor's. There were two Negroes there, too."

Frank's eyes widened. He sat up straighter and turned a little. "Your commander asked you to do that?"

"Said if I didn't they'd be suspicious."

"What the fuck's going on?" asked Frank his voice rising higher. "I'm gonna make some calls tomorrow."

"Don't," said Thomas. "I can handle this."

"If you could, we wouldn't be having this conversation."

"I talked to them for a few minutes then I went to work. Then, when I went to the lobby...."

"What?" asked Frank looking upset.

"The dead kid's brother was there wearing his Marine uniform. He confronted me about it."

"At the station house?" Franks voice rose again. "I hope he got his head busted."

"No, Dad. We can't just do that anymore."

"Goddamned police are turning into a bunch of pansies. Back in my day, he would have been taken out and relieved of some of his teeth. Can you imagine that? Right in the station house? What's the goddamned world coming to?"

"We threw him out but that's not what's bothering me really," said Thomas.

"Then what?" asked Frank. "God knows it can't be much worse."

"I don't think the investigation is over. And I feel like... I think someone's been following me after work."

Frank noticed his son's upset expression and for the first time, he realized the gravity in the conversation.

"You don't think they're gonna chase this thing, do you?" asked Frank with clear concern.

"I don't know," said Thomas.

"Don't beat yourself up over some dead kid. They come and they go."

"It's a big deal, all of this, pop. The Negroes on that committee, they just sat there not talking, like they already had some kinda plan."

"A colored kid out in a White neighborhood with a knife on him? He got himself killed and that's that."

Frank looked at Thomas and saw that there was more to the story and before Thomas could say anything: "You'd better not be thinking about talking out of turn. This kinda thing don't make a damned bit of difference to anybody that matters. And before you want to confess to me like a priest, let me tell you the code again. Nobody talks about nothing. You open your mouth and you're gonna be all alone at the precinct."

Frank tipped his beer, then, "I know what you think," he continued. "But I'm not like the bigots in this town. There's plenty of colored people I like."

"You don't have to defend yourself to me. I'm your son," said Thomas.

"Then act like it," said Frank. "There's been a Riley on the force since the beginning of the century. My father served and so did your brother, Shaun. You know, Shaunie had a situation like this once—-"

"I'm not Shaun, pop," said Thomas and the tone of his voice was forbidding.

This stopped Frank who had light in his eyes at the mention of his deceased son.

Thomas' expression grew correspondingly darker. They had clashed over comparisons to Shaun even before he was dead. Back then it seemed like normal parental favor. Thomas had his mother and Shaun had Frank. It was even.

But now that Shaun was gone, it hurt to be compared to him. No one could live up to a dead legend.

"Anyway, we got a tradition in this family," Frank continued. "Don't be the first to disgrace the uniform."

"I'm not going to," said Thomas with a trace of anger.

"The other cops, what are their names?" asked Frank.

"Don Brady and Matt Reid."

"Brady I don't know," said Frank, "but Reid, that's George Reid's boy. Good looking kid."

"They're worried, too. They talked to the same committee. They've been on my ass about keeping quiet," said Thomas.

"They should be," said Frank. "Look, it'll all settle itself out. It always does."

"It just don't feel right," said Thomas.

"Who the hell said it was supposed to?" asked Frank. "The job comes with all kinds of responsibilities. If it were easy, then every man would be a cop. It isn't about right and wrong, it's about law and order. Sometimes what's right isn't good and what's good ain't right. But does it serve the law? That's what you have to ask yourself."

Frank turned on the TV. Thomas took this to mean that there would be no more discussion. Frank's speech was good but it felt worn, frayed at the edges. Thomas felt change in the air and if he was the only one, then that meant he was already all alone.

The sounds of the television invaded the room but the silence was as loud as that of the Negroes on the committee, Thomas thought.

Thomas went home that night knowing that Sarah was there waiting for him. He stood in front of his place and started to go in and then he stopped. He went back to the front of the apartment building and sat on the stoop.

Thomas didn't want to go in and have more difficult conversation. Worse, he didn't want to go in and face Sarah's silence. He was tired of silence.

He waited outside for a while, afraid to go into his own home and feeling like a coward because of it.

How did this happen, he asked himself? Just a few short months ago he was on top of his world and now he could feel the ends of his life unraveling, tumbling to the earth.

It was the riot, he mused. That was the night everything changed. No riot, no dead kid, no riot, no Sarah having second thoughts, no riot, no regretful looks from his father.

And before he could stop himself, he blamed the Negroes. He knew they had it hard but if they just waited, things would right themselves over time. Right now, they got what they deserved, he reasoned.

Thomas walked away from his house and went to McGinty's. The patrons there were surprised to see Thomas who was a special occasion customer.

Thomas recognized the faces of several cops, some of whom were known to be heavy drinkers. The regular elbow-bending group welcomed him knowing that alcohol calls all troubled men sooner or later.

Thomas settled in to the bar and had a drink. After the third one, he began to feel at peace.

17

<u>CAL'S</u>

Robert, Yusef and Linda sat in the back of a VW van and watched the small diner across the street. The van was used and Robert suspected that it might be stolen. It was cluttered with trash and smelled of incense and weed.

After Robert accepted Yusef's challenge, the other members of The Vanguard had dispersed, except the girl named Linda who had attended the funeral.

Her full name was Linda Peoples. She had been Marcus' girlfriend. When Robert found this out, he remembered his brother's face when they'd talked about women. Marcus had said she was beautiful and he had not lied.

Linda had requested to go along with the two men. Yusef had not put up a fight. It was obvious that Yusef had affection for and confidence in the young girl.

Linda was nineteen. She wore her hair in a short afro and was fond of midriff shirts that showed off her muscled abdomen. Her skin was brown and smooth and she had the biggest brown eyes he'd ever seen. She had been a track star at Central High School and her body showed it. Robert liked what he saw and couldn't help but think that his brother did too.

The VW van sat a little down the block from Cal's, a popular greasy spoon on the east side. It was not quite as secure as McGinty's, but many cops ate there. The place was almost filled with patrons and it didn't take Robert long to see that they were all White. Two police motorcycles sat in front of the place next to a fire hydrant.

"So what's up with this joint?" asked Robert.

"We're interested in the two pigs sitting near the front," said Yusef in his crisp English.

"They on our list," said Linda and Robert could tell from her voice that she, unlike Yusef, was a real girl from the ghetto.

"So what you want me to do, kill them?" asked Robert and he smiled at his joke.

Yusef reached into a case and pulled out a rifle.

"Please," said Yusef.

The rifle had a scope on it and a crude, makeshift silencer on the end made of insulation and duct tape. Yusef handed the weapon to Robert.

Robert took the rifle and felt the weight by instinct. He balanced it on his forearm then looked down the sight. He checked it and found it unloaded.

Before he could ask, Linda's hand was sticking out with several gleaming rounds. Robert took two of them and loaded the rifle.

He rested the weapon against his chest. Yusef and Linda just stared at him with very serious faces.

"What about the other bullets?" asked Yusef.

"At this distance, I'll only need two," said Robert.

"Confident," said Yusef smiling. "I dig that. The one on the right is the worse one," said Yusef. "He beat and raped a sister six months ago and got away with it. That woman was one of our many spies in the establishment. Our code demands blood for this crime."

"So, you'll trust me if I kill a man?" said Robert evenly as he sighted the weapon.

"Ain't that the way the man do it?" said Linda. "You was in the Army, right?"

"Right," said Robert not arguing. "So, I do this and I'm in."

"All the way," said Yusef.

"How come there wasn't no revenge for my brother?" Robert asked.

"We're not sure who killed him," said Yusef. "We know there were three cops at the scene but which one did it? Or do we kill all three?"

Robert turned back to the weapon. He aimed the gun at the cop sitting on the right. Waitresses passed back and forth and he waited for a clear shot.

Robert drained himself of all compassion and logic. He took a breath and settled. He focused and tugged at the trigger.

Robert heard the hammer strike but no explosion followed. He pulled the trigger again. He was pulling the gun away to examine it, when Yusef reached out for it.

"Dummy bullets," said Yusef. Robert released the gun and Yusef put it aside.

Robert's soldier face remained. He scanned the man and woman before him unable to dial down his intensity.

"I ain't got time for bullshit," said Robert. "If this is what you do, then forget the shit."

Yusef smiled at Linda who smiled back at him. "She said you'd say that. She also said you'd pull the trigger."

"Marcus told me he was cold-blooded," said Linda. "Why you don't trust me, I don't know."

"Noted," said Yusef.

"I like this kinda work," said Linda. "Got me working at some janitor job cleaning up after White folks. I'm a revolutionary, baby."

Yusef gave her a hard look and she clammed up. Robert noticed this but did not let on that he'd seen the harsh glare.

"I don't apologize for our methods," said Yusef. "They work for us. "We were testing you just now but we do have business with that cop."

"He's protecting dope dealers in the neighborhoods," said Linda. "He and his partner even beat down the competition if they have to."

"They're dirty," said Yusef. "Got any ideas how to send a message?"

"Yeah," said Robert. "We got to get personal with them."

"What does that mean?" asked Linda.

"Well, we could expose them," said Robert, "but even honest cops cover for dirty ones."

"I know that's right," said Yusef.

"So we got to take the game right to them," said Robert. It's Monday, right? The drug boys make most of their money on the weekend. Sunday, no self-respecting cop will make a pick up, too busy in church pretending to be a good Christian. So chances are, their pick up is today."

Yusef smiled at Robert's wisdom. Linda had a look of pure pride on her face.

"Let's do it," said Yusef.

Robert covered the van's license plate with tape as they waited for the cops to finish their meal. When the cops were done, they got on their bikes and rolled off.

Yusef drove as they trailed them. It was tricky business but Yusef was very good at mingling into traffic.

The cops patrolled for a while and then headed down a street known for trafficking drugs. It was a rather nondescript little street that looked prosperous. The dealers didn't run or signal. The cops stopped outside a house that had several men sitting on its porch.

Yusef stopped the van at the corner.

"Now if we go down there we got to buy something or get our asses shot," said Yusef. "I hate a muthafuckin' drug dealer."

"So now we know where they go to get their blood money," said Robert. "We hit 'em next time."

A week later, Robert Yusef and Linda were all at the same location waiting for the dirty cops. Like clockwork, they rolled up on their bikes and went down the street.

"We do this right and it'll come back on them," said Robert. "To Linda he said: "You ready?"

"Yeah, daddy," said Linda. She was dressed in heavy makeup and a short skirt.

Yusef drove the van to the far end of the block and turned the corner. There was a lookout posted there, a man who looked to be twenty or so. Yusef rolled halfway down the block so the lookout couldn't see him.

Robert jumped out of the van and sneaked up on the lookout. Robert punched him hard in the small of his back then tripped him to the ground. He rammed the man's head into the ground several times until he stopped moving.

Robert absently thought how easily men in the movies knocked a man out. In reality it was much harder.

Robert pulled the lookout's body behind a tall bush and hid next to him. Linda jumped out and stood on the corner. She had her skirt hiked up to the crest of her ass and Robert couldn't help but look.

The dirty cops waited outside the house. One of them was a big guy, six feet about two fifty. The other was thinner but just as tall. Suddenly, a small boy came running out carrying a thick package. The thin cop took it and they rolled off.

"That's it," said Robert. "Here they come." He pulled a ski mask over his face. In the van, Yusef did the same.

The dirty cops rolled to the corner. Linda waited until they could see her and then pretended to hurry away. It was well known that dirty cops forced hookers to give them freebies.

One of the cops issued a short blast on his siren. Linda stopped, uttering a curse. She walked over to the cops who had stopped their bikes at the corner.

"Well, well," said one of the cops. "A young one."

"Get your ass over here, girl," said the other.

Neither of them saw Robert circling behind them. Nor did they give a second thought to the old van parked nearby.

Linda walked over, keeping her head turned down so they could not get a good look at her.

"Move it!" said one of the cops.

Linda walked up to them then reached into her purse and pulled a gun and leveled it at one of the cops.

"What the fuc—"

A second later, Robert put a shotgun in the back of the other cop.

"Don't move," he said.

At the same time, Yusef came flying out of the van holding a rifle. He was wearing the ski mask and stepped in front of Linda blocking the cops' view. Linda jumped back into the van and got behind the wheel.

"You can give us that money," said Yusef.

Robert took the money package from the skinny cop's motorcycle compartment. He then disarmed both officers.

"You're all dead," said the big cop. "No where for your black asses to hide."

"Get off them bikes," commanded Robert. The cops dismounted reluctantly.

"Now run," said Yusef pointing in the opposite direction of where Robert had thrown the guns.

The cops moved away from the motorcycles but did so slowly. Suddenly Robert fired the shotgun into the air.

"I said run, goddammit!" Robert said.

The cops began to run. When they were a good distance away. Yusef ran back to the van.

Robert kicked over the cop's bikes then took out a knife and slashed their back tires.

He ran back to the van. He took two steps when someone tackled him. It was the man he'd knocked out. He'd come to. Robert fell forward, the attacker on his back. The shotgun went off into the air.

Yusef leapt out of the van and kicked Robert's attacker hard in the face. The man fell backward. Robert scrambled to his feet.

Robert kicked the fallen man in the ribs and heard one of them break. The man howled in pain.

Linda ran from the van with a can of gasoline and poured it over the toppled motorcycles. She dropped a lit match on them and they burst into flames.

Linda, Robert and Yusef ran back to the van. Linda jumped behind the wheel then peeled off.

They were half way up the block when one of the motorcycles' gas tanks exploded.

18

KNOWLEDGE

"Letter for you, Riley," said Dennison as Thomas walked through the lobby of the precinct house.

"Letter?" said Thomas curiously even as he took it from the burly Sergeant.

The letter was in a plain white envelope and was addressed to him care of the station house. He opened it. The envelope contained a single piece of paper with the word "MURDERER" written on it in red.

Now Thomas was sure that he was being followed. This had to be from the dead boy's brother, what had he said his name was? Robert, he thought.

He tore the note to pieces and went in to change. He tried to calm as he dressed, telling himself that the uniform made him noble, pure and above all the trouble he sensed.

But an hour later, there was more bad news. Yet another committee was calling him and this time, it was official.

He immediately went to look for Ned. He wanted to talk to him, ask him what had happened in his meeting. Ned had told him it was quick and uneventful. He told them that he was the last on the scene and by the time he got there, the boy was dead. But Thomas had sensed there was something more, something Ned wasn't saying.

Ned had called in sick. Convenient, Thomas thought. Brady and Reid were not to be found either.

Now he could see the looks of suspicion on the faces of his coworkers. He felt the whispering behind his back. He was in trouble, a young cop's future on the line for a murder.

Thomas took off early that day and went straight to McGinty's bar and tied one on. Later, he fought bitterly with Sarah after coming in drunk.

There are times in life things seemed simple to everyone around you. People were telling Thomas to tow the line, to stick to the story but it wasn't that easy. He kept seeing the dead boy on the ground and that look of anger in the eyes of his brother. He kept seeing Shaun dying in Korea and watching his father fall to pieces because of it and he kept seeing his beloved Cahan in a big coffin surrounded by hundreds of people.

Death was all around him, guiding his destiny, changing his life. Death and all its vile products sat before him like a putrid tree, whose roots sank straight to hell.

The next day, he went into the committee. This time it had officers from the FBI and IAD. One of the FBI Agents was a Negro.

His Police Officers Association representative was there and they were recording the event for posterity.

Brady and Reid had already talked to this new panel. Thomas wondered why they talked to him last.

"Are you sure you don't want your rep to speak for you, officer?" asked the IAD Agent as Thomas took a seat.

"No, sir," said Thomas. "I can speak for myself."

"My client has nothing to hide," said John Richards, the Police Rep. He was a cop turned attorney and he was known for being good at his job. He had told Thomas not to worry with an air of confidence. But that had not kept Thomas from his concern.

"Do you know why we reopened this case, Officer Riley?" asked the Negro FBI Agent.

"No," said Thomas.

"Don't you mean, "no sir?" asked the Negro.

There was quiet in the room at this question. Thomas locked gazes with the Negro FBI Agent.

"I'm not in the FBI," said Thomas defensively.

The Negro Agent laughed at him derisively like he had scored some kind of victory.

"Some of the riot files were sent to Quantico for analysis," said the Black FBI Agent. "This case bounced back to us."

"We just have a few questions for you, officer," said the White FBI Agent.

"We read your account and the other officers' as well," said the Internal Affairs cop. "You still contend the deceased was dead on the street when you and the other officers found him?"

Thomas looked at Richards who nodded to him.

"Yes," said Thomas.

"You said he had a knife near his hand like he'd been in a fight," said the White FBI Agent.

"Yes," said Thomas not bothering to check with Richards.

"And you heard the shot prior to discovering the body?" asked the Negro FBI Agent.

"That's correct," said Thomas.

"But you and your partner, Ned Young, got separated so only you and officers Don Brady and Matthew Reid found the body first," said the IAD cop.

"That's right," said Thomas.

"And none of your weapons match the bullet that killed Marcus Jackson," said the Negro Agent.

"Because none of us shot him," said Thomas with a little anger in his voice.

"Try to keep your answers to yes or no Thomas," said Richards. "I ask this panel to phrase their questions accordingly."

"We're only stating things that are in the record," said the IAD cop. "We're just getting verification."

"If it's in the record," said Richards, "you don't need to re-verify it. "

The IAD cop threw his hand up in mock surrender. Thomas wanted to nod to Richard or something but he didn't want to make this matter any more antagonistic than it already was.

"So, officer which hand was it in?" asked the White FBI Agent.

"Excuse me?" asked Thomas.

"The knife," said the White officer. "Which hand did Marcus Jackson hold it in?"

Thomas looked at Richards who didn't know what to say.

"This isn't a test people," said Richards. "Whatever's in the report is his answer."

"Your client said the knife was near his right hand," said the Negro FBI agent. "The other two officers said the same thing in their reports and the crime scene photo shows the same."

"If the report says that, then that's what I said," said Thomas.

"Marcus Jackson was left handed," said the IAD cop flatly.

Thomas tried not to show his shock at this. Richards was as cool as ice and then he laughed. "So?" said Richards.

"The man was in danger of losing his life against an armed assailant and he used his other hand?" said the Negro Agent and Thomas saw a deadly serious look on his face.

"And that's not all," said the white FBI Agent. "We found Marcus Jackson's prints on the knife handle but not on the blade. The knife wasn't a switchblade. You have to open it like this."

The agent took out a buck knife and opened it, pulling the blade out with his fingers. He made sure Thomas and Richards saw this action.

"How the hell did he pull off that trick?" asked the IAD cop.

Thomas looked at Richards who terrified him by having a shocked look on his face.

"Nothing to say, officer?" asked the IAD cop.

"All I know is that he was dead when we got there," said Thomas. He looked at Richards who still had the shocked look on his face.

"Listen," said Richards finally. "These matters are filled with stress, maybe my client was mistaken."

"The medical team reports the knife was by his right hand as well," said the Negro Agent.

"Officer," began the IAD cop. "This case is going to be looked at further by this committee. I strongly suggest that you think about the story you gave and what it means to your career."

"People have died, officer," said the White FBI Agent. "And the government is not going to just sit around while nothing is done."

"*People* have died," said the Negro FBI Agent and Thomas caught the meaning of his emphasis.

Thomas was let go. He stepped out into the lobby with Richards. They moved down the hallway when Thomas turned to Richards.

"What the fuck was that?" asked Thomas. "Why did you just sit there like that?"

"What was I supposed to do?" said Richards. "There was nothing in the file about that kid being left handed and prints on the knife blade."

Thomas just looked at Richards then he turned and kept walking. Richards followed him.

"You want to tell me how that knife got opened without his print on it?" asked Richards.

"No," said Thomas. "I can't." He looked away before he could stop himself.

"Well, you and your friends had better find an answer to that question," said Richards. "If this thing goes to a Grand Jury, it'll be a count of perjury if they catch you in a lie."

"No one's lying," said Thomas. "Look, thanks for your help. But next time I'll get myself a real lawyer."

Thomas walked off and he could feel Richards' eyes burning a hole in his back. He knew it was wrong to take out his frustrations on the lawyer but there was no one else around.

Thomas rounded the corner and ducked into a men's room. He went into a stall and pulled out the little flask he'd started carrying lately. His heart was beating fast and he could feel a dull ache building just behind his eyes.

He opened the flask and the sharp aroma of whiskey greeted him. He took two hits from the flask then returned it to his pocket. Then he stuffed his mouth with Juicy Fruit chewing gum and walked back to the lobby.

19

<u>BLOWBACK</u>

Robert and The Vanguard's actions had immediate effect. The theft of the drug pay off money from the dirty cops had started a gang war and ended in the death of a rival dealer. Apparently, the cops had made the dealers get them more money.

"All the better for the ghetto," Yusef had said.

Robert spent the rest of his time watching Officer Thomas Riley and gathering information on him. He found out where he lived, where he went to hang out, his friends and whom he was sleeping with.

Robert saw his woman, a beautiful white girl with blond hair. She was a hippie and a radical, one of the good ones. . He wondered if she knew what kind of man she was with.

He also discovered that Thomas was developing a drinking problem. He'd go to a cop bar and hang out and had taken to keeping a flask on him. Robert smiled at this. The man was guilty and it was eating away at him. Soon, he would break.

Robert decided to send him the letter with the one word on it written in red. He knew Thomas would know he sent it, but Robert was hoping to provoke the cop into doing something stupid.

If he came at him then he'd kill the bastard and his brother could rest in peace. But he'd have to confront him with plenty of witnesses or none at all, he thought.

Robert began to wonder how Riley had avoided the draft. He was young and able-bodied and should have been called. He vowed to find out.

Robert also asked questions about Marcus within The Vanguard. Somewhere between Riley and The Guard was the truth. Marcus was well known and highly respected on the street and within The Guard itself. Marcus often spoke to kids after school and even tried to turn a few dealers away from their occupation. Robert was proud of his brother's reputation but this only brought on more sadness.

Robert's activities caused him to miss a few days at work and soon he was forced to quit his job at the Faygo plant.

"Why did you quit the job, Bobby?" asked Denise.

"I ain't got the time for it," Robert said.

"You need more time to run with those wannabe militants? How's that going to help us?"

"You mean *you*, don't you?" said Robert. "All women care about is some man busting his back for them. Well, I got shit to do and it don't got nothing to do with buying you stuff. You got a job. Work it."

Denise had just glared at him with rage and frustration. She walked out on him and he was surprised to find that he didn't care. In fact, many things that he should have been worried over, he didn't care about anymore. He needed a job and he certainly wanted the love of his parents. But since he'd started on the trail of the killers, none of this mattered.

"This thing's gonna kill you," his mother had said. "God took your brother but this anger's gonna take everything else."

Robert became a stranger in his home. He stayed out later and later doing his work. Some nights, he didn't bother to come home at all.

Denise cut him off in bed, fearing what he might be doing with other women. Robert didn't complain or argue; he just accepted this as the price of his newfound undertaking.

Yusef became a big part of his new life. As he suspected, Yusef had attended Michigan State but dropped out when The Movement called to him.

They spent hours together exchanging ideas and talking about the future of their people. Yusef believed that the Black revolutionaries would some day be as important to America as the Founding Fathers. He even joked that he'd be on the dollar bill some day.

Yusef Muhammad had been a follower of the Black Muslims. After hearing Malcolm X and Elijah Muhammad speak in temple number two on Linwood, he had converted to the Muslim faith and changed his name. Gerald Robinson was gone forever.

Yusef became a bodyguard for the Nation in Chicago and once even protected Malcolm X who pushed for the end of nonviolence as a way of dealing with White America. After Malcolm was killed and other Muslims implicated, he left the fold.

Yusef fell in with various Black radicals and ended up in The Vanguard and was tapped to start a chapter in Detroit.

He jumped at the chance to go back home and continue the revolution. It was here he felt that he was meant to make his mark on the world.

Yusef ordered Robert to teach the other members everything he'd learned in the Marines. Robert held weekly marksman classes and taught hand to hand. Linda was one of Robert's best students. She was tough, mean and possessed a strength that belied her size.

Linda worked as a part-time domestic for a White lawyer in the city. She told her bosses that she was a junior college student but that was a lie. She hadn't even finished high school, dropping out in her junior year.

Ben Kilmer, the lawyer she worked for, was connected in city politics. Linda used the White lawyer's connections to get information that had sometimes been useful to The Vanguard. When the city was planning a crackdown, she informed Yusef and none of their activities were affected.

She hated working for the White people, smiling and acting subservient, but so far, it had been beneficial.

Robert tried not to think about his attraction to Linda who subtly flirted with him all the time. She wore tight jeans or miniskirts and made a point of standing where he could get a good look.

Robert and Denise were not seeing a lot of each other and arguing when they did and their sex life had tapered off.

So Robert fantasized about having the young girl. He'd take her into one of the back rooms and watch as she peeled off her clothes. Once she was naked, he'd taste every part of her until she was begging him to make love to her. Then he'd attack his occupation, feeling the sweetness of her youth and longing with his own.

Such thoughts were dangerous, he knew. A married man was best left to his sexual confinement, where he was safe. Thinking was always the beginning of trouble, he reasoned. So he made it a point to always have someone else around when he saw Linda.

That didn't stop other men from trying to get next to Linda, though. They all seemed to want her but as far as he knew, none of them had any success. Secretly, this made Robert happy.

Yusef encouraged relationships between the members. He himself was sleeping with two of the women as well as a white girl across town.

That was another of Yusef's laws. He told the men that it was their duty to have sex with as many white girls as they could. He knew the white girls all wanted what their fathers told them they could not have and this was an opportunity for the cause.

The men were encouraged to sleep with the white girls and then get them to give them money which found its way into funding operations against their race. It was the sweetest revenge he knew.

Of course, this was a secret between all the brothers. The women were not to ever know about it, Yusef reasoned. Women could be possessive and no one needed that shit. And any woman caught sleeping with a white man would be dealt with severely. They could hustle and scam them but that's all. In Yusef's view, white men had taken all the Black women they were ever going to get.

Robert read the sports page this day in The Vanguard's safehouse that was located in the heart of the inner city. The neighborhood was bad but the people were loyal to the cause. Yusef played Robin Hood amongst the locals and in return they kept quiet.

Linda came in with Bohan, carrying bags of groceries. The safehouse was fully functional and there was always food. Robert missed his mother's meals but lately the home cooking wasn't worth the conversation that went along with it.

Linda smiled at him and immediately put down the bags and walked over. She was wearing a light summer dress and Robert thought that it had been unseasonably warm. It was a sheer burgundy number and it hugged her hips. Her hair was curly today and it crowned her nicely. She wore no bra and her breasts swayed gently beneath the fabric of her top.

Robert fought the swell in his pants. He could not do what he was thinking. Linda was, in a way, his brother's widow.

"Hey," said Linda sitting next to him on a chair.

"Hey yourself," said Robert.

"Hear Yusef's cooking up something big this summer," said Linda.

"Hasn't told me about it yet," said Robert.

"He will. He's got his way about being dramatic."

"Yeah," said Robert not knowing how to respond.

"How come you never asked?" said Linda. "About your brother, I mean."

"Ask about what?" said Robert.

"He was with me that day, you know."

"I didn't know that. He got killed at night."

"Yeah, but, there's more to it," said Linda. "It's kinda personal."

Robert put down the newspaper and turned to her. She was so beautiful that he blinked when he looked directly at her. She smelled of Ivory soap and hair grease. He smiled a little. All the Black girls had the same endearing smells, soap, cocoa butter, Vaseline or Royal Crown and the like.

"Me and Marcus was together that day," she said and she smiled a little. "We always did it in the basement of the house. No one ever goes down there much. He said he was working on something for Yusef but wouldn't tell me what it was. Said it was a secret. I thought maybe that's what he was doing in that white neighborhood that night."

Robert was a little surprised by this. Yusef had been very candid with him about Marcus' activities, but there was never any mention of a special assignment.

"Anyway," Linda continued, "Mrs. Kilmer came back early and Marcus had to hide for about an hour. Then he left."

"What time was it?" asked Robert.

"That was four or so."

"In the summer, there was still four hours of light left," said Robert. "What the hell did he do for four hours?"

"I don't know," said Linda and now her voice sounded sad. Maybe Yusef can tell you."

"I'll be sure to ask," said Robert.

Silence enveloped them for a moment and Robert could tell that the attraction he was feeling was mutual. Linda looked at him and he could see it in her eyes, the desire to be approached.

He thought about Denise and being cut off from sex. He grew ever so slightly angry about it. That was some bullshit, to be denied sex in a relationship where you couldn't get it anywhere else without going to hell.

"I don't want you to feel funny around me," said Linda as if sensing his thoughts. "Me and Marcus we liked each other and all, but we wasn't married or nothing."

Robert looked into her eyes and now they both acknowledged it openly, what they felt and what they wanted.

"I don't." He lied.

"We're all family, you know and it's dangerous to go outside the group when you need to be with somebody."

"I don't know what to say," said Robert. "I'm married, you know—-"

"You ain't listening Robert," said Linda smiling beautifully. "I ain't trying to take you from her."

"I heard you," said Robert. "But it's not that simple. I have to live with it, with her if I... if we do something."

"You're saying a lot of things, but I ain't heard "no" yet," said Linda.

"Linda, you know I want to," said Robert, "I dig you and all but I got too much to lose. Too much," he added.

"Can't say it, can you?" asked Linda. "Okay, then let's call it a maybe. Things change, people change, you know."

She patted his hand and squeezed it a little. She got up and walked across the room and Robert sighed a little watching her ass toss the dress around.

"Shit," he muttered to himself.

Yusef came in and began talking to Vince about something. Robert waited until Yusef was finished and then he asked to speak to him privately.

They moved away from the others and Robert told Yusef what Linda told him about Marcus then waited for the leader to speak.

"Damn," said Yusef, "I told Marcus not to tell anyone. Look Robert, your brother was on a special assignment for

me and I guess you got a right to know. In fact, come on
with me."

Yusef got up and walked outside. Robert went with him.
It was nice out, a bright and sunny day. Some kids played a
game of stickball on a rundown playground.

"We might have a rat in the group," said Yusef flatly.
"The feds may have planted him. I got a friend, a sister in
the government who told me. Your brother was helping me
out, trying to find out who it was."

Robert was a little angry but remained calm. He didn't
want to blame Yusef for anything yet.

"What did he find out?" asked Robert.

"We had a suspect."

"Who?"

Yusef didn't answer right away. He stopped walking and
Robert followed suit.

"I guess I have to trust you," said Yusef. "I mean, you just
got in and we had the problem from before. It was Vince we
were looking at. My government contact told me she saw
him at the federal building once. Vince ain't from Detroit.
He's from Philly but we had him checked out. But you know
the cops, they can make a cover for you."

"But you guys haven't been busted," said Robert so
maybe he's cool."

Yeah, I thought of that. But I keep my activities
fragmented. There's never any one big thing, you know.
The feds, they need a murder or something big to get us all.
They like to do things big. They won't blow their cover for a
little thing."

"So maybe Marcus got burned by Vince?"

"Could be," said Yusef and he seemed to be saddened
and angered by the notion.

"Why didn't you tell me?" asked Robert and now there
was anger in his voice.

"I was going to," said Yusef soothingly. "I didn't want
you to go off half-cocked and hurt the man. I wanted you to
get acclimated first. Besides, I'm not a hundred percent sure,
you know and the group is more important than any one
soldier."

Robert knew this was wisdom. He would have gone after
Vince when he'd first joined and he knew from the Marines

that when you put one man above the platoon, you were fucked.

"I want to take up where Marcus left off," said Robert. "Put me on it."

"You're too close," said Yusef. "I don't know what you might do."

"Then give it to me and another man. He can watch me."

Yusef thought for a long time and then, "Okay, fine. You'll be with Linda."

"Cool," Robert said too quickly. He knew this was potentially trouble but he didn't want to draw attention to it.

"Cool," said Yusef. "Just stick close to him for a while and let me know what you see."

They headed back to the safehouse and for the first time, Robert thought that the murder of his brother might be more complicated than he first believed.

He had no doubt that the cops killed him but now he wondered if the traitor among them had led Marcus to his doom.

It was not difficult to see scenarios under which an informant could have gotten Marcus killed. And what about Yusef, he thought? What if Yusef himself had suspected Marcus or worse sent him into danger knowing what might happen.

Robert tried not to look at Yusef too much. He was a smart man and Robert didn't want him to know what he was thinking on this subject. If he had to take action, he didn't want him to know what was coming.

In Memphis, at 6:01 pm, Martin Luther King Jr. was shot dead by an assassin.

20

<u>RECKONING</u>

There was reaction all over the nation after King's death was announced. Blacks took to the streets in peaceful protest or violent uprising. It was clear that the ethnic minority was still divided on the best course of action.

There were skirmishes and violence in just about every major urban city in the country. The nightmare of a Black revolution, a *defacto* civil war was being felt in every community. The country, already burdened by Vietnam and the rising power of Communism had another terrible problem on its hands.

Thomas was again called into the streets to keep the peace and again he answered the call, only this time he did so fueled in part by alcohol.

Ned was still out sick and Thomas was starting to worry. He called but got only a busy signal. During this time, he had taken on another temporary partner; another old vet named Clark Pierson.

Two days after King's death, Thomas and his temp partner were called to a disturbance at a local pawnshop. They found a group of Black suspects looting the place. Pierson, a balding man with a bushy moustache called in the incident and asked for back up.

They pursued the fleeing men on foot. They ran in several different directions. Pierson and Thomas split up after individuals.

Thomas tracked his man who could not move fast due to the small TV set he carried. Thomas caught up to him in an alley. It was a dead end with a high wall. Thomas drew his service revolver.

The suspect, who could not have been more than eighteen, was caught cold. He placed the TV set on a trashcan and raised his hands in surrender.

"I'm cool," said the suspect. "I'm cool."

"Lock your hands behind your head," said Thomas.

The suspect did and Thomas moved toward the man, taking out his handcuffs.

As he approached, he saw the man change. The skinny dark boy's face turned into those of all the death and loss in his life.

Thomas stopped walking. His legs felt heavy and his stomach lurched. He looked at the frightened man before him who had blessedly turned back into himself. Thomas straightened up and focused on the man. He lowered the cuffs and the gun.

"Run," Thomas said.

"What?" asked the man who looked scared and confused.

"Go," said Thomas. "Get out of here, just leave the TV."

"Uh uh," said the man. "I run and you shoot me in the back. Naw naw, my mama didn't raise no fool. You take me in. If you gonna beat me, go on and do it, but I ain't runnin', not tonight."

For some reason the man's response enraged Thomas. This man had no idea that he was being given a gift. "You stupid--" said Thomas. Then he holstered his gun and snapped in it in. "There. Now get out of here or I *will* shoot you."

The suspect lowered his hands. He backed away, testing the promise and then he turned and ran off, jumping the high wall.

Thomas grabbed the TV set and turned around. When he did, he saw Pierson standing there looking at him with accusing eyes. Thomas was sure his own eyes were filled with guilt.

Before Thomas could say anything, Pierson turned and walked off.

Robert watched the news in his parents' house with heat in his belly. Even though he felt that Dr. King was misguided in his approach, he knew what he meant to Black people. He may have been a fool, but he was *our* fool, he thought.

Abraham watched in silence, his eyes were red from holding back tears. Denise and Theresa were still sniffling, dabbing handkerchief's in their eyes. Robert just watched TV with a cold expression on his face.

The depth of White arrogance always surprised Robert. Dr. King's death was like losing a loved one for every Black American and yet White people only seemed to care about how it affected them. They worried not about the loss of a legend but about the imminence of retaliation. Robert wrung his hands hard as he watched the images on the news.

"I'm going out," Robert said standing up. Later, he would realize that he announced it on purpose, wanting to stir up his family.

"No," said Abraham. "We're going to church and you're coming with us. I've had all I can take of you and this nonsense."

"What I do ain't nonsense," said Robert.

Theresa and Denise watched wanting to comment but knowing that if they did, the argument would only escalate. In a way, they each had been waiting for this for different reasons. There had to be an end to it and the assassination was as good a reason as any.

"You think I don't know what you do out there?" said Abraham. "I'm not blind, Bobby. You quit your job, abandon your wife and give yourself to a worthless cause. Dr. King is dead and now is the time for us to choose."

"What me and my wife do is our business," said Robert.

"Not when it's in my house," said Abraham.

"I am so damned sick of you and your house," said Robert. "You been holdin' that up over me all my life."

"Then get a house of your own," said Abraham. "Go back to work, support Denise and stop acting like a fool."

"I'm not a fool, daddy," said Robert. "If it's time to choose anything, it's time to choose our own destiny."

"If we do what they do, then we're all lost," said Abraham.

"I ain't lost," said Robert. "I'm making a difference."

"How? Doing violence? Following that White cop?" asked Abraham.

Robert looked at Denise accusingly. "So she told you about it, so what?"

"You're playing with fire," said Abraham.

"No good can come of it, Bobby," said Theresa finally. "You've got to find some peace. The church is the way. It's always been there for us."

"I'm going to find out who killed my brother."

"*Your* brother, *your* brother," said Abraham scornfully. "You act like none of us loved him. *He was my son!* And we're all angry about it, too. But anger will not undo what God has done. Only forgiveness will."

"*I ain't got no forgiveness!*" Robert screamed and the statement cut through the moment like a revelation. Robert's eyes were wide and seemed to burn with the truth of his confession.

"Then you have to leave," said Abraham. My house is God's house and there is always forgiveness here."

"Fine," said Robert and he turned away.

"No!" said Theresa grabbing Robert by the arm and moving between father and son. "No. I'm not losing another son, Abraham. I'm not!"

Abraham looked at her and the fact that she said his name and not Robert's told him where she stood. He looked at his wife and all that they were passed between them. Abraham threw up a disgusted hand and he walked out on heavy feet.

"Thank you, mama," said Robert.

The slap that followed was loud and cold in the silence of the room. Robert was stunned. He could remember every time his mother had raised her hand to him. It was not her way and he knew that her intention was not to hurt him but to show how hurt she was inside. He hung his head a little and touched the stinging side of his face.

"Your father is right and you know it," she said. "And even if he wasn't, he's still your father. Some things are bigger than we can know, Bobby. All this hate between Black and White is gonna end as soon as the Lord gets tired of it. You can believe in Him or not but I know in my faith that He is God."

Robert was about to speak but Theresa cut him off. "I'm not the one to argue with tonight about the Lord, Bobby," she said. "You do what you want, but just remember what I said. Then, to Denise, she added. "Sorry you had to see this, baby."

Theresa walked out. The side of Robert's cheek was still burning when he turned to the angry face of his wife.

"What? You gonna yell at me, too?" asked Robert. "Want me to turn the other cheek? I can't believe you told them our business."

"We're all worried about you, Bobby," said Denise. "I'm not going to apologize for what I did."

"I can take care of myself," he said in a frustrated tone. Y'all just need to leave me alone——"

"I'm pregnant," said Denise.

Robert forgot about his mother's anger and his father's disapproval. He looked at his wife and was filled with joy and shock. He pulled his hand from his face and felt the corners of his mouth turning up into a smile.

"When?" he asked.

"This week. I just had to make sure."

Before she knew it, Robert had covered the distance between them and taken her into his arms. He kissed her and she hugged him tightly.

"This is great, baby," said Robert. "This is great."

"Now you see why I told your father?" she said. "We need you, Bobby. This changes everything."

Robert moved back a little so that they could see each other.

"What's different?" he asked with caution.

"Everything," Denise said. "I supported you but now, we have a family and I can't have you out there risking your life."

"And so I'm supposed to just forget about my brother, about the movement, go get a job from the enemy and do what I'm told. I made a baby, Denise. I didn't cut my balls off."

"Why does everything have to come down to that for you? You're not less of a man if you care about your baby."

"I care but there's work to be done on our conditions here, can't you see that?"

"Don't give me that shit about Marcus," Denise folded her arms defiantly. "I know you, Robert Jackson. This is about you. You're thinking that you gave Marcus the knife and you got him mad at you that day. You're thinking, 'If only I had done something.' You're doing all this revolutionary stuff for yourself. Listen to your mother. Let it go before it's too late."

Robert hung his head a little and Denise knew she'd gotten to him some. But he was a bull-headed man and baby or no, Robert had his calling.

"I ain't gonna deny what you said but what's done is done," he began. "Don't matter what my reasons are. My cause is righteous. If my daddy don't want me here, cool. We can move out. Get a little place across town. Maybe move in with The Guard."

"No," said Denise.

"I'm your husband, woman," said Robert with anger and some incredulity. "That don't mean nothing to you?"

"Mother and father come before husband and wife," said Denise. "I may not know what it means to be a man but I know what it means to be me. And it means putting your child before revenge. It means a Black family is good for the movement and another dead father isn't. So, if you're moving out to keep on doing violence, we won't follow."

Robert moved closer to her with pain in his eyes. It was these times that she found him the most attractive, when he dropped his battle armor and showed what was underneath. Denise steeled herself against her own emotions.

"You ain't gonna leave me," he said.

"I'll stay here with mama and daddy while I'm pregnant. If you want to stay with us you can but your activities have to stop."

"You gonna use my baby to make me do what you want?" There was real hurt in Robert's voice.

"You don't know what it means to be a woman," she said.

Robert watched as Denise walked out of the room, leaving him alone. The TV continued to report on Dr. King's death and soon he turned it off when it got to be too much.

He sat alone for along time, debating the issues in his head: a baby, a gift from God versus the earthly causes of men. No matter what his choice, he'd lose.

He asked himself what his son or daughter might want him to do. Would they respect him for leaving and going on with the cause or would they see him as a deserter to their young life? Denise wouldn't have the baby until some time next year, he thought. By then, he could be done with all of this.

He sat for another hour thinking and then he went into his bedroom and kissed his wife. She turned to look at him and before he said anything, she knew he had made his decision.

"I gotta go," Robert said to her. "I'll be close and I'll check on you everyday."

Denise reached over and grabbed his face and kissed him. Robert couldn't tell if it was a good luck kiss or a goodbye one.

21

<u>EVIDENCE</u>

The irony that the leader of the nonviolent movement was killed by the ultimate violence was not lost upon anyone. Now the question was, what would win the souls of Negroes, Dr. King's religious-based philosophy or the radical, violent militancy?

H. Rap Brown and Stokely Carmichael both visited Detroit after King's death. Massive crowds turned out to see both dynamic speakers. Their fiery rhetoric inflamed an already angry people and projected fear into the hearts of Whites. They each spoke of King's death as a call to arms against an enemy that showed no mercy.

Thomas and other police had been assigned to protect the speakers and they received a chilly reception. Brown and Carmichael taunted police and spat fiery words of revolution into the air, making a thankless job even more so.

The only good news around town was the Tigers had taken first place in their division and showed no signs of slowing down.

Thomas had been talking about baseball the night before at McGinty's but that was the last thing he remembered at this moment. Right now, he didn't know how he'd gotten into the room he was in. In fact, he didn't *know* what room he was in. The last thing he remembered was going to McGinty's after his shift ended and having a good time.

Pierson had moved on since Thomas let the Negro suspect escape. Thomas didn't care. Ned would be back soon and he'd have a real partner again.

Thomas was on the floor of the room and it didn't seem familiar to him. He was on his face and looking into a hardwood floor. The floor was dark brown and seemed to be well kept. It was polished and he could see his own eye in the dull reflection. He felt a cold draft on his legs and then something else.

He was naked.

He turned over and felt himself. Shit. His genitals felt cold and doughy. Thomas lifted himself off the floor. He looked around the room and now he was sure that he was not home. As he righted himself, a sledgehammer hit inside his head and he almost fell back to the floor.

He sat up straight and just breathed for a moment. His balls hit the cold floor and he winced. Sarah popped into his head and he winced again. Then he began to remember.

After his shift ended, he'd run into Brady and Reid. They were confrontational as usual but this time there was more. They were scared. The talk of Grand Juries and indictments was everywhere.

The death of Dr. King only made things worse. Negroes wanted blood and heads on platters. White heads. Police heads. Brady and Reid were afraid and they leaned on him about keeping quiet in their most threatening manner.

Thomas had gotten into a bitter argument with the two men and it had almost come to blows. But cooler heads prevailed and the three men parted company without incident.

Thomas went home and found Sarah there with some of her college friends. He hated when they came over to his place and she didn't tell him.

All the guys she hung out with wanted to fuck her and Thomas wasn't sure about some of the women's motives in that regard. The radical student movement was filled with perverts.

Thomas wanted to unwind but was forced to listen to talk about peace and how the Negroes were oppressed and how White people needed to stop it. He went into the kitchen and poured himself a drink, then another.

After he was intoxicated, Thomas had said the wrong thing. Actually, he had said many wrong things and Sarah had corrected him in front of her friends and demanded an apology.

Thomas refused to apologize. He was still a man after all, not like these long-haired queers who thought reading books made them men.

Sarah made him feel like a stranger in his own home, so he said more nasty things. The friends had excused themselves and headed out.

And then the real fight began. He and Sarah went over all of their problems again, rehashing all the pain, broken promises, mistakes and incompatibility issues.

She started in on him about his drinking, telling him that he was becoming a stereotype, a drunk, Irish cop. He just ignored her, lying about how much he drank and what a problem it was. He struck back at her with her balk on the marriage and her excuses for it. He called her a snob and he knew that hurt. And then Sarah went for the deathblow.

She said he was just like his father.

Thomas had heard a train coming. Sarah kept talking but the train's noise filled his ears with its deafening rumble. She was turning red as she spat his sin at him. And then he saw a fist traveling toward Sarah's face. The train wouldn't let him hear what she was saying and that fist, it was just going to hit her all on its own.

Sarah stopped yelling at him when she saw the trembling hand. It meant to strike her, to hit her in her lovely mouth and shut her up.

She looked at Thomas with fear and shock in her green eyes. It was his hand and it was going to smite her like a god would a nonbeliever.

Thomas stopped the arc of the blow. He turned his head toward the hand and unclenched his fist and dropped it to his side, hoping it would fall off and roll into a corner.

He was about to say something to Sarah, something magical that would make this ugly moment fade from her memory but Sarah flashed a look of pure fear from her green lights then ran off. She went into the bathroom and he heard the door lock loudly.

He went to the door and was about to pound on it but then he would be the monster that she obviously thought he was. He called her once, but she didn't answer.

The regulars at McGinty's welcomed him like the prodigal son later that night. A few drinks and he had told the entire story. He was surprised by the sympathy he received. These were learned men, men who had been through much in life and they understood.

"Is that all, boy?" said one man. "Shit, you're all worked up over nothing. A real woman needs a good smack in the chops at least once a week."

"You should go back and finish the job," said another learned drunk."

"Hell, I hit my first wife," said yet another. "Second one, too. "I'll get married again, when I find one that can take a punch!"

Laughter rolled and the liquor flowed like a soothing river.

Something had told Thomas that this was wrong but for the life of him, he couldn't remember what it was. The sweet, thick haze of whiskey blocked that knowledge. It blocked everything and that's why he loved whiskey. It never questioned or doubted and it never ran out. One regular always said if they put some tits on a bottle of Johnny Walker, he'd marry it.

"Barbara," Thomas said out loud in the little foreign room.

There had been a woman at the bar. She was a regular, too, a female regular. She had dyed reddish hair and wore tight dresses. All the men knew her and they all acted like they knew some secret.

She was a whore, Thomas had thought and she was looking at him all night. He remembered thinking that he was probably the only man who hadn't had sex with Barbara.

He looked around the room now and saw the unmistakable touch of a woman.

"Jesus," he said.

He was so drunk that he couldn't have had sex with the woman and God only knew what she really looked like. Barbara seemed to be a fairly attractive woman but whiskey tended to improve a woman's pulchritude.

Thomas got up and looked for his clothes. He found them and began to dress. He smelled food cooking and it made his stomach lurch. He was going to be sick and he ran out of the room. He saw a small bathroom across the hall and went into it. He fell to his knees and heaved over the toilet for about a minute but the sickness passed and nothing left his body.

He waited for a few moments and then went downstairs. The house was fairly big. It was nicely done and he saw a picture of a handsome man in his twenties on a wall next to a stunning and shapely redhead that had to be Barbara as a younger woman. As far as he knew, Barbara wasn't married and if she was, he hoped that that man in the picture was not at home.

Thomas got into the kitchen to find Barbara preparing breakfast. He was relieved to see that she was indeed nice looking. She was ten years older than the woman in the picture but still a looker. Her waist was narrow her hips round and her chest ample. She was in a pink robe and her red hair was tied in a ponytail.

"You look like shit," she said.

"I kinda feel like it too," said Thomas.

"It's almost done," said Barbara. "Have a seat."

"Barbara I... I should get going."

"Please. Let's not do the 'Oh what have I done' act." She put some eggs onto a plate. "I knew you were sauced when I took you home. You took your clothes off and really, I might have done it with you if you was able but sadly your soldier was out of commission."

Thomas sat without thinking. The food was starting to smell good and he didn't want to be rude to someone who had seen him naked.

"Who's the man in the picture on the stairs?" asked Thomas after drinking some juice.

"My dead husband," said Barbara and her mouth turned into a flat line. Died and left me bubkus. Jim was an asshole alive and a bigger one dead."

"I'm sorry," said Thomas and Barbara's pretty little smile returned.

"I live around the corner from McGinty's," said Barbara. "Makes it easier for me."

"Sorry I tried to have sex with you," said Thomas reaching for some food."

"Me too," said Barbara. "I should have got to you after your second shot. You were already pretty lit up when you walked in." She smiled a little then added: "But you know, it's a new day."

Thomas tasted some toast and it was good. He waited for his stomach to rebel but it didn't.

"Barbara, I don't want you to get me wrong but—"

She opened her robe, revealing her breasts. They were large and quite beautiful. Barbara grabbed one and played with it, squeezing and kneading it while smiling at him.

Never had he seen a real live woman do such a thing. He
was transfixed as she fingered her nipple and it became firm.
She unloosed her thick red hair with her free hand and it fell
around her face making her look even more beautiful.

"Everybody already thinks we've done it," she said. "So
if you gonna get the sin, might as well get the fun."

"Thanks but no," Thomas heard himself say.

"Thomas, I usually charge the men I sleep with but I like
you. This is like getting a free car from the car dealer,
honey."

Thomas said no again and Barbara closed the robe and the
delicious flesh was gone. Thomas sighed and Barbara
laughed a little at the compliment.

"Can I ask you something?" said Thomas.

"Since I've seen your cock, "I'd say yes." Barbara smiled.

"Do you think Whites and Blacks can ever live together, I
mean stop all this killing and shit?"

Barbara put her fork down and looked up for a second.
Her brow furrowed a little and then she grabbed her glass of
orange juice.

"No," she said finally. Before he could ask why she
continued. "I think we hate each other, it's like we're
opposites. The Coloreds they just ain't got enough pride
about themselves, you know and White people, we just got
too much."

Thomas just nodded and kept eating. They finished their
breakfast mostly in silence. Barbara never asked him why he
posed the strange question. Thomas guessed it was all
people talked about in Detroit lately and so it was no big
deal.

Barbara teased and flirted with him some more and gave
him a sweet peck on the cheek when he left.

He walked out of the house and stood a moment on the
front porch. A tiny breeze hit him in the face and he
stiffened. He could still smell it, the odor of burned wood,
destruction and death.
Part of him wanted to go back in and take Barbara's offer
and become lost in pleasure, away from life's terrible choices.
Instead, he descended the stairs and headed down the block.

When Thomas got home he was not surprised to find Sarah gone. A handwritten note greeted him on the door. He didn't read it. He checked the house and sure enough, most of her things were gone. He sat down hard on the sofa.

Thomas called out to his grandfather with his troubled heart. He imagined Cahan coming in and sitting with him. Thomas was a boy again and Cahan was bouncing him on his knee and favoring him over Shaun. Everything was sweet, simple and good again.

Suddenly, the phone rang. He snatched it up thinking it was Sarah.

"Gonna get you, muthafucka," said the Negro voice.

"Who is this?" Thomas asked stupidly.

"I'm gonna get you if it's the last thing I do."

"Who the fuck is this--?"

The line went dead.

Thomas slammed the receiver down in anger. He was not going to take this laying down, he thought. He was going to find the Negro and settle this when he could.

He sat for a moment, seething in anger. Then he opened Sarah's note and found just what he knew was there. A break up along with her fear of what he was becoming. But there was a bright spot. A phone number.

Sarah had left a phone number to her friend Elizabeth's place. To him, that meant hope. She still cared and wanted him to know where she was. He called several times but the line was busy.

Thomas went into work a little late. As he hit the lobby, he saw a gathering of cops. Dennison and a few others stood looking somber.

"Riley, " said Dennison motioning him over.

Thomas walked to the big man wondering what was going on. These days it could be anything.

"Yeah sarge?" said Thomas.

"Got bad news, son," said Dennison. "Your partner is dead."

"What?" Thomas said but he had heard him clearly. His partner was dead. "I knew Ned was sick but—"

"No," said Dennison. "He was murdered. We're pretty sure. There are detectives at the scene, his place." Then he added: "I wasn't supposed to tell you for a while."

Thomas ran out of the building, grabbed a cruiser and headed to Ned's house. Ned had lived alone after his second wife left him. Cops never had good luck with women, he mused.

The gravity of this settled on him as he approached the crime scene. A crowd of neighborhood people was across the street from Ned's place. He recognized newspaper and TV people who were being held at bay by uniformed cops.

Sarah, his drunken night and the sexy redhead were erased from his mind as he jumped out of the cruiser and pushed his way into the house.

"You don't want to see this," said a detective Thomas recognized as Bernie Mandeville.

"Move," said Thomas and he stepped around the officer into the small livingroom.

Thomas stopped short as he saw the body of his partner laid out between the livingroom and the entrance to a kitchen. Ned had been shot twice, once in the chest and again in the head. The head wound was delivered after he fell, and there was a large splatter on the floor and lower wall.

Ned was dressed only in his bathrobe. An unopened beer sat in a far corner, obviously dropped when he was shot.

A hit, thought Thomas, heart and headshots, like a professional.

"Pistol," said Mandeville behind him. "One in each area."

"But... he called in to the station," said Thomas with disbelief

"Yeah," said Mandeville. "But we think this was done a day later, after the King assassination. Retaliation. Everyone around here knew he was a cop."

Thomas stepped back as he felt himself becoming a little nauseous. He turned into the living room and saw something that made his heart stop cold.

A bottle of scotch and a glass on a coffee table.

Slowly, he walked over to it and only after asking if prints had been taken did he touch it.

It was full. The glass next to it was empty.

"Detective," Thomas called. Mandeville walked over to him.

"You really shouldn't be here," said Mandeville. "You're practically family, officer."

"This drink," said Thomas ignoring him. "Why was he pouring it, if he was getting a beer?

"He was having a beer and a shot," said Mandeville casually. You think we didn't think of that? Us gold shields are awful smart, officer."

"Ned was a good cop. No way some lowlife broke in here and caught him by surprise."

"So what are you saying?" asked Mandeville.

"He was getting the beer for a guest, someone he knew."

"And that's who killed him?" Mandeville laughed a little.

"I don't see anything funny here, detective," said Thomas. "My partner is dead. We need to do something about it."

"Okay officer," said Mandeville. "I know you're upset but this is a homicide and we're on it. We'll consider your theory but right now, we're thinking some agitator type did this."

"That's what they want you to think!" yelled Thomas and several cops turned in their direction.

"They?" asked Mandeville.

"Whoever did this," said Thomas knowing he'd said too much.

"You should go," said Mandeville. "We got it covered. I'm sorry for your loss." Mandeville nodded to another officer who placed a gentle hand on Thomas' shoulder.

"Come on, sir," said the officer. "Please," he added.

Thomas went to McGinty's and found it full of cops. He was consoled and managed to resist drinking for the first hour. Finally, he took a shot of whiskey and it rested his troubled mind.

Someone had murdered a cop and there was already talk of vigilante justice. But what troubled Thomas the most was that Brady and Reid were not attendance.

The next week, the funeral was held. It was so big that it had overflow in Ned's little church. Both his ex-wives were there and a daughter that Thomas only heard about once.

Brady and Reid came with their wives and Thomas could have sworn that they intentionally avoided him.

Thomas was already working on proving that the two killed Ned. The pressure of the Marcus Jackson investigation was heavy and Brady and Reid found out something about Ned's testimony and had him eliminated. Or maybe Mandeville was right and it was an agitator or maybe even that pest, Robert Jackson.

Whatever the truth, Thomas saw dark days coming and for this he was not happy.

The next day, he called the number Sarah had left but got Elizabeth on the phone. Thomas liked Elizabeth generally but she didn't seem to feel the same way. She was short with him telling him that Sarah was out. He didn't believe her but he didn't start an argument. He promised to call later.

As he walked to the door there was a knock. He hung his uniform on a coat rack, then grabbed his service revolver and went to the door.

"Who is it?" asked Thomas careful to stand to one side of the door frame.

"FBI," said a man's voice.

Thomas opened the door, revealing the FBI agents who had questioned him.

"Thomas Riley?" asked the White agent

"You know who I am," said Thomas.

"Thomas Riley?" the White agent repeated in a flat, all-business tone.

"Yes," said Thomas relenting.

"You've been subpoenaed to testify in connection with the death of Marcus Jackson," said the Black agent.

The Black agent handed Thomas the paper and smiled. It was the most evil smile Thomas had ever seen.

The White agent just looked at him like he smelled something foul. Then they turned and walked off.

Thomas stared at the envelope. He opened it and looked at the thing. The official court heading, the scrawl of a judge and the noble pronouncements made his knees weak.

Thomas closed the door and turned. He caught sight of his uniform hanging on the coat rack. It teetered on its wire hanger and rocked back and forth like a man on the gallows.

PART THREE

DARK TOWN REDEMPTION

June 1968 – October 1968

"Man must evolve for all human conflict a method
which rejects revenge, aggression and retaliation.
The foundation of such a method is love.

- Martin Luther King Jr.

22

<u>GHOSTS OF MOTOWN</u>

Robert Jackson was now living two distinct lives in the changing city. He continued to harass Thomas Riley and followed Vince when he could do so safely. He now felt that part of the mystery of his brother's death involved The Vanguard, the mole inside of it and the White officers.

He lived in a little apartment near The Vanguard safehouse. It was a modest place with only five other tenants, most of whom were working families. He kept to himself, didn't talk much and generally minded his own business. The owner was a Guard ally and so the rent was low.

The death of the cop named Ned Young had surprised him. When he'd read it in the news, he'd wondered if the police would come looking for him officially or off the clock. Either way, he was ready.

No good end comes to a man who was no good, he thought. If the cops did bring him in, he'd make sure he had plenty of witnesses and a lawyer.

Yusef had asked him if he had killed the cop. Robert said nothing, simply reminding Yusef of the conspiracy laws. Yusef had only laughed and patted him on the back.

But Robert had not killed the old cop. He was pretty sure the one called Ned had nothing to do with Marcus' death. But maybe the resolve between the conspirators was weakening. Maybe the other three had iced him for wanting to tell too much.

Robert smiled at this thought. He might not have to do anything but wait for them all to self-destruct.

White people were leaving Detroit in droves now. The riot, Dr. King's death and growing violence were too much for them, he guessed.

Negroes on the other hand, seemed to be doing well in some quarters. Motown's success was growing. Berry

Gordy moved his headquarters to the Donovan Building on Woodward Avenue in the middle of downtown Detroit.

Now here was a Black company in the same neighborhood with the titans of the city. White people would see Black men wearing nice suits and driving fancy cars and Black women coming to work in offices like their White counterparts.

The Guard and other radical groups were also doing well. Many people tried to get in The Guard but Yusef was very selective and still very worried about moles. They had added some members but not nearly as many as they might have.

The Guard's activities were becoming more sophisticated. They still dealt in civil disobedience but they also began to undermine the establishment's financial institutions as well.

To Robert, this was a fancy name for fraud but he went along with it in the name of the cause. Bank scams; check kiting and out and out robbery kept the coffers full. He got a small cut of the funds, as did they all.

Yusef also used the money to buy weapons, black market explosives and to influence local politicians. These funds helped change a city council vote on zoning and saved a Black neighborhood.

Yusef was particularly happy these days. The White people were leaving the city and soon, Blacks would have a clear majority. They'd take over Detroit, D.C., Baltimore and other cities and turn them Black. And then America would have to bargain with the brothers for power. He could see the end of the revolution and it was beautiful.

Robert's other life was at his former home where he checked in regularly on his unborn child and wife.

Denise and Theresa made him feel guilty each time he showed up and as Denise's belly grew, she had only to look at him to break his heart.

Abraham was noticeably absent when Robert came by. The Tigers were in first place and his excuse was that he was needed at the stadium. Robert knew this was a lie but it kept conflict out of his visits and that was a blessing.

So it was no shock to Abraham when two uniformed cops visited the family saying they wanted to talk to Robert. But the family didn't know where their errant son was. Robert had never given them his new address fearing just this kind of situation.

Abraham was embarrassed that everyone on the block saw a police car outside of his home. Robert knew the cops had come to question him about the murder of Ned Young.

They had not come with an arrest warrant, only with the flimsy need "to ask a few questions." If he had been home, there's no telling what the officers might have done.

Even though the riots had made cops more wary, they still had their violent ways. Maybe he would have been taken for a ride downtown for questioning that would never happen. For once, he was glad that he'd left home.

A Grand Jury was looking into Marcus' death as well as other riot deaths. Theresa and Abraham had applauded this action and thanked God.

Robert wasn't fooled. The White man was just putting the finishing touches on the cover-up just like Kennedy and King. When all was said and done, there would be no one held accountable. Still, he secretly harbored hope that someone would be arrested and it would all be over.

Robert and Linda were following Vince around town this day. Vince was with Bohan and one of the new recruits, a tough, sharp-edged woman named Bernia.

Robert and Linda watched the trio as they talked to some young kids outside of a high school. Bohan was an incendiary speaker and he held the crowd in his hand. Meanwhile, Vince and Bernia stood in the audience and led him on.

"So what you gonna do?" asked Bohan. "Now that the white man is afraid of us, are we going to just say 'good' and go back to drinking whiskey, shooting dice and taking White people's shit? That's what our fathers would do. But we're the new generation and it ain't happening! We have an obligation to our children to discourage White people of the notion that they can ever take anything from a Black man and walk away without a foot in their flat asses!"

The kids laughed and clapped for Bohan. But it was not the ones who enjoyed the speech that Vince and Bernia watched. In the crowd, there were several young men and women who just nodded their heads and listened. These were the probable future Guard members, the ones who were not moved to easy emotion but understood the message, the ones with inner rage.

"When is Yusef gonna drop this shit," said Linda with frustration. "We been on him for a long time and we ain't got nothin'."

"We got something," said Robert. "We just don't know what it is yet."

"What we got?" asked Linda sounding like an innocent child.

"Who is he calling from them pay phones all the time?" asked Robert. "He always looks suspicious when he does it. So who's getting the calls?"

"His mama?" said Linda jokingly.

"His mama is dead," said Robert. "Or at least that's what he said. And whenever we've followed him on foot, we lose him because he shakes us. Why is he so good at that? It's like he's worried about something more than being followed. That's why we each have a car today. We're gonna find out where the hell he's going."

"Well, I think we ought to give up," said Linda. "We could be working on hitting that Jew store with the others."

Robert turned to her with a serious face. "This man might have caused Marcus' death. If there's any chance to find that out, I'm gonna do it."

Linda flashed an ashamed look. "I'm sorry," she said. "I didn't mean to—— I'm sorry."

"No problem," Robert said and he gave her a smile. She returned it and she looked so sexy that he felt that immediate need to compliment her and get a dialogue started in that direction. Instead, he asked something that had been on his mind since the night at Cal's.

"So why are you working at that janitor service?" asked Robert. "That's a shitty way to make money for the cause."

"I ain't supposed to talk about it," said Linda. "But I really can't because I don't know."

"Well, maybe it's better you didn't," said Robert. He hoped this would prompt her to tell him more, but it didn't.

Robert turned and kept watching as she put her hand on his shoulder warmly. He noticed that whenever he was aggressive or strong that it seemed to turn her on. She rubbed his back a little and he was reminded that he had not had sex in a while.

"I don't like that Bernia," said Linda. "She's always looking at me funny."

"You think she's a dyke?" Robert asked.

"Seems like one to me," said Linda then she made a disgusted noise.

"Maybe she sees something in you," Robert joked.

"That ain't funny," said Linda. "My cousin is like that and I stopped speaking to her, nasty bitch."

"Sorry," said Robert.

They watched for a while longer then the trio left the gathering after taking time to talk to the serious faces in the teen crowd.

Vince, Bohan and Bernia walked down the street and had lunch at a little rib shack. Robert and Linda took this opportunity to move their cars closer to them.

When they got back, they saw Vince walk to a pay phone and place a call. When lunch was over, Vince split from the other two then went on by himself.

"Okay," said Robert. "Let's get on him. Every time he heads to the Westside. There's two main ways to get there from here. You take Six Mile and I'll lay in at Seven Mile. One of us should pick up on him. If you find him, follow and then come back with what you see."

Linda agreed and they each set off. Vince traveled the east side ducking into alleys and generally making sure he wasn't followed and then he jumped on a westbound bus. By the time he got to Woodward, Robert was a mile or so ahead of him.

Robert waited on Seven Mile waiting for the bus to come by. This area was very White and Jewish and he stood out. Luckily for him, there was a car wash nearby. Robert hung out with some of the other Blacks at the wash and waited. When he saw Vince go by on a bus he hopped back into his car and followed.

Vince got out at Greenfield and headed north toward Eight Mile. Robert left his car in Detroit and crossed the avenue that separated the city from the northern suburbs.

Vince seemed nervous and Robert couldn't tell if it was guilt or fear from being out in whitey land. He kept a distance from Vince, knowing that two Black men too close together would be seen as a danger.

Robert watched Vince duck behind a trampy looking motel. The Black prostitutes who worked the northern part of Detroit took their White johns into such places.

Robert waited and then he followed. He found the back of the place clear. He checked the individual windows.

Suddenly, he saw a police cruiser coming his way. The back of the motel faced another street and he was exposed. The traffic was going so fast that he hadn't worried but the cop car was cruising slowly like they always do.

"Dammit," he cursed. His heart started to beat faster and he told himself to calm down.

Robert dropped down behind some garbage cans and held his breath. This was it, he thought. He'd be caught and jailed or worse. He thought about Denise and the baby and saw her telling him again that he was wrong for what he was doing, that he was putting himself in unnecessary danger.

Robert peeked between the cans and saw the police cruiser come his way. He was prepared to run for his life but the car stopped and finished executing its turn and moved on.

Robert waited for a while and then stood up. He continued to check the rooms, peeking around drawn blinds and shades.

And then he heard the Temptations and voices from a room. But the voices were not conversational; the couple was in the throes of passion.

Robert went to the window where he heard the sounds coming from and tried to get a look inside. Vince must have climbed in the window through the back, he thought.

Robert struggled to see around the blind that had been drawn. He saw two bodies writhing on the bed and the voice of a woman grunting and moaning. On a little table, he saw a small radio from which the Temptations' voices came. Why had Vince come way out there to get laid? He thought.

Robert got some of the garbage cans and blocked the view from the street while he waited. He crouched there listening to the couple moan and curse. He tried not to think about Linda but it was all he could think of.

He entertained more fantasies of having sex with the young girl. He saw her taking him to bed, lying down and that wonderful moment when a woman first surrenders her precious gift to your power.

The couple's moans reached a crescendo and soon they were done. Robert moved back to the window and peeked inside. He saw the covers fall away revealing a naked Vince. Next to him, was a White woman.

She was about thirty or so and had dark hair. Something flashed in the dull light and Robert saw that she wore a huge wedding ring.

Robert remembered what Yusef had told him about compromising White women. Now Vince's actions made sense. Unless that woman was with the FBI, Vince was just covering up the affair.

Robert waited a while longer and saw the woman give Vince some money. When they started to make love again, he moved off, taking the garbage cans away so as not to make Vince suspicious when he came out.

Robert went back to his car, careful not to attract too much attention in the White neighborhood. He thought about Marcus and how darkness had caught him on his way home.

Suddenly, he hated White people and all of their shit. The simple act of walking from one place to another was a life-threatening action because of them. They truly were the devils the Black Muslims said they were.

When Robert got to the safehouse, he found Yusef gone. Robert asked where he was and was told Yusef was at a local park. He found Yusef there watching a kids' game of baseball.

Robert got his attention and then he and Yusef moved off by themselves. Robert told Yusef about Vince and Yusef just laughed.

"Was she a good looking White bitch?" asked Yusef.

"I didn't get that good a look," said Robert. "I saw she had on a wedding ring, though."

Yusef laughed again showing his perfect teeth. "Man I love it. Some White oppressor is going to bed with that bitch every night not knowing that he's following a Black dick."

"Thing is," said Robert, "I didn't find nothing suspicious on that other thing."

"Yeah," said Yusef, "so now I really don't know what the fuck is going on. If it ain't Vince, then who?"

"What about Bohan?" asked Robert. "He's all militant and shit but there's something about him I don't trust, almost like he's working too hard, you know."

Yusef's face darkened. "Look man," said Yusef. "I'm gonna tell you something because I trust you but I don't want you to judge, okay?"

"Judge Bohan or you?" asked Robert

"Either one of us," said Yusef.

"Okay," said Robert. "You got my word."

"Bohan's a punk," said Yusef. "That's what you sense from him, why he tries too hard. He's a faggot."

Robert didn't know what to think about this. He didn't see any signs that Bohan was a sissy but he had to take the information on its face.

"How do you know?" asked Robert.

"I busted him," said Yusef. "I got suspicious of him when I did a check. My friends in Chi Town told me he was suspect, so I confronted him and he copped to it."

"What did he say?" asked Robert.

"He denied it at first and then he just said that he struggled with his sexuality sometimes," said Yusef. "I had a decision to make. The brothers ain't too keen on that shit, you know. They feel like any man who gets down like that is weak and can be turned. So, I let him stay but I told him that if he was found out, that I'd have to let him go. He's a good brother and a strong leader. I don't really care where a man puts his dick as long as he's loyal."

"If you cool with him, then I am too," said Robert. "I just never thought he was like that."

"You can't tell these days," said Yusef. "Faggots are some of the most manly muthafuckas I ever met, especially the Black ones. Yusef thought for a second, then "The sooner I find this rat, the sooner I can tell everybody about my plan to put us on the map."

"What you gonna do if you find the mole?" asked Robert.

"Kill him," said Yusef. "Same as the White man does for treason."

Robert left Yusef and went to visit Denise but called first so that Abraham would be warned. He made the trek across town and found both his mother and father gone. He wondered for a moment if Theresa was avoiding him as well.

He and Denise had pleasant conversation over some cold chicken and then the talk got serious as it usually did.

"I'm not coming to live with you, Bobby," said Denise. "Stop asking."

"If I stopped, you'd think I didn't love you anymore," said Robert.

Denise didn't respond she just tore into a chicken thigh and washed it down with a Faygo pop.

"I know you think I'm doing what I'm doing for myself," said Robert but I'm not. I mean I am messed up about my part in Marcus' death but there's more to it. I don't want my son growing up and getting lynched because he looked at a White woman or was in the wrong part of town. I don't want my daughter raped just because some White man got a notion. I'm making this world better for our baby, can't you see that?"

"No," said Denise quickly. "I don't see it. All I see is a man obsessed with a ghost and regrets he can't do anything about. The world ain't yours to save, Robert Jackson. Come back home, get a job and raise your baby; that will make the future much better than anything you can do out there in the street."

Robert just shook his head. She didn't get it. Denise was like most women, only concerned about their own safety, their own little piece of the world through a man's effort.

"This revolution is bigger than you know, Denise. This whole country is going to fall. White folks are tearing themselves apart and when it all comes down, you gonna see I was right and I had to do what I'm doing."

Denise fell silent and continued to eat her chicken. Robert got up and kissed her on the forehead and rubbed her belly. He pronounced his love for her again.

"I'll be around," he said. And then he told her where he was living and not to tell anyone.

Robert left his former home and had a sense of sadness as he always did. The little apartment where he lived now was a house but certainly no home. But he didn't head there. He had one piece of unfinished business today.

He headed downtown and went to Cadillac Square. There, he waited until a plump Black woman of about forty or so walked up and sat next to him.

"You late," said Robert.

"I got a job," said the woman. "Anyway, it takes time to do what you wanted. I had to get by a lot of people. These things is secret, you know."

She just looked at Robert and then he remembered. "Oh," he said, "here." He handed her some money.

The woman counted it and then she reached in her purse and handed Robert a manila envelope.

"How's the fight going?" asked the woman.

"Good," said Robert. "I appreciate this."

"Don't know why you care so much about this one," said the woman. "He's pathetic if you ask me."

"I got my reasons."

"Okay," said the woman. "It's been a pleasure." She got up and turned and walked off.

"Thanks," Robert called behind her.

After the woman was gone Robert opened the envelope and lifted the first document, the draft records of Thomas Riley.

23

GRAND BOULEVARD

"I wanted you to know that I'm not coming back," said Sarah, as they walked along. "I know you've been hoping I would, but I'm just not sure about it."

The flat, almost business-like quality of her tone hit Thomas hard. Sarah had agreed to meet him in the shopping district on Grand Boulevard. It was overcast out and the sidewalks teemed with people. They walked near the intersection of Woodward Avenue, the literal heart of the city.

"You seeing somebody else?" asked Thomas with a tinge of anger.

"No," said Sarah. "But I don't want you waiting for me."

Thomas felt light-headed. What should he do? Ask more questions; try to engage her in conversation in hopes of getting her to open up? Or should he yell his frustration and preserve his male dignity? In the end, he settled for silence.

"Okay," he said dejectedly. "Okay."

"I know this is hard," said Sarah. "I've been turning it over in my head for a long time but after what happened at your place—"

"I said I was sorry about that," he said and it didn't sound pleasant. He immediately regretted the tone and quickly apologized for it. "I'm sorry," he said.

"Seems like everything is so hard right now," she said. "They killed Dr. King and you and I fight over nothing. I feel silly, you know, like it shouldn't matter but it does. In a way, our problem is the same one the country has."

Thomas didn't know what that meant but he didn't want to say it. He just nodded a little and tried not to look angry.

"My partner is dead," he said. "And he knew there was a pathetic plea behind it. "It's like losing a brother all over again."

"Thomas, don't...." Sarah's voice cracked a little.

"I don't know what I'm gonna do without you," he said . "I feel like no matter what I say right now, that it's gonna be wrong, like I can't ever please you."

Sarah moved closer to him and for a moment he thought she would kiss him. "Maybe you shouldn't think about me so much," she said. "I'm moving in with Liz so you know where to reach me. I gotta go, really."

She walked off. He watched her move off and waited for her to turn around and look back at him, an act that might have given him hope. But Sarah walked on and out of his life like there was a great power pushing her away.

He saw the world swirling, spinning in the fetid water of his life, headed into rank inevitability.

Just then, he caught the scent of alcohol. But there was none around. It was in his head, he reasoned. The drink had taken charge of his brain and could call him anytime it wanted. He desperately wanted a drink. No, he reasoned, this time he *needed* one.

Thomas got to his apartment just after dark. The low-rise building looked ominous as a streetlamp flickered on. The shadows around the place were growing long as he approached.

Sarah's statement encouraging him to date was her way of trying to get out of their relationship, he thought. If he dated someone, then she could date without guilt and then once they were both on the market, it was over.

Maybe she had lied, Thomas thought as he climbed the stairs to the second floor. Maybe she was seeing a man and didn't want him to know. His first thought was to follow her and find out, but if she discovered him, then it really would be over.

Thomas couldn't stop the images of Sarah having sex with a stranger from entering his mind. He saw her naked, being kissed and stroked by the man, touching those places that were meant only for him. Maybe this new man was even licking her between the legs, which was something Thomas hadn't done with her yet. It was a taboo and he was still getting used to the idea of oral sex.

And then he had a worse thought. What if the man was Black? Sarah had always said that the races needed to mix. What if she was screwing some big Negro with a big Negro penis? His head ached at the thought.

The horrible thoughts were quickly replaced with the urge for a drink. He opened the door to his place with the intention of turning right around and going to the bar.

The first thing Thomas noticed was that the lights were all on. He had left them off but someone had been inside. He was reaching for his gun when his eyes registered the wreckage in the room. Someone had turned his place upside down.

His little TV was busted. The sofa had been slashed and everything in the little kitchenette was broken.

Thomas quickly went from room to room, his gun out in front and surveyed the damage. All of his clothes had been ripped to shreds and they had even unspooled the toilet paper in the bathroom.

He cursed under his breath. Was it Brady and Reid or that Negro? The cops that were sent to his home had not found him or scared him away from his harassment. He would have to take more drastic action.

And then he saw it. On the wall near the bathroom door, there was a message. He guessed it had always been there but he was too shocked, too mad to have seen it. He forgot about Robert Jackson. The enemy was closer. The message read simply:

PROTECT AND SERVE

He checked the door and saw that the lock had been jimmied. He cursed and kicked things that were already kicked over. He'd find no prints or any other evidence. Cops knew about such things. Thomas sighed and sat in the middle of his living room floor, defeated.

His father had told him this would happen. Frank tried to warn him about not picking the right side in the force. The investigation was coming and he'd have to make a choice then. But this, what they had done tonight, was clearly a declaration of war.

Thomas buried his face in his hands. He found the phone, which was one of the few things that hadn't been broken and called Sarah. The line was busy. After trying to reach her a few more times, he got up and left the ruins of his life and went to McGinty's.

At the same time, Senator Robert F. Kennedy was headed to the Ambassador Hotel in California, where an assassin would end his life.

24

<u>VISITOR</u>

Robert watched the funeral services for Robert Kennedy at Vanguard headquarters with mixed emotions. He was pleased that the power structure was crumbling but he did not like its choice of victims.

Malcolm, Dr. King and now both Kennedys were gone. Great men were rising up for change and the powers that be were killing them as fast as they could. America was going to be dragged into the new age kicking and screaming, or it would not make it at all.

Yusef had been excited about the assassination. He saw the death of Robert Kennedy as a last gasp for America. The racists were trying to hold on to power by murdering off their own leaders while Lyndon Johnson, the southern bigot was in the White House and Nixon; the compliant weasel was planning to run in the next election. In his mind, it would not be long now.

Yusef had come to Robert after Kennedy was shot and informed him that they had to step up their agenda.

Robert saw Linda walk out of the main room. She was a fan of the Kennedys, often wearing t-shirts with their faces on it. The death had hit her as hard as Dr. King's.

He followed her out and found her in a back room near tears. Robert went to her and they embraced.

"I know this is supposed to be good for us," she said but I don't see how. He was a good White man, a good one."

I don't know where this country is going," said Robert but I just know it's gonna be a better place when all this is done. I gotta believe that."

"I don't know," said Linda.

"I can't argue with you," said Robert. "But there seems to be a big price for the kind of freedom we want. I guess we all gotta pay it."

And then he knew it. Knew what had been in the back of his mind since Marcus died and he saw Thomas Riley at the graveyard.

All of his detective work, the harassment, the digging was all preparing him for the inevitable moment when he knew what he had to do. Whether The Vanguard had drove Marcus into the night or not, he had to take revenge because that was what America was about. Power taken by force.

Robert became aware of the woman in his arms again. The smell of her, her tiny heart beating against his chest.

They just stood there a moment, holding each other and Robert could feel the heat rising between them. He wanted to let her go but he couldn't. His arms were locked tight.

"You ever regret killing them Viet Cong in the war?" she asked him.

"Sometimes," said Robert. He didn't know where the question had come from but he wanted to console the girl. " I try not to think about it."

"It's bad, ain't it?" she was talking near his ear and her breath was warm on his skin.

"Yes," said Robert. "Once it's done, it changes you and you can't take it back."

"I got a feeling that more people are gonna die because of what we do here," said Linda. "I don't know if I can live with it."

"Then don't. Stay away from that part of what's coming."

"Don't know if I can," said Linda. "If I do it, do you think you can forgive me?"

"Of course I can," said Robert.

She pulled her head back and kissed him hard on the mouth. All of the thoughts telling Robert to stop were burned away by the fire under his skin. Linda licked and bit at him, pulling at his clothes and he was doing the same to her.

She opened her top and pulled her bra down and pulled his head to her breast. He bit her dark nipple and she moaned loudly. He grabbed at her ass and squeezed it hard. He would have her now at last, he thought.

Robert rose up and looked at Linda's face and was about to kiss her again but the face in his hands was not Linda's. It was Denise's. He was holding his pregnant wife's full cheeks and looking into her brown eyes.

Robert pushed himself away from the heat of the young girl. He was breathing hard and he could feel his heart pounding the walls of his chest. He shook his head slowly and pulled his arms to his side.

"She's pregnant. Denise. We're having a baby," he said. "I'm sorry. I didn't mean to...." He stopped talking because he was about to tell a lie. He had meant to do everything he'd just done. "I do this and I don't know who I am."

Linda didn't say anything she just looked at Robert with longing on her face, her blouse open and her breast still wet from his mouth. She backed away from him, fixing her clothes.

"It's okay," she said. "I'm not mad at you." And then she rushed from the room.

Robert wanted to call after her but it was too dangerous. He fixed his own clothes and left the safehouse.

He walked the short distance to his apartment and his head was filled with images of death. He saw JFK's head blown open, Malcolm X shot by a *de facto* firing squad, Dr. King hit on that balcony and then Robert Kennedy shot down in a crowd at close quarters.

Then he saw images of the war, the men he'd killed and the American soldiers who had died. He saw the riot victims and the fires of hatred. And finally, he saw his brother die and somehow it was all the same sick nightmare.

Death was changing the world, death with its finality, power and deep mystery was laying waste to everything and no force on earth could stop it.

Robert got to his apartment house and headed for his place, which was on the ground floor near the back. He reached for the doorknob and heard a noise inside. He did not have a gun but he always kept a knife on him. If there was someone inside, he had picked the wrong night and the wrong man.

Robert took out the knife and flung the door open.

Denise jumped up as fast as she could for a pregnant woman. She actually screamed a little and lifted herself sideways from the old sofa.

"Denise?" Robert said and his voice seemed to bounce off the cheap walls.

"You scared me," Denise said. "What you doin' with that knife?"

Robert put the blade away, a little ashamed. "Didn't know who was in here."

"The super, he let me in," she said.

He went to her and as he got closer he could see that her eyes were red and she'd been crying. Robert hugged her and he felt the bulb of her belly against his. It felt like joy.

"I didn't know what to do," said Denise. "I saw Bobby Kennedy dead and I thought about what you said and I couldn't stop crying and thinking about the baby."

"It's gonna be all right," said Robert. "They won't win. I won't let them."

He held her and was surprised that his bold statement did not sound hollow to him. He meant it. He would not let these forces ruin his life or that of his child.

Robert glanced next to the sofa and saw a suitcase that looked heavy and full. He smiled.

"I should be here, with you," she said.

"Thank you. He kissed her then grabbed the suitcase and looked for a place to put her things.

The next day, Robert got to the safehouse just after noon and found it filled with members. He mingled and tried not to have awkward moments with Linda but to no avail. She cornered him and made pleasant talk. He chatted with her and breathed easier when another member came and joined them. Robert extricated himself from the conversation and moved on.

Yusef arrived and the members assembled. They stood around Yusef in a big circle, as was their custom. Yusef had told them that this was the way tribesmen met in the Motherland, standing as equals. Yusef quieted the crowd and began to speak:

"My beautiful brothers and sisters," he began. "Troubled times are upon us. The Black man still fights for his dignity while the White man is killing his own like dogs, trying to hold on to the racist status quo he created."

There was applause at this and Yusef quickly quieted them down.

"If we are not careful," Yusef said, "the movement will fall into the hands of the pacifists, the apologists and others in league with our enemies. The same tired ass niggas who take promises instead of truth, the same niggas who take laws instead of realities, the same niggas who take an ass-kicking and then open a Bible to heal it. If we want freedom, we must be willing to pay the ultimate price. I will not ask you to do anything that I wouldn't do myself and I am asking you for your life in service of our cause."

The room was stock-still and Robert could even hear the breathing of people near him. This was it, the moment when every soldier learns his worth.

"I have a plan to put our group in the forefront of the movement and focus the eyes of the nation on this city," Yusef continued. "Detroit, home of the worst race riot in American history will be the cradle of our new movement! We will attack on three fronts, the paramilitary police, the government and the center of economic power. We will not follow the weak ways of dead leaders. We will force them to come to the table with a real bargain for freedom or we will burn this muthafucka down!"

The members were starting to applaud again when the doors to the room burst open and the place was flooded with police. They brandished automatic guns, pistols and shotguns.

The room fell into chaos.

Some of the members tried to run, others fought but the cops were well-armed and organized.

Yusef struggled against two cops and his face held an anger which none of them had ever seen.

Soon, all of the members were facing the wall spread-eagle and the cops were patting them down and removing knives from their person. Yusef insisted that the guns be kept away from the members in the safehouse for just this reason. They could avoid a weapons charge if they were raided.

The two Vanguard members who were posted outside to guard the meeting were hauled in handcuffed and thrown to the floor.

The leader of the police, a thin, hard-looking cop walked over to members lined up against the wall. He went down the line, and then stopped at Yusef.

"You the leader?" he asked. "I saw you standing in the middle of this gang."

Yusef didn't answer he just scowled at the cop. The cop hit him hard in the ribs and Yusef fell to one knee.

"I'm only going to ask you one more time," said the cop. "Are you the leader?"

"Fuck you," said Yusef.

The cop hit him with the butt of a rifle and Yusef fell to the floor. Robert jumped away from the wall only to have a gun placed at his temple. He threw up his hands and was shoved back to the wall.

"Cuff 'em!" yelled the leader. "We know who you are and your little game is over," he said to the members. "Fucking ungrateful traitors. I suspect my men will find drugs on these premises and you all will be charged."

"Ain't no drugs in here!" someone shouted.

The cops began to handcuff the members when Robert saw movement from the corner of his eye. He turned his head toward Yusef who was moving on the floor beside the cop leader. He didn't yell at him to stop. He wanted Yusef to do what he was obviously doing.

Yusef was reaching for the cop's service revolver.

Yusef grabbed the gun and the cop leader turned just in time to see him take it from his holster.

The cop was too close to Yusef to get a shot with the long-barreled rifle and so when Yusef raised the gun, the cop would be dead.

Yusef leveled the barrel and a shot rang out. But it was not a pistol shot but the big bang of a rifle from another cop who saw Yusef and reacted. Yusef was hit in the chest. He flew backwards and the gun was lifted into the air. Yusef fell on his face and lay there, dead.

The other members were shocked. Some cried and others even tried to fight but the cops beat them back or intimidated them with guns. He was gone and there was nothing they could do about it.

"Fucking bastard tried to kill me," said the leader incredulously. He was breathing hard obviously shocked by Yusef's attempt. "Did you see that?"

"One less to worry about," said the man who had shot Yusef.

The leader took the cop who had killed Yusef and went to another cop and whispered something. This man took it to several others who nodded.

The cops then took four of the men, including Robert and lined them up on the wall away from the others.

"I guess we're gonna have some casualties here," said the leader. "Turn them around."

Robert and the others were turned around and several cops leveled their weapons at them. The remaining members looked on in horror. Some cried, others prayed.

"Stop!" said Bohan. "I'm a cop!"

"Get your black ass back on that wall," said the leader.

"No," said Bohan. "I'm undercover and if you shoot me, your asses are going down. You just blew a year of work here."

Bohan's voice was different now. His Black inner city dialect was gone and he sounded more proper and educated, more like Yusef actually but not like whom he had presented himself to be.

The cop leader thought about this. He looked at another cop, and then turned back to Bohan.

"How do I know you're telling me the truth?" he asked. "And if I think you're lying, I'll shoot your black ass myself."

"You can check with Agent Thomason at the FBI and the local liaison, Detective Dietrich at Detroit PD. My UID is 13970."

The leader dropped his rifle. The other cops did as well. Bohan dropped his hands and sighed a little.

Suddenly, Yusef rose from the floor.

"There's your mole," said the leader. He took off his police cap and a cascade of long black hair fell out onto his shoulders.

Robert stepped away from the wall and stood next to Yusef and the cop leader. Bohan's mouth hung open as he looked around at the cops who were all smiling.

"Let my people go," said Yusef deadpan. The phony cops began to release the members.

"They're friends," said Yusef to his followers. "They are from the Dark War Front. Do not hurt them. We're all friends here. To Bohan, he said: "Except you."

Suddenly, a man charged at Bohan. It was Vince. He hit Bohan with a running punch and toppled the big man to the floor.

"Muthafuckin' rat!" said Vince. He kicked at him on the ground.

Bohan jumped to his feet ready to fight but he met the barrel of a gun in the hand of Yusef.

"This one's not loaded with blanks, Bohan," said Yusef. "Handcuff this nigga," he said to Vince.

Bohan was handcuffed as the rest of the cops took off their disguises.

"You owe me big for this," said the leader. "I had to shave for you."

"And I will repay you, David," said Yusef.

David and Yusef shook hands and hugged as the White men started to leave the room.

The Vanguard members huddled around the traitor and glared at him. Robert saw the look of hate in Linda's eyes and it froze him.

"You all can thank brother Robert for this," said Yusef. "He brought us a little trick the man used in Vietnam. I've suspected that we had a mole for a long time and now we know."

There were murmurs of approval and applause and Robert felt someone clap him on the back.

"Now, you little faggot," said Yusef. "We want to know what you've told them about us."

"You can't kill me," said Bohan. He was looking right into Yusef's eyes and surprisingly showed little fear. "They know I'm in."

Yusef hit him hard in the face. "Answer my question!"

"Let me," said Vince who clearly felt more betrayed by the man he had called friend.

"I'm not telling you anything," said Bohan.

"Our friend here is a faggot," said Yusef to the crowd. "The cops sent us an undercover cocksucker to do a man's job."

"You fool," Bohan laughed. "I used that story to throw you off my trail. Figured you'd hold on to that and stop looking at me."

"Well, it worked," said Yusef. "You had me fooled but you didn't fool brother Robert."

Then Yusef kicked Bohan in the balls, dropping him to the floor.

"And I got your fool," said Yusef.

Bohan caught his breath and stood. It took him a while and Robert was actually impressed by the effort. He was tough; there was no doubt about it. "You're crazy, all of you," said Bohan breathlessly. "This so-called movement will fail."

The members cursed and spat on him. Yusef stopped this with a hand held high.

"Hold on people," said Yusef. "We're not communists. Let the man speak. Go on, say your peace."

"The government is too big," said Bohan. "It's too rich, too powerful and you don't have enough support to win."

"We don't need to win," said Yusef. "Tell him, Robert." He looked to Robert who didn't know how to feel about Bohan now. He was a rat but he had attained a respect for him over the last few months.

"The Viet Cong know they can't win the war," Robert began. "But they'd rather die than live under our boot. So, they fight to weaken us, hoping that others will join the fight and take us down. That way, they can't lose."

"And that's what we're doing," said Yusef. "We ain't got to win. We just gotta survive long enough for this country to fall."

"You're crazy," said Bohan. "People are tired of all this violence. In the end, you'll die and nothing will change. If you let me go, I'll work with you for leniency."

Yusef laughed and the others joined him. Robert just looked grimly at Bohan knowing that he would soon be dead.

"Okay, I's be seeing yo' point," said Yusef in a fake drawl. "We's caints beat da White man. He be too big an' strong fo' us little Black chil'lins." This drew peals of laughter from the members. "Your days are numbered," said Yusef in his normal voice. "I oughta burn you right now."

"Yusef," said Robert. "We need to think here. First, we got to leave this place and find another one. It's not safe here no more. Second, we got to get him to talk. We can't know how much they know until we get it out of him."

Yusef thought only a moment about this. There was undeniable wisdom in what he had just heard.

"We gotta move, people," said Yusef. He gave orders issuing assignments off the top of his head, coordinating teams and leaving no detail unattended. He was masterful and Robert could see how he had become the leader.

Yusef was one of the ones that got away, a brilliant man who had not reacted well to the limitations associated with his skin color.

Yusef gave Vince the assignment of transporting their prisoner away. Yusef walked over to Robert and put a friendly hand on his shoulder.

"I can see who'd take my place if I should fall one day," said Yusef.

"It's bad luck to say stuff like that in a war," said Robert.

"I was a little worried about you, Robert. I didn't really know if you had ambition beyond justice for your brother but I can see I was wrong. I apologize for that."

"No need," said Robert.

"Just know that I'll always remember what you did here today, man. It was brilliant."

"Just playing on the team, boss," said Robert and he smiled.

Yusef's face suddenly turned very serious. "I really meant what I said about putting myself in danger in this plan. I might not come out of it alive so I need to know that you'll step up. After what went down today, no one will question it."

Robert didn't answer. He extended his hand and they shook on it. Not any of the cool handshakes the brothers did these days, just a plain, old-fashioned deal binder.

Vince hit Bohan one more time for good measure then he and two other men dragged him off after tying his feet together.

Robert walked through the chattering excitement of the moment. He ignored the slaps on the back and the handshakes from his comrades. He headed to the door, back in soldier mode.

25

<u>POLAROID</u>

Thomas' mood had been somber for days. The death of Bobby Kennedy had not touched off riots, but it had thrown the nation into an abiding depression. The flag was at half-mast and it seemed to Thomas that it had been there for the last year.

The reports were that one man had committed the assault but there were already rumors of a conspiracy and talks of a family curse. The eldest Kennedy, Joe had also died young. When you added Jack and Bobby to that, it seemed like terrible fate.

So many great men had fallen. America was becoming like many of the banana republics around the globe. Don't like a leader, kill him. Don't like the government, wait a day; there's a new one coming.

He thought about Sarah as he walked to McGinty's. Sarah and her friends wanted to change the country. Everyone talked about the Negroes but young White kids were rebelling too. They defied the draft and burned their cards and bras. They protested the war and questioned the honesty of their government.

It was unheard of and Thomas just didn't see the logic in it. The government had always taken care of its people. If you didn't trust your government that meant you didn't trust yourself.

McGinty's regulars had stopped giving Thomas a big reception when he arrived. Thomas didn't know that this meant he was now a regular too and their corruption had been completed. The regulars only loved you until you became like them and then they resented you because you were like them.

Thomas pulled up to the bar said nice hellos and then poured liquid redemption down his throat.

He toasted Ned on the first round. A big picture of him had been placed behind the bar. As Thomas raised his glass so did everyone else.

He avoided the advances of Barbara who was wearing a low cut dress that left little to the imagination. She rubbed, flirted and swung her cleavage under his reddening nose all night but he resisted.

Thomas was sober enough after a few hours to go home. He got there and walked inside ignoring the mess. He hummed and old Irish song, one of the ones Cahan had always sang to him as he slowly fell asleep amid the debris of his life.

The next day, he got up and cleaned up the place, salvaging as much as he could. When he was done, he was left with a lot of emptiness. It matched his insides, he thought. Losing Sarah and the respect of his coworkers had drained him like the city was being drained of White faces.

He didn't go into work that day. He didn't trust himself not to jump Brady and Reid on sight and with cops; you never knew how bad the fight might be.

Cahan had often told the story of a cop who had lost it on the job and ended up shooting up the station house, killing two men and injuring several others before he was himself gunned down by his brothers in blue.

He thought of Ned, fat, lovable and dead on his livingroom floor with a shot and a beer. He didn't care what the detectives said; he knew no vigilante had killed him. It was a hit and a cop had done it.

He wondered what they were saying about him at the station behind his back. He'd refused the bluepact and he knew that Brady and Reid would spread it all over the station that he was disloyal, a rat who would sell out his friends.

Thomas spent the rest of the day trying to reach out to Sarah. He called and got no answer. He swung by her place but saw no one.

He retired to McGinty's where he had another night of drinking.

The next day, he went into work and realized that he did not have a partner. He sat at his locker after he dressed, not wanting to move.

"I think it stinks," said Dennison to Thomas as the latter sat at his locker looking glum. "Ned was a stand up guy."

"Who's my new partner?" asked Thomas.

Dennison's face fell and he averted his eyes for a moment and before he said it, Thomas knew. "Well, you don't have one yet," he said. "None of the regular guys will ride with you while this thing's hanging over your head."

"What do you mean regular guys?"

"The colored cops don't have a choice of partners. Many of them want street assignments to get away from the baby duty they have to do."

"No, thanks," said Thomas and he was not at all shocked by the venom in his voice.

"Didn't think so," said Dennison. "So for now, you can fly solo."

"I thought the department didn't like that sort of thing," said Thomas.

"They don't," said Dennison but nobody's saying nothing about it. If you want, I can put you on desk duty and—-"

"With the washouts and the old timers? No fucking way," said Thomas.

"Didn't think you'd wanna do that either," said Dennison. "Well, then you got no choice. Look Riley, for what it's worth, I don't think you ratted anyone."

"Is that what they're saying?" Thomas spat.

"Some guys around here are just paranoid, looking for somebody to blame, that's all," said Dennison apologetically.

Thomas felt his heart sag as Dennison walked off. He'd reached into his locker and had the flask in his hand before he knew it and it was to his lips a moment later. The warmth of the whiskey was soothing and it burned away some of his pain.

Thomas walked outside to a police cruiser. He could feel the eyes of the other cops all over him, like he was walking toward a firing squad.

Thomas got into the car and looked at the key in the ignition for a long time. He felt that if he turned the car's engine over that his humiliation would be complete. Finally, he started the car and it seemed to be an insult to his ears as he pulled away.

He spent his first day doing close patrol to the precinct. He did not see Brady or Reid and was glad of it. He could not have taken their smug looks.

The Grand Jury was making headlines and it felt like their influence came closer to him each day. The secret nature of it was maddening, he thought.

Thomas missed Sarah desperately and called her place as many times as he could but he did not reach her.

He didn't want to go home and he didn't want to drink either. He found himself driving over to Sarah and Liz's place as the sun was setting and soon he had the house they rented staked out.

He could go over and say he was in the neighborhood, he thought but no one would believe that. He sat there a long time, listening to a rebroadcast of a Tiger game on the radio.

Thomas saw the front door of the little house open and Sarah and Liz walked out. They were dressed up nicely and they walked down the street away from Thomas. He waited a while and then he followed them on foot.

Sarah and Liz walked about a half-mile to a local bar frequented by the college kids. Thomas peeked inside after them and saw them go over to two men. One of them was a fireman he knew. The other was a tall thin man he did not know. The thin man hugged Sarah and kissed her on the lips. Sarah had looked surprised at the kiss and turned red after he did it.

Thomas felt his hand curl into a fist. He saw himself running inside and grabbing the man and beating him bloody in front of Sarah.

"You going in?" said a voice from behind him.

Thomas turned with a start and saw a big, beefy man standing a few feet from him. He must be the local bouncer, he thought.

"No," said Thomas.

"Then you have to go," said the bouncer.

Thomas was about to flash his badge but thought better of it. What if this buffoon went back inside and told someone that a cop was outside looking through a window? What if Sarah heard and put two and two together?

"Sorry," Thomas said and he walked off.

He felt the bouncer watching him as he rounded a corner. When it was safe, Thomas went back and stood watch across the street from the bar in the doorway of a closed shop.

When they didn't come out for another hour, he walked off, went back to his car and drove home.

What the hell was he doing he asked himself. He was like some kind of pervert who followed women around trying to watch them undress. He had to get Sarah back or else get her out of his head and his heart.

Thomas turned onto his street and pulled up to his apartment. He parked and got out of the car. He dreaded going back to the empty place. Brady and Reid had put a good one on him. Every time he went home, he was reminded of the consequences of his impending testimony.

He walked toward his building slowly. The street was deserted and his edifice looked lonely, desolate.

Something moved ahead of him.

The apartment house was in the middle of two other buildings and there was a big shadow being cast by the one to the right. The walkway had a row of hedges along both sides; just the kind of place a man could hide if he wanted to surprise you.

Thomas didn't stop walking or otherwise indicate that he had seen anything. As he moved closer, he reached for his service revolver, placing his hand on the snap and undoing it. He stepped on the pathway to his building and saw the vague figure of a man hiding in the hedge to his right.

Thomas' heart sped up and his grip tightened on the pistol. His mind filled with all his troubles and through the clutter one thought arose, clearly and cruelly: someone would die tonight.

Suddenly, a car's headlights went on across the street behind him. The light bathed him, casting his shadow before him. In that instant, Thomas saw more than just his own outline. He saw the man by the hedge was just a jacket hanging from a cord with a skullcap perched on top.

Before he could sense him, another man was upon him.

Thomas was knocked to the ground. His service revolver skidded away from him, landing on the edge of the lawn.

He saw instantly that the man on him was Robert Jackson. Robert placed a knife to his throat.

"Now, you and me are gonna have a real conversation."

He was about to say something else but Thomas had already lifted a knee into his groin. Robert tumbled to one side, yelling out.

Both men quickly got to their feet and squared off. Robert's knife was gone. Thomas guessed he had dropped it. Robert was doubled over a little. The blow to his balls was still hobbling him.

Thomas knew where his gun was but he'd never be able to get it in time. He also knew that he could not beat the Marine in a fair fight, even with his police training.

Robert waded in. The men traded blows and Thomas got the worst of it. Robert smiled knowing he would win this confrontation.

"That all you got?" said Thomas, trying to bait him into a mistake.

Robert swung again but missed. Suddenly, another pair of headlights illuminated the scene. Robert's eyes were caught and for a moment he was blinded. In that instant, Thomas shoved him to the ground. When Robert got up, Thomas now held the lost police revolver on him. Robert froze, not looking at the gun but into Thomas' eyes. Thomas could see it; Robert was ready to die.

Thomas cocked the weapon. Robert was silent. He just stood there watching, judging.

"I could kill you," said Thomas.

Robert said nothing. He just looked at Thomas. In those eyes, Thomas saw no anger. There was something worse. Emptiness. The Negro had an abyss in his eyes that frightened Thomas even though he himself held the gun.

"I came here to get the truth," said Robert finally.

"To cut it out of me?" asked Thomas

"If I had to," came the reply with calmness.

"Nice little trick by the hedge," said Thomas. "Almost had me fooled. But tonight just isn't your night, is it, boy?"

"Big man for somebody who washed out of the Army," said Robert flatly.

Thomas' eyes widened. Robert smiled a little.

"What the hell are you talking about?" asked Thomas trying to cover.

"You know what the hell I'm talking about," said Robert. "You washed out of the service and said it was a hearing problem. You had a nervous breakdown, crying about your dead brother and grandfather. And here you are, a cop, holding a gun and covering up a murder, still a washout."

"You stay out of my life, you fucking—-" Thomas stopped himself again.

"Go on, say it," said Robert. "Say nigger, then kill me like you did my brother."

"I didn't kill your brother!" Thomas said. The gun shook in his hand. He sighed a little as if unburdened by something.

"Then who did?" Robert said.

Now it was Thomas' turn to fall silent. He felt the gun waver again, suddenly heavy. He saw lights coming on in some of the apartment units.

"You look like you could use a drink, Thomas," said Robert. "Go on, I know you keep a bottle on you."

"Jesus, you *want* me to shoot you, don't you?" asked Thomas suddenly realizing.

"You or me," said Robert. "Makes no difference to me now. Just like your partner. Which one of you panicked and blew him away?"

Robert reached into his pocket and Thomas shifted the gun in response. But Robert produced a Polaroid picture. He held it out and moved it toward Thomas' face. It was a picture of Marcus, the dead boy. In the picture, Marcus looked happy and full of life, wearing a Tiger's cap.

"This was Marcus Alexander Jackson," said Robert. He was born May 4, 1950. He was a good student, an artist and football player. He loved Captain Kangaroo and Marvin Gaye. He was in love with a girl and he was murdered for going to see her and staying out after dark because his skin is black."

Thomas lowered his weapon and didn't care if Robert took it from him.

"You look at this picture, dammit!" Robert shouted. "He was loved! He was my hope. You look at him and know he was just as good as you and them other two cops. Just as good."

Robert didn't make a play for the dangling weapon. He threw the photo into Thomas' chest, then turned and ran off.

Thomas put his gun away then looked at he awful picture on the ground and took it. He wanted so badly to rip it apart but could not didn't have the strength to do it.

26

<u>BOMBS</u>

On September 14, 1968, Denny McLain won his 30th game, making him the first major league pitcher to do so since the great Dizzy Dean in 1934. Three days later, the Tigers clinched the American League Pennant and won a trip to the World Series.

Robert was happy but the game did not offer him peace from his troubles. He'd failed with Thomas Riley. He had not taken revenge and didn't learn anything new about his brother's death except that Riley had been believable when he'd said that he didn't kill Marcus.

Thomas looked into the man and beyond his grief he saw truth. But that didn't mean Riley wasn't covering for the other two, he thought. And it didn't mean he was going to leave the White cop alone.

Yusef saw the baseball joy in Detroit as an opportunity for a strike. He had been vague about his big plan to put The Vanguard into the national consciousness.

They were safely moved to a new location, a big two-story building in a declining area of the city. Now he felt it was time to tell everyone his scheme. He was going to strike the major oppressor force of the city. He was going to bomb police headquarters.

Robert had known of the plan for some time now. He thought it was extreme and dangerous but he'd helped to set it all up.

Robert made two devices from the government's own new synthetic explosives, procured from a black market source recommended to them by David, one of the phony cops who'd helped to expose Bohan's treachery.

The plan was simple yet elegant. Two of The Guard's members had been posing as janitors for months and would plant the device. And when the time was right, they'd detonate it. And while the cops mobilized after the explosion, Yusef planned to rob a bank in broad daylight. He was going to man this operation himself. Then he'd send his manifesto to both newspapers.

Yusef had at first wanted to detonate the device during the World Series, but Robert had vetoed this idea. Baseball had never harmed anyone, he thought. Robert was surprised to find that most of The Vanguard held this opinion as well.

Robert fashioned a remote device that would detonate the bomb from a distance.

Linda and another woman named Ruth were given the job of planting the device. It was agreed that Black women weren't as suspicious as men these days and that no one even looked at Black faces when they were cleaning up.

"Fine piece of work that bomb," said Yusef. "But why do we have two of them?"

"Standard procedure," said Robert. "You always have a back up if you have the materials. And if we get caught, what better way to destroy the evidence? Getting the stuff to make it was the hard part."

"You can thank David and his gang from Chicago," said Yusef referring to the men who had posed as cops. "Those boys do not play."

"Why don't we just let Bohan go?" asked Robert. "I mean, he ain't giving up any info and he don't know where we moved to."

"We could," said Yusef, "but then he'd bring a lot of heat down on us. I can't have that. Not now. Besides, he's a traitor to the race. In the tribe, they'd kill him."

"So, how you gonna do him?" asked Robert.

"I was hoping you could assist me on that," said Yusef in his proper way. "I mean, you're good at these things. Vince wants to do it, but he's so mad at Bohan, I don't trust him, you know."

"Not me," Robert said and he surprised himself at how fast he'd come to the conclusion. "I don't wanna do it."

"That's cool," said Yusef. "It ain't like you don't pull your weight around here. We'll take care of Bohan at the same time we detonate the device. They'll be so much confusion, that no one will care about another dead nigga, especially if we shoot him up with dope first."

Robert was solemn at this. He didn't like it but at heart he was still a soldier and there were always casualties. If this were Vietnam, he would have cut Bohan's throat himself and then had dinner.

"We still have to test it," said Robert, "the bomb materials."

"How do we do that?" asked Yusef.

"I made a little one," said Robert. "I want to test the detonator, too. I mean, if we hit it and it don't go off, we're fucked."

"Solid," said Yusef. "When we gonna do it?"

"Tomorrow, after the game," said Robert. "I know a place. It's way out but it'll be worth it."

"Okay, but just me and you," said Yusef. "I want to keep access to the detonator at a minimum."

"Cool," said Robert.

"I suppose you're rootin' for the Tigers to win," said Yusef.

"Ain't you?" said Robert.

"No, and I'm taking all bets," Yusef smiled

"I got fifty on the Tigers," said Robert proudly.

"Fifty?' Yusef smiled. "I'll be happy to take your money."

Before he left, Robert looked in on Bohan who was being kept in a back room of the new place. He was chained to a wall and blindfolded. It stank inside. There was a bucket there for him to evacuate himself. Robert was reminded of the Cong they took as prisoners in the field.

"Who is it?" asked Bohan in a frightened voice as Robert entered.

Robert didn't answer. He just turned away from the doomed man and closed the door, leaving him in darkness.

27

<u>THE SERIES</u>

The World Series opener took Thomas' mind from his other problems. He still had the Polaroid that Robert Jackson had given him. It was in a drawer in his kitchenette but even from there it spoke to him.

The Grand Jury had to be working their way toward him, he thought. It was only a matter of time before he'd be called. What would he do? He could hold fast to the police code, or he could come clean with it all.

Neither choice was good. One left his life in shambles; the other left him a damned soul.

He was still a pariah at the station house. The story had been told and retold and as he understood it, he was no better than some junkie dropping a dime on his supplier. Very few men took his side publicly.

Brady and Reid were still well liked but they had many detractors as well. But no detractor would denounce the pair openly. It was clear who the department was behind.

Thomas saw for the first time how rare strength was. Most people, even cops, just wanted an easy life, to get along with others and not be singled out.

This made it simple for guys like Brady and Reid to control things. They were forceful, opinionated and unafraid to do what they wanted. They were aggressors amongst the aggressive and it had given them armor in this fight. You almost had to respect them for that.

The death of the Negro boy had changed his whole life, he mused. It would force him to become like Brady and Reid or would crumble him under its power.

And the homicide detectives still had no clues to Ned's murder. They were officially still investigating the case. Unofficially, they'd decided a Negro radical killed Ned. Thomas didn't buy this and knew that the killer would never be found if he didn't force the issue with Brady and Reid. It would be dangerous to do so but these days, everything was.

Robert put the tiny practice bomb inside the makeshift structure and counted off footsteps as he walked back to Yusef. The device was about the size of a shoebox and the charge as big as a golf ball.

They were in the country near I-75. Robert remembered his uncle taking him there, hunting for rabbits when he was younger.

He and Yusef had driven off the interstate, careful not to be seen by anyone. They found a clearing and had built a little structure from loose wood and fallen trees.

The remote was good for several hundred yards, which meant that they'd have to be fairly close to police headquarters in order to detonate it effectively.

Robert had spent the previous night nursing Denise who was sick all the time, it seemed. He'd sent her back to his mother's house for a while out of his fear of what would happen when he wasn't around. She did not argue. The baby was coming, he thought. With all the things going on in the world, his child was coming and he had such mixed feelings about it.

"Okay," said Robert. "I'm ready."

"Some game yesterday," said Yusef referring to the Tiger's loss in game one.

"It's just one game and it wasn't even at home," said Robert. "All the Tigers have to do is take one in St. Louis and then we kill them when they come to Detroit."

Robert had taken the loss hard and it did seem like the Tigers were horribly outmatched by the mighty St. Louis Cardinals and their ace, Bob Gibson

Robert took out the detonator, a crude and evil looking box about the size of a transistor radio. It was a slate gray metal box with lumpy, soldering marks on the corners. There were two buttons on the faceplate, which he had colored red and black. The red button armed the unit and the black one brought the thunder.

Robert took a little breath and then pressed the red button. "Armed," he said. He looked at the structure and thought a second and then said. "We'd better move back some more."

"Oh come on," said Yusef. It can't be—"

"Just move back a little," said Robert.

They did. Yusef now had a disbelieving look on his face.

Robert took another breath then pressed the black button.
    "Fire in the hole!"

The structure literally disintegrated. The sound was deafening. Chunks of wood flew into the air and Yusef and Robert both jumped backwards from the force of the explosion. Debris fell around them in clumps.

"Whoo shit!" said Yusef.

"Damn," said Robert. "It was bigger than I thought.

"That's okay," said Yusef excitedly. "It worked. So, compared to this one, how is the actual device?"

"I'd say at least twenty times as powerful."

"Then you'd better give the detonator more range," said Yusef. "We don't wanna get blown up when it goes off because we're too close."

They ran back to their vehicle and quickly returned to the city. Even out here in the sticks, someone might have heard a blast that loud.

Robert sat in the passenger seat as they pulled onto the interstate. Yusef turned on the radio and heard Mary Wells' silky voice rise.

Halfway to Detroit, a police cruiser began to follow them. Yusef reduced his speed. He switched lanes. The cops followed him, keeping pace.

"Shit," said Robert.

The cops sat there trailing and Robert knew they were calling in the plates. If they were pulled over, the cops might find the detonator and somehow put two and two together.

"Be cool," said Yusef. "The car's clean."

The Guard made it a habit never to drive hot vehicles or carry guns on their person unless they were working. Yusef knew the laws and tried to stay a step ahead of them. After a few minutes, the police cruiser passed them and took an exit.

"Fuckin' pig," said Yusef. "It's gonna be so good to watch them burn."

Yusef had a smile on his face that wouldn't go away.
Robert knew it was not that he had out-smarted the cops.
Yusef was seeing visions of destruction and adulation.

Thomas tried not to let the empty passenger seat make
him feel naked. Riding without a partner was like going to
the prom alone. You felt unwanted and lonely.

The Tigers had stolen game two in Missouri and were
now home with the series tied. Frank had some connections
for tickets but it looked pretty dry out there.

He hated working nights alone. Thomas sat on a street
doing nothing. He saw shady types but didn't feel like
hassling anyone. He just wanted the shift to end and then go
home and sleep.

The police radio crackled and brought him back to the
living.

"Unit requests back up... Twelfth Street near Clairmount,"
the female voice was barely audible and there was a lot of
static."

"Copy," said Thomas.

There was another blast of static and he heard the voice
again. He knew the dispatcher on duty and so he spoke to
her.

"Claire, your channel's shitty tonight," he said with a
smirk.

There was no response as he drove off. The address he'd
gotten was in a very bad area near the heart of where the
riots were.

Thomas got to the area, a bleak, ravaged sector. He saw
no other officers. He waited a moment, then got out of the
cruiser and looked around. Nothing. He reached into the
cruiser and grabbed the radio mic.

"Unit nine at scene, no officers in sight," he said.

"Unit nine, clarify," said the voice on the other end this
time, it was crystal clear.

"You sent a back up request," said Thomas, "but there's
no one here."

"I didn't send a request," said the voice on the radio.

"You didn't—-"

A shot rang out in the night, breaking the stillness wide open.

The windshield of the cruiser shattered.

Thomas fell to the ground but he wasn't hit. He pulled his gun and reached for the radio mic, which dangled from the window of the cruiser.

"Shots fired! Shots fired!" he screamed as he scanned the area looking for the sniper.

Thomas opened the cruiser's door and got behind it. He heard the dispatcher calling for back up as he continued to search for killers in the darkness.

He saw nothing and heard nothing. Then from somewhere, a dog barked and then stopped. The stillness loomed around him for several minutes. Thomas' heart was pounding and he heard his owned strained breathing.

"They tried to kill me," was all he could think of. First Ned and now it was his turn. They could not silence him with guilt or their fake nobility and so they tried to silence him the old fashioned way, just like Kennedy.

The stillness was cut by the sound of sirens. His heart slowed and he felt his confidence begin to return.

As the other units arrived, Thomas stood, lowering his weapon. This was totally against police procedure but he was no longer afraid of being shot.

He stood beside his cruiser waiting to answer the inevitable questions that would be asked. But he knew it would be to no avail. His assailant was gone.

The rain had been coming down all day. Abraham and the grounds crew had worked overtime trying to keep the field playable and for the most part they'd done a good job. The team had lost the third game and now they might have to play in the mud in game four.

Abraham sat in the grounds keeper's service area on a stool. He had his food and some cold beer. The team wasn't doing well but he had a feeling things would turn around.

After all that had occurred in the last year, they needed something good to happen in Detroit.

"He ain't coming," said a voice to Abraham's right.

Abraham turned to see Otis Young, one of the other grounds keepers. He was a squat man with big arms and a bald head. His eyes gleamed and Abraham knew why.

"Go on Otis, my boy is coming."

"They're gettin' ready to play the anthem! Let me sell his ticket"

"No," said Abraham, "for the last time, no." Normally, Robert could come to the game for free but during a World Series everyone had to have a ticket. Abraham had gotten one for him and left it at the gate.

"Do you know what I can get for that ticket, man? I told you I'd split it with you."

Abraham turned, his face all business. "Me and my son have been seeing games all our lives. No matter what problems we might have, it ain't bigger than the World Series. So, I don't care if God and Jesus himself wants the ticket, I ain't giving it up."

Otis made a disgusted noise and walked off. Abraham turned and watched the players warming up. He said a silent prayer for the team and for all the broken things in his family's life.

How did it come to this, he thought. He was young once, vital and could control his kids with one harsh look. Robert had always been a handful but even he was manageable back in the day.

He hoped the Army would change the boy, but that hadn't happened. The only thing that could save Robert now was God and Robert had all but renounced Him.

Abraham heard footsteps behind him but he didn't turn around. They came closer and still he didn't move. He heard wood against the ground as another stool was pulled next to his and Robert sat down.

Abraham turned his head and looked at his son. Robert looked at his father and something like a smile played on his lips.

Robert turned and looked at the field like a kid at Christmas as the players returned to their respective sides.

Abraham said nothing. He turned to watch the game munching on a big bag of peanuts. He held them out to Robert who absently took some.

The national anthem began to play. Abraham stood and placed his hand over his heart. Robert just sat and waited.

Linda and a woman named Ruth Smith, one of The Guard's oldest members entered police headquarters with dread. They had been assigned to join a janitorial service some time back and now they were trusted faces. They headed into police headquarters through the rear, carrying a large box marked "CLENSER."

They quickly went to the janitorial service area and grabbed a cart. The women carefully slid the box in the bottom of the cart and loaded other supplies onto it.

Ruth was a big woman with wide hips who was fond of braiding her hair. Others said it made her look too harsh but she said the look was from the Motherland and they could kiss her considerable ass.

"Wegottabe quick 'boutdis," said Ruth. She talked fast and had a habit of running words together.

"No doubt," said Linda.

They rolled their service cart down a long hallway. The White cops and office staff walked by them oblivious, not speaking to or even noticing the two Negro women. They were invisible, just like Yusef said.

One of the wheels on the cart twisted and the whole thing turned into a wall with a thud.

The box containing the bomb dislodged and tipped out onto the floor.

Linda gave an audible gasp. For a second, they were both paralyzed with fear.

"Need some help?" asked a voice from behind them.

They looked around and saw a young Black officer. He was kind of handsome Linda would later remember.

"Oh no weokay," said Ruth.

The young cop lingered on Linda. He was obviously interested in the pretty girl.

"Here, let me," said the cop. And he bent and helped Ruth put the box back.

"Thank ya," said Ruth.

"No problem," said the cop. "Don't think any of these other officers would ever help you." Then to Linda, he said, "Do you talk?"

"Sometimes," said Linda and she couldn't help giving him a pleasing smile.

"See you around?" said the cop and it was a question to Linda filled with intent.

"Probably," said Linda.

The cop moved on and Ruth pushed the cart back into the hallway.

"Why you gotta flirt wif da man?" asked Ruth angrily. "We supposed ta be invisible."

"How did I know they had Black cops down here? I couldn't just ignore him."

"You needda turnit off sometimes," said Ruth.

"We ain't got time for your jealousy, old woman. Just do your job."

"Ain't nobody jealous of yo' skinny behind."

Linda bit her tongue. Black women like Ruth thought that anyone who was a normal size was skinny. You had to be some big ass heifer in Ruth's mind.

Linda had several unkind things she could have said but she had visions of an argument and the bomb tipping out of the cart and killing them all. She glared at Ruth and said nothing.

Ruth pushed the cart around a corner. They made their way down another hallway and stopped to do some work according to the plan.

They cleaned several rooms and bathrooms, which always made Linda sick to her stomach. Men were such pigs, she thought. Finally, they made their way to a supply closet down another hallway and went inside.

Ruth and Linda entered and then quickly put on rubber gloves. Yusef had made sure everything on the bomb was wiped clean and that no one ever touched it with a bare hand.

They uncovered the bomb. It was heavy and they took care when they removed it. They had it halfway out when they heard a massive cheer and celebration outside the door.

"Guess they won" said Ruth.

"Who cares?" said Linda.

"I do," said Ruth. "We down three games to two. I got money on this thang."

Thomas entered the precinct house and immediately his nerves jangled. He had taken some time off since the shooting incident but felt good enough to come back in. Officially, it was reported as an unidentified sniper.

Within the ranks, it was whispered to have been a militant group trying to kill a cop. Some even said it was retribution for something Ned and Thomas had done while partners.

But Thomas knew better. It was Brady and Reid at their worst.

Frank, Esther and Katie had rushed to the stationhouse to console him. Esther was near tears and Katie was as well. Frank was silent and had a concerned look on his face. He was too strong a man to show emotion even for something like this.

Thomas spent the night at his parents' house. He lay in the bed and dreamed of better days. He closed his eyes and thought of innocence and complete families, of love and fulfilled desires.

He saw all the Riley men, the living and the dead, throwing the baseball around and making the soul-deep connection through the game.

Sarah read about the story in the newspaper and had rushed to meet Thomas. She was very concerned and seemed genuinely happy to see him. Thomas didn't press her on anything of a personal nature and there was no kiss at the end, still he entertained notions of them being together again.

Thomas moved into the lobby of the precinct and found more people there than usual. There were even some women from the clerical staff.

Thomas waved at Dennison and headed for the lockers when he saw them all start clapping. His first thought was that something good had happened to the Tigers. The team needed to win the last two games in order to win the World Series. But the game wasn't going to be on for hours, he thought.

Then he realized that the ovation was for him, for what had happened on the street, for facing the sniper alone. Thomas blushed visibly and couldn't fight the smile forming on his lips.

He walked into the locker room and headed towards his locker.

Thomas saw Brady and Reid standing together. They looked at him and shared a laugh about something and then Brady looked at Thomas and winked. Or did he blink? It didn't matter because as soon as he did it, Thomas launched himself at the pair.

Thomas now understood what it meant to "see red" because that's just what happened. He had crossed the room before he knew it and grabbed Brady by the front of his shirt. He shoved Reid out of the way as the first punch sailed at Brady's jaw. It caught him flush and dropped him.

A second later, Reid hit Thomas in the small of his back and Thomas dropped to one knee. Reid was about to deliver another blow when Thomas swung with his right arm and caught Reid in the groin. Reid toppled to the ground in a heap. The whole fight had lasted about twenty seconds.

Other officers scrambled over and broke up the attempts to keep fighting. In the end, no one would say how it started. They were all told to just cool down.

Thomas got a paid day off from the commander who didn't like the fact that he was back to work so soon after the incident anyway.

Thomas left the precinct and drove to his father's house. The streets were empty and the city looked deserted. Then he remembered that a game was coming on.

He found his father watching the game alone, sitting in front of the old black and white TV.

"No party this time?" he asked, sitting down.

"It's at Donahue's place," said Frank.

Thomas was about to ask him why he hadn't gone but Frank had one of those looks on his face that told him not to. Frank was brooding about something.

Thomas told Frank about the altercation at the station house and was surprised to find his father upset. He thought his Frank would be mad about the fact that he'd struck another officer but there was something else on his mind, something that had unsettled him.

"Heard you refused to sign a bluepact," said Frank.

"Yes," said Thomas. "Is that why——?"

"I know the bluepact is nonsense and truth be told, they don't really mean anything like they used to but it's a loyalty sign, a test and you failed."

"Did Brady's dad call you?" asked Thomas sensing a conspiracy. "I know he's a friend."

"It don't matter who told me. What matters is you do the right thing."

"They might have killed Ned," said Thomas. "And they probably took that shot at me, do you realize that?" Thomas' voice had risen.

"If they did, they had a right!" said Frank loudly.

Thomas looked around. He didn't want his mother and Katie to hear this.

"Your mother and Katie are out shopping or something," said Frank reading his expression. "They didn't want to watch the game with me."

Thomas wanted to ask his father if he had heard him right but he knew that he had. He got out of his seat and turned to the old man.

"How can you say that? They had a right to make an attempt on my life? To kill another cop?"

"You don't know if they killed Ned. And they only wanted to scare you," said Frank. "Any good shot could have——"

"What? Killed me? Do you even know what you're saying?" asked Thomas loudly.

"It's the way things are. Cops have to look out for their own," said Frank not flinching at the tense look on his son's face. "You can't just go your own way. How will that make me look?"

"My life isn't about you," said Thomas moving closer to his father. "It's not for you to impress you old cop buddies while you talk about the good old days when you could beat defenseless Negroes and not get in trouble for it."

"Who the hell are you talking to, boy?" said Frank.

"When I go to the Grand Jury, I'll make my own decision and I'll make it for me, not for you."

"You gonna be a rat, turn on your brothers and washout of the force like you did the Army?"

His father looked like a stranger now, a nasty little man who had broken into the house and claimed the face of the man who'd raised him. Thomas felt none of the love or respect that he'd given to that face.

"Go to hell," said Thomas.

Thomas headed for the door but didn't make it before Frank had a hand on his shoulder and was turning him around. He pushed the older man from him. Frank gained his footing and lunged at Thomas. Thomas stepped to one side raising his fists.

The two men turned to each other, ready for the fight. A moment passed and then Thomas dropped his hands. He walked to his father and then by him. He grabbed the doorknob and turned it.

"You get back here!" Frank yelled but Thomas flung the door open and headed out. "I mean it, don't come back if you leave, Shaun!"

This stopped Thomas where he stood. He turned to face the old man who was just realizing what he had said. Frank's face was his own again but it was sad and embarrassed. But there it was, the truth, as real and awful as it always was.

"I'm not...." said Thomas and then he stopped; a small click sounded in his throat as though something had shut off a switch. His eyes burned with emotion, filling with liquid.

There was no need to finish the sentence, no need to exert his existence by denying his brother's identity and then he realized the two words that he did utter had another, more awful meaning.

Thomas turned away from his father and moved through the door.

The cool air outside tingled his skin. Thomas walked away from his former home. He felt the presence of his father behind him, slipping into a long, dark silence.

28

GAME SEVEN

October 10, 1968.

The city streets were empty again. Everyone was getting ready for the game. The series had been one of the best that anyone could remember.

And there was so much more than baseball glory riding on it for the little city by the narrow river. Many would say later that the fate of Detroit hung in the balance. Others would write that perhaps it was the soul of a nation that was at stake.

Robert was at home with Denise who was feeling better lately. Even she had gotten baseball fever and was in a rooting mood. Her belly swelled and her face had taken on thickness. She looked so different from the lithe girl who used to fly around the track and Pershing, her brown legs a blur in the summer sun.

Every time Robert looked at her, he had dreams of his child. He hoped he was bringing him into a better world.

Yusef had informed Robert that after the game was over, they had to strike as soon as they could. They'd wait until the team came home.

In victory or defeat it would be a big deal and the city would be distracted. If they won, then The Guard would bring the city crashing town. And if they lost, then their call to action would plunge the city into the abyss of their darkest despair.

Robert had agreed but his heart was not completely in it. The attack on the cops would rip the ailing city open. And then what? How many more people would die, how many homes burned after this violent act? How much more death would he see before life changed?

He realized with a sudden jolt that he never understood what he was fighting for in Vietnam and the fight at home was looking even more nebulous.

Denise smiled at him from across the room and his heart filled with a river of swirling emotion.

Thomas was at home amid the nothingness he'd built in the tiny apartment, accompanied only by the beer he was drinking and the picture of the dead boy.

He had not talked to his father since the fight and he didn't care to. They were all that was left of the Riley men and the gulf between them seemed impossible to cross. He wondered what Shaun and Cahan would do if they could see the disgrace they had become.

Thomas' Grand Jury subpoena was delayed. Like everything else, the World Series had put it on hold. He was somewhat relieved though he knew it was only a matter time. The series would end and then the wheels of justice would go back into motion.

Brady and Reid had already been called. The two would not say anything about what had happened. They kept to themselves and away from Thomas.

Thomas tried to get some information on their testimony but he was no longer trusted at the station and so after a few attempts, he'd given up.

Thomas guessed that he was always called after Brady and Reid because the Grand Jury considered him to be the prize of the investigation. They wanted to trap them all with any inconsistencies they found and they sensed that he was not nearly as good a liar as they other two men.

He wondered why they hadn't killed him. If Frank was right then they had surely had a chance at the phony police call. Ned was a loner, old and had been really angry. Thomas was young and a department legacy. He had so much more to lose by talking than Ned.

Still, he felt like a trapped man. He only wanted to do an important job, get married, start a family of his own, have kids and not repeat the mistakes that had been made by his father. But somehow, it had all gone to shit and he'd been left with nothing. No job, no family, no love.

Fate had taken away so much from him the last year and now it seemed all he had was the game, the game and his hope for a win.

Throughout Detroit, the citizens replaced their racial struggles with the struggles of their team. The pain of the last year was great and the fight to find harmony had not ended.

Now victory for Black and White Detroit did not look any different from the battle being fought on the baseball diamond. Everyone watched with rapt attention, seeing redemption in each pitch and hope in each swing of the bat.

The game traveled into the ninth inning with Detroit leading. Tim McCarver came up for the Cardinals with two outs in the ninth, their last chance. He popped up the ball.

Bill Freehan, the catcher frantically waved his teammates away as the ball crested and began its plunge back to earth.

Time and hearts stood still as the little white orb fell. The convergence of fate filled hearts with pure energy. The ball landed in the thick folds of the catcher's mitt.

It was over.

The Tigers poured onto the field. The players hugged, cried and shouted their victory.

And in Detroit, the people Black and White, ran from their houses into the streets in celebration.

29

<u>WOODWARD</u>

Thousands jammed Woodward Avenue as the heroes rode down the street, smiling and waving to the faithful amid showers of confetti.

Robert, Denise, Abraham and Theresa were among the crowd at the parade downtown. Robert couldn't help but notice the races, so long against one another, mingling effortlessly. No one seemed to remember a city on fire and cluttered with death and chaos.

Yusef had urged Robert to strike during the parade, but Robert had stayed away with the detonator. This was history and he wanted to be part of it before he got back to business.

"You'd never know there was a riot here," Robert said to Denise.

"Makes you wonder why we can't do it all the time," she said absently.

"God is good," said Theresa.

"God loves baseball," said Abraham with a big smile.

"Marcus would have loved this," said Robert and for the first time, no sorrow followed the invocation of his brother's name.

"Yes, he would have," said Abraham.

Theresa agreed and Robert could see none of the grief and sadness his mother's face used to hold whenever his brother's name was brought up.

"There's Willie Horton!" said Abraham and he waved.

"He's handsome," said Denise.

"He sure is," said Theresa smiling. It was very uncharacteristic for her to comment on the attractiveness of any man. Robert's head jerked around at the comment and then he uttered a small laugh.

"Never seen so many people in one place," said Denise. "It's gonna take days to clean up this mess."

They watched as the heroes kept rolling by and the crowd cheered their favorites.

Suddenly, Robert pulled Denise close to him and put his face to her ear.

"If we have a boy, let's name him after Marcus."

Thomas worked the crowd with his new partner, Zack Wilson, a young Negro officer. Zack was earnest, hard-working and very thankful to be on the street.

After the shooting incident, Thomas allowed himself to take a Black partner. He didn't know it but his action would have an effect on the entire force in the coming years.

"I'm a basketball fan myself," said Zack, "but this is great."

"The greatest," said Thomas. "I'm never going to forget this."

Thomas waved to Mickey Lolich, who tipped his hat to him and Zack. As the vehicle carrying the pitcher moved away, it revealed Robert, Denise and their family on the other side of the wide street.

Thomas saw Robert and his family, but they did not see him. Robert hugged a very pregnant woman. That had to be his wife, thought Thomas. There were two older people, who favored Robert. Mother and father, he reasoned. Thomas was filled with a subtle envy. His tormentor seemed to have everything that he wanted.

Zack told Thomas that they had to move on, keep pace with the procession. Thomas moved off and as he did, he realized what had been taken from Robert's family. The brother was gone, just like Shaun, a gaping wound in a family's love. And yet they had gotten over it.

Thomas thought of the Polaroid at his apartment. He thought of Sarah, her fiery green eyes and he knew finally what she had meant. A person who could not adapt to the changes in life was doomed to unhappiness and would bring grief to all he loved.

That was not a future.

Much like the riots, it was oblivion.

Thomas moved on, looking at the elated, racially mixed crowd and understood that the people had embraced something larger than race, politics, hatred, and the ignorance that is sometimes humanity.

Detroit had been plunged into a chasm of inhumanity and it took a simple game, a simple metaphor for life to remind the people of their capacity to forgive and their power to heal.

It was implausible really, he thought, the kind of thing a child wishes for in his earnest heart, but somehow it had been enough. The city had been redeemed.

30

<u>RED BUTTON</u>

As Robert and Denise got close to the apartment, he saw Thomas Riley in plain clothes, waiting for them near the entrance.

Robert froze. He did not have a weapon on him but he vowed that no harm would come to his wife and their baby.

The cop saw them and sensing some apprehension, Thomas held up his arms in surrender.

"Who is it?" asked Denise.

"That cop," said Robert. "Riley."

Denise stopped in her tracks and gripped his arm tightly. He reassured her and they walked up to the man.

"What do you want?" asked Robert.

"Just to talk," said Thomas pulling his arms down. To Denise he said, "Hi, ma'am."

Denise didn't respond. She looked at Robert who told her to go inside the apartment and wait for him. Normally, she would have protested but given her condition, she did not.

"So, you here to arrest me?" asked Robert.

"No," said Thomas.

"Then get to your business. I got things to do."

Thomas' face turned serious and he took a deep breath. "My older brother, Shaun was killed in Korea. My father took it hard. I think he buried a piece of his heart that day. Our family has never been the same since then."

"So does that make us even or something?" asked Robert but there was no anger in his voice this time.

"No. I just know how you feel, I think," said Thomas. "My family— we've spent our lives trying to make up for that loss." Thomas stopped for a moment and it was clear that he'd come to some kind of finality in a long struggle. "I'm going to the Grand Jury and tell them the truth."

"Did you kill my brother?" Robert asked.

"No," said Thomas. "But I think I know who did."

"The other two cops?"

"Yes," said Thomas. "And they may have killed my partner and took a shot at me the other night."

"Damn," Robert said under his breath.

"Brady and Reid got to your brother first. I heard a shot and ran toward it and they were already there over his body. I saw Matt Reid take out the knife, open it with a handkerchief and then place it by his hand."

Robert seemed close to tears as he took this in. "If you're looking for forgiveness, I ain't got none."

"I don't want it," said Thomas, "but I'd be happy if you could take this back." Thomas reached into his pocket and took out the Polaroid. "I think he'd be happier in your house."

Robert took the photo and pocketed it. The smiling face on it didn't break his heart now; it only invoked memories of who Marcus had been.

"So, what's gonna happen to you after you testify?" asked Robert.

"I don't know," said Thomas. "They could suspend or fire me. No matter what happens, I won't be able to work with the cops in that station again."

"Too bad," said Robert. "I'm thinking even a half- honest cop is kinda rare in your profession."

"Not really," said Thomas. "I gotta get going now." He turned to go and then he asked: "So when is she due?"

"Soon," Robert managed a smile.

"Congratulations."

Thomas walked. Suddenly, he stopped, turned and asked: "Hey, how about them Tigers?"

"Yeah," said Robert. "How about 'em?"

Robert went inside and checked on Denise and filled her in. She asked if she could give the good news to his parents and he agreed.

As Denise called, Robert grabbed the detonator from its hiding place and checked the battery inside.

31

<u>BLACK BUTTON</u>

When he arrived at the new safehouse the next day, Robert found an angry Yusef waiting with most of the members. Bohan had been transferred to the main room and Robert knew this did not bode well.

The membership stood in a circle around Bohan. Vince, his former best friend was looking particularly happy.

Linda was there wearing a Tiger's hat. She smiled at Robert and he returned it.

"Glad you could join us," said Yusef.

"Sorry but I told you I couldn't do it while the celebration was going on," said Robert.

"Well, now it's over," said Yusef. "And we have plenty of unfinished business. First, this traitor, here."

Bohan looked a little better. Robert supposed that they had cleaned him up for his execution. How humane, Robert thought.

Bohan still had the blindfold on and now Yusef removed it. The light stung Bohan's eyes as it was removed. Bohan looked around with true fear on his face.

"Get it over with," Bohan said his voice sounding distressed. "I'm tired of this shit."

Yusef responded by taking out a .38 from his waistband and holding it to his side. Yusef didn't look around to anyone and Robert understood that he had decided to do this himself.

"Don't I get a last request?" asked Bohan thickly.

"Hell no!" yelled Vince.

Robert had never liked the idea of killing the cop. But if he tried to help Bohan, surely they would all rise up against him. Still, he felt that he had to help, maybe make it easier on the man. And then he heard Bohan speak.

"I want to tell Robert something," said Bohan.

The room fell into silence. Everyone turned and looked at Robert with anticipation or surprise.

Yusef looked afraid for some reason. He adjusted the gun in his hand as Robert took a step closer to the condemned man.

"Me?" said Robert stepping forward a little. "What is it you want to tell me?"

"I don't have to die with this on my conscious," said Bohan. "I want you to know what happened to your brother."

Thomas was feeling good as he walked toward the federal building. He wasn't nervous for the first time because he knew how this would turn out. He would go in and surprise the stone-faced feds by telling them what they suspected. They would be made speechless by his actions.

Cars rolled by noisily on Michigan Avenue. Not far away, Thomas could see Tiger Stadium, still draped in post victory garb. He smiled a little. Why did it feel so good?

He'd told his family about his planned testimony and got the expected reactions.

Frank yelled and accused him of being a disgrace and his mother had played referee in the short match.

Thomas left the house feeling good about himself but wondering if his father could be trusted to keep quiet. What meant more to him, his son or the brotherhood? The answer to that question would hurt his father one way or the other, he thought.

He hadn't told Sarah about it. She would think he was doing it to get her back. In a way he was, he thought. He hoped that she would see his action as those of a man who had accepted the present and turned away from the past. It had been a long, painful journey and he had plenty of battle scars.

Thomas' smile faded as he moved closer to the building. He saw a group of men standing in his way. They were far off but he was close enough to see that they all had something in common.

They all wore police uniforms.

"I already know how Marcus died," said Robert to Bohan. "One of the cops told me everything that went down."

"They don't know," said Bohan, "but I do. I was there."

"He's lying!" said Vince. "Shoot his ass, Yusef. We're wasting time."

"Let the man speak," said Robert moving between Yusef and Bohan. "It was my brother. I got a right."

Yusef nodded and Robert turned to Bohan.

He'd lost some weight due to his incarceration but he was still bulky. His skin was ashen and his face looked grayish around his yellowed eyes. And his hair had grown back in, stubbly and flecked with gray.

"I was out that night," Bohan began. "Your brother was making his way through a White neighborhood where I met my police contact. I saw him running from the cops and I didn't want to be seen. So I ran, too."

Bohan coughed violently for a second, choking on phlegm. He spat and Robert felt a pang of disgust. He looked over and saw Vince whisper something to Yusef. Yusef nodded, glancing over at Robert briefly.

"The cops started following us both," Bohan continued. "Don't think they really knew there were two of us. Finally, I hid in these bushes. Your brother, he just kept coming my way and then he ran into someone else. Linda. She started yelling at him about screwing some White girl. Linda pulled out a gun and shot him. When the White cops got there, they panicked, thought no one would believe they didn't kill Marcus so they put his knife next to his hand and then the last cop showed up."

"Linda, do you—" Robert turned and looked for Linda but she was gone.

Thomas stopped on the street for a second. Would they dare come here in broad daylight and try to stop him? He had his service revolver on him and thought about reaching for it. But he was out-numbered. There were at least six men standing on the sidewalk about a block from the federal building.

Thomas started walking again. Whatever they wanted, he would not let them keep him from what he had to do. His life would never be his again if he didn't—-

Thomas stopped suddenly again. Now that he was closer, he saw the face of some of the officers. It was Dennison and his partner, Zack Wilson and a few others he called friends. Thomas moved closer and they smiled at him.

"What are you guys doing here?" asked Thomas.

"Patrolling," said Dennison.

"Yeah," said Zack. "Nothing wrong with keeping the city safe, partner."

"Just making sure you know we're not all blind or assholes," said Larry Weathers, a ten-year man.

Thomas wanted to hug them all. Instead, he saluted and they all stood at attention and snapped a salute back.

"Protect and serve, right?" asked Thomas.

"Damned right," said Dennison.

Thomas went to the building and walked up the stone stairs. He went inside and through security. They took his weapon and held it for him.

Thomas had called back John Richards, the POA rep and apologized for his behavior. Richards had agreed to represent him. Thomas didn't know what kind of trouble he'd be in for supporting Brady and Reid's story but he wanted someone who would give it to him straight.

He got onto the elevator and went up to the fourth floor. Thomas promised himself that today would be the beginning of a new life. He'd sworn off drinking and was even thinking about going to one of those new groups for men with drinking problems he'd heard about.

He got off the elevator and walked toward the room where the hearings were being held. He saw John Richards there in his expensive-looking suit. Next to him, he saw his mother with Sarah.

He moved toward Sarah and it felt like a dream. He got to her and they kissed not needing to say the things that both of them being in this place meant. Esther just smiled and dabbed at her eyes.

"She insisted after I told her you were coming," said Esther.

"It's okay," said Thomas. "I appreciate the support. This is John, my lawyer."

"We've all met," said John. "It's great for you to come but I'm the only one who can go in," said Richards. "You two will have to wait."

"We don't mind," said Sarah.

"As long as I know they're out here," said Thomas.

Thomas didn't ask where his father was. He knew. He was at home holding onto his old ways, and hoping that the world would never change. Thomas looked at Sarah and smiled.

"Good luck," said Sarah.

Thomas and Richards went into the hearing room. It was more ordinary than he'd imagined. No great seals and expensive grandeur.

Thomas looked around and saw the familiar faces of the men and women who had reopened the investigation and the new faces of the Grand Jury.

"We are here in the case of Marcus Alexander Jackson," said the U.S. Attorney, a straight arrow type. "Specifically we are to hear testimony from Officer Thomas Riley, one of the three Detroit police officers at the scene of the death. I'm Walter Lincoln for the government. Officer Riley, you may be seated."

Thomas took the witness stand and was administered the oath. He looked into the faces of the gallery with confidence.

"John Richards representing the witness," said Richards.

A stenographer got it all down, her fingers moving furiously.

"Now Officer," began Lincoln. "This body has reviewed your report on the events of July 28, 1967. And we have also reviewed your statements to two different investigating committees subsequent to this report. You are now under oath. Do you still hold to the statements you have previously made?"

"No," said Thomas.

The room buzzed and Lincoln seemed unprepared for this, the most unlikely of things, the truth.

"Well, which parts would you, uh, what sections would you like to repudiate?" Lincoln stumbled.

"My client has a statement," said Richards. "You may examine him after he says what he came here to say."

Lincoln looked at another man, an older White man and Dana Von, the pretty Black attorney who were in the back of the room. They both nodded and he turned back to Thomas.

"Okay," said Lincoln. "Proceed."

Thomas cleared his throat and began to speak.

Robert hit the front door of the place and heard Yusef yelling something behind him about the detonator but he didn't stop.

He saw Linda down the block. She had a big lead on him. Robert ran as hard as he could after her and soon he was closing the gap.

Now, it all made sense to him, Linda's instant love for him, her asking him about forgiveness for killing someone in the revolution. Guilt for what she had done. She'd murdered his brother over petty jealousy. He would not let her get away.

Robert saw her running for a bus and increased his pace. If she got on it, he'd lose her.

Linda missed the bus, cursed the driver then cut down another street. Robert moved after her, keeping a steady pace. Soon he was close as she ran onto a busy street. There were lots of people and they were slowing her down.

Robert closed in on her and he heard Linda yelling to people to help her and pointing to him. Most people got out of his way but one man tried to block him. Robert sidestepped him easily.

Robert was in striking distance to her now and he leapt at her and tripped her up. Linda fell onto the ground hard. Robert grabbed her and pulled her to her feet.

"You... killed him!" Robert said breathlessly. "You killed him!"

"Let me go!" said Linda.

"*Why?!*" Robert was crying now and he couldn't stop himself. He shook her and wanted to keep doing it until she stopped breathing.

"He was fucking her!" said Linda. "A *White* girl! All that bullshit about Black power and Black queens and he was doing it with her. And he loved her!" she hissed. "He told me. I followed him and I saw them together, my man between the legs of that whore. I felt like nothing, don't you see? I was nothing to him." Her voice cracked and her eyes overflowed.

"You're going to answer for this and not to The Guard, to the police," said Robert. "I'm going to drag you down there and turn you in myself."

Robert yanked her hard then felt strong arms clamp his own to his sides. It was the man who had tried to block him, grabbing him from behind. Robert lost his grip on Linda as the man pulled him away from her.

"Goddammit!' said Robert. "Let me go."

"You okay?" the man asked Linda.

Linda didn't answer him. She just looked at Robert and said, "I'm sorry."

Linda turned and ran into the street still looking at Robert's anguished face.

She never heard the yells of warning from the people on the scene. Linda was lifted from the ground by the speeding car. To Robert it looked like a sick ballet as her arms spread in an arc and her body tilted in the air, her feet replacing her head.

Linda crashed back onto the hard pavement, her beautiful face hitting the ground and the rest of her body's weight falling down and breaking her neck and spine.

The crowd gasped loudly and someone screamed. The man released Robert who cursed at him and shoved the man away.

Robert ran to the fallen woman and saw her empty eyes. She was gone.

Robert ran off as the crowd gathered around the driver of the car, a middle-aged Black woman who screamed at what she had done.

Robert headed back to the new safehouse. He saw his brother's face surprised by the killer who had been his lover and friend. He thought about Linda and the irony of it all, her hatred of the White girl fueled her rage, which was used to kill.

At the safehouse, Robert found Yusef and the rest of the members. He informed them of what had happened. Linda was gone. Yusef looked guilty for the first time and Robert let him stew in it a moment.

"Did you know?" he asked Yusef. "About the White girl?"

"Yeah," said Yusef, "but I didn't think Linda knew."

"But you encouraged it, didn't you?" Robert spat. "It was for the cause, right?" Robert glared at the man.

"Yes," said Yusef with strength. "Robert, there are things here bigger than us. You know that. You fought in their war and look what they did to——"

"White men didn't kill my brother, a Black person did. What do I do with that?" His hand had raised and an accusing finger was pointed at Yusef.

"But if it wasn't for them and their racist oppression, none of this would have happened," said Yusef calmly.

Robert shook his head slowly. "They ain't God. They can't be responsible for everything we do. We can't have it both ways, Yusef. *We* control what we do." Then as if to make sure he knew it, Robert said: "A Black person killed my brother."

Yusef was silent. He had something on his mind but he didn't have the willingness to say it.

"Where's Bohan?" asked Robert noticing for the first time that he was gone.

"Who's that?" asked Yusef. "No Bohan in this organization."

"And Vince!" Robert grabbed Yusef by his shirt. "Where are they?!" Vince and several of the others were gone.

"Let me go," said Yusef.

Robert released him. "I get it now," said Robert. "We kill, they kill. And it's all justified by words, speeches and bullshit."

"I know you're hurting," said Yusef, "but we have our cause and it's just. Now, give me the detonator and let's go."

Robert looked around. There were still members present, about fifteen or so. They looked at Yusef, ready to assist him if he needed it.

Robert took out the detonator and handed it to Yusef. "I'll be ready in a minute," he said and he walked off. Robert returned to find Yusef and some of the others getting ready to leave.

"You might want to stay here," said Yusef. He held the detonator in his hand like a toy. "I don't know if I can trust you right now. When you get over this Linda business, I'm sure you'll be better."

"That's not right," said Robert advancing toward Yusef. "I made it and I deserve to see it go off. Besides, what if something goes wrong?"

"You made a back up," said Yusef. "We can try it again somewhere else."

Robert just kept moving toward Yusef. He was almost close enough now.

"Not good enough," said Robert. "I want to see it."

Yusef thought for a moment, assessing and then, "Okay, but I'm going to be the one to push the button."

Robert got to Yusef and stopped. He would only have one chance at this.

"Thank you," said Robert.

"You're wel——"

Robert's arm flew out so fast that Yusef had no time to react. Yusef thought it was a blow but Robert grabbed the detonator from him and jumped away.

"What the hell was that?" Yusef laughed. "We'll just take it from you."

"I armed the other bomb when I went off just now," said Robert. "I am going to blow up this place in thirty seconds. I suggest you and all these people get clear."

Robert placed his finger by the black button.

Some of the members ran immediately. Several of the men stayed, looking at Yusef for guidance.

"I don't believe you," said Yusef.

"It stops here," said Robert. "Bohan will be the last casualty of this war. But on the bright side, you can keep the money you owe me for the World Series."

Robert pressed the red button then he began to count backwards. His face fell into the familiar look of the soldier/killer. Yusef had seen that look and it frightened him.

"Think about what you're doing," said Yusef. "What this means to the movement."

"Twenty-seven, twenty-six...."

The men who were left were getting nervous and one of them ran. Yusef looked at the others and told them to go. They happily ran off.

"You do this and there's nowhere to run from me," said Yusef. "Nowhere!"

"Twenty-five, twenty-four..." was Robert's answer.

Yusef cursed and then ran out of the building.

He was still running outside when the building blew up behind him. The place was on a short block and there were no occupied homes close to it. The explosion started in the basement and the building collapsed on itself in free fall, like a planned detonation.

Still, the blast shattered windows a block away and a yellow-red fireball rose into the sky like an angry god.

Yusef and the others were so shocked that they couldn't move. It was the end of their home and there was a sense that something had been irreparably broken. The irony weighed heavily on Yusef. His realm had been shattered by a violent act in the name of nonviolence.

Yusef and the others mingled into the crowd as the fire raged and the fire trucks began to arrive.

Through the smoke and flames, none of them saw Robert one street over, calmly walking away, headed home.

32

<u>RICE AND SUNLIGHT</u>

Thomas was still not used to the scratchy beard he wore. He'd grown it as his hair grew longer. He liked the look but the damned thing itched all the time. He tried not to scratch as he stood before the minister with his new bride.

They had just taken their vows in the little church. Thomas wore a black tuxedo and Sarah wore the traditional white dress.

There were over a hundred people there, including Sarah's parents, a couple so handsome, that they looked like the pictures that came with store-bought frames.

Sarah had surprised everyone by moving back in with Thomas. The attempt on his life had awakened her. And his confession to the Grand Jury proved that he was indeed a changed man.

But the thing that had impressed her the most was the day she and Liz stumbled across Thomas at a restaurant, laughing and joking and eating from the same plate as his new Black partner.

Thomas for his part had not questioned her or himself. He welcomed her back into his life as though it was always meant to be.

Robert Jackson had exonerated Brady and Reid after Thomas' damming testimony. The police found the murder weapon in Linda's apartment, tucked in the back of a closet.

Thomas had been shocked to find that the two cops had been telling the truth. Still, he reasoned their lack of faith in the system had condemned them. They were so afraid that they'd framed themselves.

About a month after the World Series parade, Brady and Reid were at McGinty's celebrating, when an agent from IAD and the FBI walked in and arrested them for the murder of Ned Young.

The bar was deadly silent as they were read their rights and walked out in shame. A week later, Brady would agree to testify against his partner, confessing that they'd gotten into an argument with Ned about the boy's death and killed the older man.

Two other things damned them. One was a partial fingerprint on a counter in the kitchen and the other, a new cop at the science lab who touted something called forensic fiber analysis.

Thomas hadn't been fired from the force but he was suspended for a time. He transferred to a new precinct and was surprised when Zack followed him.

He hadn't had a drink in many months and was now meeting with a new group of regulars called Alcoholics Anonymous. A strong group who had the novel idea that drinking was a disease that could be passed down from father to son. Not the best news for the Irish, he mused.

Thomas kissed Sarah making the ceremony complete. He turned to leave, walking down the aisle. Thomas smiled broadly as he pulled Sarah behind him.

The couple moved past the happy faces in the gallery. Thomas saw his new partner, friends like Dennison and others from the old precinct.

His mother and sister stood together. Katie was growing up and looked dangerously like a woman to him. Esther cried of course and dabbed at her face with a handkerchief.

They were almost out of the room when Thomas saw Frank at the end of a pew. He was turned away from him about to leave. Thomas had a smile building on his face when the man turned back and he saw that it was not his father but another man he did not know.

Sarah went to the man and kissed him, calling him uncle somebody.

It would have been nice, Thomas thought if his father could have found some measure of forgiveness in this moment but life was not so neat. Life was far more complex and that kind of absolution did not fall from the sky like God's rain; it grew from the tended earth of a man's toil.

Thomas took his bride from the church as the crowd threw rice on them. He pulled Sarah into the bright sunlight and he thought a day had never looked so beautiful.

33

CAIN'S DELIVERANCE

Robert held the brown baby in his arms at the hospital and was a little afraid. Newborns seemed so fragile you think that if you sneeze you're going to break something.

Abraham and Theresa chattered at him, telling him to hold the child higher as Abraham tilted a camera in front of them.

"Your first picture, Marcus," Robert said to his son and smiled.

Denise was getting dressed for the trip home and she was happy to be going. The labor had been long and hard and she muttered something about "never doing this again." Robert just kept his mouth shut. He was happy but he was no fool.

Robert told his parents what he discovered at The Vanguard about Marcus' death. They had all agreed to go to the investigators and tell them what they knew.

Some days later, the Detroit police received an anonymous call and found the bomb in the storage room. There was a big panic as they called in the bomb squad who easily diffused it.

It was never reported in the press. Things were good and no one wanted strife to return. The police changed all of their security measures after the event.

The feds took the case, and although they suspected a link to a bizarre explosion some weeks before, no one was ever charged.

Bohan's body was never found and Robert thought about going to the police, but Yusef, Vince and many of the other members of The Guard had disappeared. And without a body, there was really no crime. He wondered if the cops would look for their missing agent and if it would all come back to haunt him one day. Only time would tell.

"I'm ready," said Denise.

Robert handed her the baby and Denise sat in a wheelchair. Robert pushed her out, supervised by a nurse. They went outside into the parking lot and soon Denise and child were in the back of Abraham's car. Robert did not notice but he had never stopped smiling.

That next spring, Robert stood at his brother's graveside with the child. Denise protested but Robert had countered that the baby would never know he was in a graveyard. Still, Denise was upset and stayed in the car waiting for him after paying her respects to Marcus.

It was a cool day and not a cloud in the sky. Marcus was buried in the northern corner of the place and they had erected a headstone, which read: "Son, Brother and Friend."

"I used to think talking to dead folks was crazy," Robert began. "So, this is your nephew, Marcus. Eight pounds when he was born. Big fella. Make a heck of a first baseman one day."

Robert adjusted the baby in his arms. He was waking up and he'd probably start crying, he thought distantly.

"I know you been watching me and saw all the things I did," Robert continued. "I'm not proud of them, Marcus. Change is hard, and it don't pay to push it, but at the same time, you got to stand up. How far you go is the thing. We went too far. Anyway, I'm renouncing my ways again and I wanted you to witness it."

Robert took the detonator from his pocket and placed it near the headstone. All of the wiring and the buttons had been removed and so he had no fear of leaving it.

Robert turned and walked away from his brother's grave carrying his son.

They left the cemetery and drove into the city. Detroit was still draped in Tiger orange and blue, filled with banners and signs praising the team.

Robert felt pride but the victory he celebrated had nothing to do with baseball.

EPILOGUE

April 9, 2010.

Thomas and Robert walk into Comerica Park in Detroit alongside their grandchildren. Security is very tight this day and so it takes a while. People are searched and there is extra security around the stadium.

The old men disliked the new stadium. It is too clean, too... new.

But no new stadium would have been good enough for them. Their baseball hearts would always be at the corner of Michigan and Trumbull. Tiger Stadium still stood just across downtown, like a monument to all things past.

It is Opening Day for the Detroit Tigers. The temperature is warm and the skies clear, a perfect day for baseball.

Like all baseball cities, Opening Day is a grand tradition. The stands were filled with people, many playing hooky from their jobs.

And today is about more than the game, more than sport and team loyalty. The President is throwing out the first pitch of the game and the world is watching.

The old men settled into their seats with the two young kids. Thomas was with his thirteen-year-old granddaughter, Jenny and Robert was with his namesake, a boy everyone called Scooter.

They had good seats, several rows up from the opposing team's dugout. Robert smiles and thanks his father for that.

"Where's Sarah?" asks Robert.

"Gone shopping with Denise and the women," says Thomas. "Let's hope we still have bank accounts when they get back," he laughs a little.

"All rise for the singing of the national anthem," says the announcer.

The crowd buzzes as it gets to its feet. Robert rises and places his hand over his heart. The more than fifty thousand people sing as the anthem is sung.

"And now to throw out the first pitch," boomed the announcer, "The President of the United States, Barrack Obama!"

The crowd erupts into a deafening cheer.

Robert and Thomas share a look over the noise and Thomas sees water in the eyes of his old friend. He feels a lump in his own throat as well.

In their lives, this moment is so much more than its obvious historical significance. They each think back to the road that has brought them here and feel the full measure of their years.

Theirs was a fateful and unlikely meeting, which yielded, after a time, a friendship that had lasted four decades. It would have been easier to forget their history but both men were strong and stubborn. So they held on to the bond if only to prove that they were made better by their shared ordeal.

The moment passes quickly as the pitch is delivered and the crowd cheers again.

"Didn't know he was a southpaw," says Robert absently.

The crowd sits but for a moment, Thomas and Robert linger.

"How about them Tigers?" asks Robert.

"Yeah," says Thomas. "How about 'em?"

BOXSCORES

The Detroit Tigers celebrated their status as the best team in baseball in 1968. That World Series would be remembered as one of the most exciting ever played, one that exhibited the truest spirit of the game and the life from which it springs.

The league instituted playoff games for the first time after the 1968 series. No longer would pennants be won solely by a team's winning percentage. To baseball purists, the Tigers would be the last real champions of the game.

Motown Records became one of the most successful record companies in history, making billions of dollars and creating music that defined a generation in the most troubled of times. It would come to conjure memories of the best and worst of our nation's heart.

The civil unrest ended in Detroit and the political landscape changed with the formation of New Detroit and Focus Hope multiracial committees that were designed to bring Blacks and Whites together in the spirit of cooperation.

But Whites continued to leave their beloved city and the Black minority grew to a solid majority.

President Lyndon Johnson did not seek reelection in 1968 and Richard Nixon was elected President. During his tenure, Nixon escalated the Vietnam War but protests at home and the uncanny resilience of the enemy eventually doomed the war effort.

Citing progress in peace negotiations in 1972, President Nixon announced the suspension of offensive action in North Vietnam and unilaterally withdrew troops.

Nixon proclaimed victory, American war protestors proclaimed victory and the North Vietnamese claimed victory. But with over 58,000 Americans and 100,000 Vietnamese dead, no one had won anything.

Nixon had a few other troubles in this second term and by the time he resigned in disgrace in 1974, Detroit had elected its first Black Mayor, the fiery politician, Coleman A. Young.

He would hold office for over twenty years.

READING & VIEWING

1960's St. Louis Cardinals World Series, 1968 vs. Detroit Tigers (2005) DVD (Q-Video)

A City in Racial Crisis, Leonard Gordon, Wm. C. Brown Company Publishers, (1971).

The Black Crusaders: A case study of a Black militant organization, William B Helmreich, Harper & Row, (1973).

Detroit Divided, Reynolds Farley, Sheldon Danziger, Harry J. Holzer, Russell Sage Foundation Publications, (2002)

The Detroit Riot, Hubert G. Locke, Wayne State University Press, (1969).

Violence in the Model City: The Cavanagh Administration, Race Relations, and the Detroit Riot of 1967, Sidney Fine University of Michigan Press, (1989).

Whose Detroit? Politics, Labor, and Race in a Modern American City, Heather Ann Thompson, Cornell University Press, (2004)

Layered Violence the Detroit Rioters of 1943, Dominic j. Jr. Capeci and Martha Wilkerson, University Press of Mississippi Jackson & London, (1991).

The Tigers of '68: Baseball's Last Real Champions, George Cantor Taylor Trade Publishing, (1997).

The Detroit Tigers: A Pictorial Celebration of the Greatest Players and Moments in Tigers' History, by William M. Anderson Wayne State University Press; (Updated Edition), (1999)

COMING SOON:

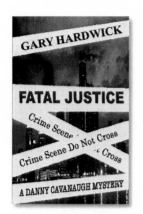

Fatal Justice by Gary Hardwick

Police Detective Danny Cavanaugh, the explosive hero of *Supreme Justice* and *Color Of Justice* is back on the case in a riveting mystery that unites Gary Hardwick's Detroit Novel Series.

A hooker with a deadly secret is murdered. Danny Cavanaugh, a white cop raised in the heart of the urban landscape is assigned the routine case and uncovers a conspiracy that reaches from Detroit's dangerous inner city to the corridors of power.

The city's new mayor, a young, brash and arrogant leader assigns Chief of Police Tony Hill (*Cold Medina*) to back Danny off the case.

When Danny won't let go, he's removed but not before incriminating digital messages between the mayor and the murdered woman are uncovered.

The sex-laced missives give political enemies the evidence to push a felony charge against the mayor.

Jesse King (*Double Dead*) prosecutes the case and the mayor hires reigning defense attorney Marshall Jackson (*Supreme Justice*) to stave off a municipal *coup d'état*.

As the fate of Detroit hangs in the balance, Danny is caught in the eye of the storm, at odds with powerbrokers, his best friend and a vicious new street gang.

He will have to use all of his talents to solve the case, even though justice may be fatal.

FATAL JUSTICE

A DANNY CAVANAUGH MYSTERY

Gary Hardwick

PROLOGUE

CITYCIDE

Someone murdered Detroit.

It hadn't died like they said in the news. The city didn't pass from a natural cause. It was "got" as they say on the street, like it had been killed by the dead-eyed drug-fiend with a jagged pipe or the cold hitter who'd pop you, then go to Popeye's for a combo.

Detective Danny Cavanaugh thought this every time he looked at a street and saw the lost youth waiting to die or the missing homes that dotted each block.

He thought it when he could see three streets over through the gutted body of a dying neighborhood.

He thought it when he saw the prostitutes, dealers and night people push their way from the inner city to its borders. Only a true, old time Detroiter could understand the tragedy of a hooker walking boldly on Telegraph Road in broad daylight.

Danny is a tall man, with an easy-going handsomeness framed by reddish hair that he keeps cropped short. His eyes are intense, piercing some would say and a shade of green that would make any Irishman proud. His shoulders are broad, flowing into thick, muscular arms and torso.

But it is when he speaks that people get a full measure of him. His intonations belie the white face and bring to mind a man of color, a black man specifically. He has come by this voice naturally, having been born and raised in Detroit.

It is an odd combination that has sometimes been a gift and at other times, a nuisance. He is enigmatic and so people think many things of him but one perception is common. He is not someone to fuck with.

Tonight Danny is sure his city is dead as he watches the paramedics take the injured boy from the incident house.

He'd seen this one before, a single mother barely holding on to her sanity and life, raises a sweet little boy who receives his philosophy of love and manhood from street life. He grows into a vessel of anger filled with hopelessness, always one moment away from igniting.

Then one night, the mother pulls a controller out of a videogame because she needs to get some sleep and a few minutes later, someone is on the floor bleeding.

Only this time, it was the son being loaded on a gurney. Maybe the mother just lost it or maybe she knew it was only a matter of time before her little boy would find her useless in his violent life and try to take hers.

The woman had argued her dominion and adulthood to the young man but he refused to recognize these respectable truths and then made the mistake of calling her a vile name. So the mother made her point again, this time with a baseball bat wrapped in duct tape.

Then standing over her now unconscious son and smoking a no-brand cigarette, the mother called the cops and waited to be taken to jail.

Danny talks with a young uniformed officer who'd stepped out of the house looking rattled. She reacts a little hearing the black man's voice coming from the white face of a man in his thirties. Danny hardly notices as he is used to it by now.

Danny comforts the young officer and sets her to an assignment away from the house. This is good because at that moment, the morgue attendants bring out the injured boy and it is clear that if he recovers, he will never be normal again.

This was the kind of crime that brought Detroit more unwanted press, Danny thought. The city was a media fascination but not the good kind. The news outlets quoted the staggering unemployment rate, the murder rate, the poverty rate and the shrinking population. They talked incessantly of leadership gone bad and government gone wrong. So, whenever some talking head wanted an example of the failure of America, they had only to invoke the name of the city.

Detroit's new mayor hadn't helped the situation either. Everyone held so much hope for him when he was elected. Sure he was young but youth was what the city needed, they had all said. He would be the one, the messiah, the man who saved Detroit.

But it had not happened.

The young leader turned out to be just another arrogant bully, trampling on good intentions and incapable of living up to the nobility of the city he led.

All the celebratory fireworks anointing him had quickly turned to crap and rained down on everyone.

So the media have their joke, Danny thought. But they don't know the city was murdered, killed by neglect and sins that fester.

Danny loved his city. He couldn't explain it to a person who didn't live there. It was like an old dog. It was loyal and loving and you respected it for the innocence and greatness it harbors inside.

And when anyone dared assail his city, he was ready to defend, if not fight for its honor. To mess with Detroit was to taunt that old, sweet dog and find its mouth full of sharp teeth.

The paramedics roll off as police finish taking their witness statements. The little crowd that dared to come out starts to go back inside their homes and Danny wonders if any of them will sleep this night.

The female uniform comes back to him and says that the officer in charge is done and thanks Danny for coming out. He waves at the officer in charge who he knows from work.

Danny turns and walks the short distance between the crime scene and his home, which is just across the narrow street.

RASHIDAH'S ESCAPE

Rashidah Watson hated Seven Mile. This was true even though streets were not people. They were dirt, concrete and lines of colored paint but if there was ever a street that deserved to be reviled, it was Seven Mile Road.

The night rose around her and she could sense the last of winter was leaving Detroit. The wind still held onto the last of its chill but you could smell spring just beneath the odors of the city.

Rashidah had made sure she parked below a working streetlight. And she had done so without a moment's thought. She was born and bred in the city and so her head was full of the mantra of street survival. Do this and live, do that and take the risk.

She sat in her warm car not too far from Greenfield and waited for her friend. Boy was always late, she thought. A Mary J. Blige song murmured under the sounds from the street and her lungs were filled with the sour sting of the joint she'd just finished.

"I'm gon' kill him," she said out loud to herself as she checked the time again and turned the song up louder.

In Rashindah's brief twenty-five years, Seven Mile had become a symbol for everything she despised about the city.

First, there was always some bullshit going on. If it wasn't the lowlife drug boys, slinging dope and shooting folk, it was the random thieves who might hurt you just for a damned cell phone.

Second, the street itself was whack. It was narrow and always in need of repair. The long winters left potholes big enough to eat your tires and cracks so long and wide that you felt like you were driving on a tightrope, her mother used to say.

At least, that's what her mama, Donna, said before she was gunned down on Van Dyke near Seven Mile. Fool never even gave her mother a chance. He didn't say, "Get out the car," or nothing. He had just shot her and tossed her body aside, like she was garbage. Goddamned crystal meth made crack look like a puppy, she thought grimly.

After her mother was gone, Rashidah went to live with her aunt Joyce, a Bible-thumping disciplinarian with a bad drinking problem.

Rashidah noticed that a lot of religious people drank too much. She could remember pastors with a liquor smell wafting from their smooth-talking mouths and acolytes with their cute white gloves and silver flasks in their purses. She wondered how many smiling Sunday morning faces and Holy Ghost Riders were really just inspired by the power of Johnny Walker. The only question was, did the drink drive them to God or did God drive them to drink?

She missed her mother. But Rashidah was used to loss. The first time she saw her father he was in a casket. She had only been five but the memory was burned into her. She saw a friend get stabbed in a fight at school and knew at least ten other people who had died or been killed. Yes, she new loss and it knew her too.

Rashidah's Aunt Joyce would drink herself silly and then play Aretha Franklin gospel records and scream to God to forgive her sin. And the only sin Aunt Joyce ever committed besides getting shit-faced was Juwan Jenkins who lived three streets over. The two had been screwing for years even though Juwan had two kids and a wife.

Many nights Rashidah lie awake listening to the bed thump in the adjacent room and her aunt's muffled moans of pleasure. Once Rashidah had summoned up the courage to peek through the door and saw her Aunt Joyce bent over with the big man behind her.

The sight of it had hypnotized her twelve year-old eyes but her stomach was hot and it felt good somehow. That's what sex was, she thought. It was silly-looking and yet it was fascinating.

Her own sexual awakening had come a year later with Sean, a local boy who had given her things and taken her to the movies for a whole year waiting to get some.

She gave in to Sean in his basement while his parents were away. She didn't remember much about it only that it hurt for a while and then it was better.

The best thing about it was the power she had over Sean after it was done. The fifteen-year-old boy followed her around like a puppy dog and did everything she asked. She could be mean, sweet or dismissive and he'd just keep following her with that eternal longing in his eyes.

It wasn't long before Rashidah realized that her power extended to all boys. Soon, Sean was gone, replaced by older and richer boys who bought her more than McDonalds and movies. She was getting watches, jewelry, electronic gadgets, clothes and of course, cash. All that and for what? Letting them pleasure her. Hell, half the time she would have got with the boy for the fun of it, but that wasn't how the game was played.

While Rashidah was learning, she had to go to church three nights a week and all day Sunday. She did it because Aunt Joyce would beat her ass if she even looked like she didn't love the Lord. Rashidah's mother had been gentle sweet and kind. It always puzzled her how her sister could be so evil.

Going to church kept Joyce happy and distracted. She never guessed that Rashidah really didn't have a part-time babysitting job that paid for all the things she suddenly had.

Rashidah endured five long years of forced sermons and playing the local boys until she became of age.

When she was old enough to leave her aunt, the evil street claimed her.

Barely eighteen, she moved out of the house and in with an older man named Nathan, who gave her money for sex but came so quickly that it hardly seemed like work. It wasn't a perfect life but she had a car, and all the current clothes. He bought her a Coach purse and even though it was a high-class fake, none of her friends could tell.

When she thought about it, this was the best time of her life. She was popular, satisfied and for the most part, happy. Then coming home from a party one night, Rashidah was robbed and assaulted near the hated street. Thank God there was only one man because she managed to fight him off and escape with just a few bruises and a stolen purse.

After this she'd gotten a gun, learned to use it and now never went anywhere without it.

Rashidah moved on from Nathan after getting a job as a waitress in one of the strip clubs on Eight Mile, a street that was Seven Mile's retarded brother.

At the club, a very clean and rather elegant place called Mr. X, Rashidah watched the dancers shake, grind and bend over for strange men. They made a lot of money but that could never be her thing, she thought. It was dishonest, a low-rent tease. She was much more noble. She would do you straight up if the price was right.

It was better to be a waitress, she found. She tipped around on her high-heels in a short skirt and a sheer top. When she saw a man who looked like a baller, she'd make herself available. The truth was, many men liked to look at strippers but felt that they were dirty and didn't trust having sex with them.

So Rashidah would let them get horny off the show and then she'd close in for the kill.

She sidelined as a hooker and always kept her business tight. She slept with men and would even go down on them if they were particularly nice.

She hooked up once with an NBA player from Philly and thought briefly that he might change her life. This dream was dashed when he suggested that she have sex with him and one of his teammates.

She knew then that no man would be her salvation and she closed her mind to it and along with it, her heart.

Men were just to be used for as long as you could play them. All they cared about was their need to get off. This defeated every notion of decency and morality they possessed. Whether it was some father of three getting head behind his wife's back or some businessman who wanted to bang you on his lunch break, they were all weak-minded freaks that could be had for a little fleshy fun.

Rashidah dreamed of getting out, going to New York or somewhere glamorous like that, starting over a new life as a model with a nice, darkly handsome man who could keep it up and who would love her despite her sin.

This dream was reinforced every time Rashidah looked in the mirror. She was beautiful. The only thing her father had ever given her was his genes but they had help transform her into a gorgeous specimen.

She was five nine with long legs. Her breasts were big and her ass was plump and firm. Her eyes were light brown. She wore her hair straight and long and had recently purchased a high-end weave that was almost undetectable.

Her mother had been a good-looking woman also but had squandered it on worthless men. In fact, her mother's whole life had been one big struggle, a fight between the strong gravity of fate and hope's slim promise. In the end, some half-assed addict with a big gun and a tiny brain stole her mother's life and the world just kept turning.

Rashidah's life would be different. Her Big Mama, Bessie had been a cook and maid all of her life. Her mother had been not much more, working for the county in a low-grade job.

To Rashidah it was evolution: Bessie was an old southern name linked to the bondage of their past. Donna, her mother's name was a feeble attempt by black folks to give their kids whiteness. But her name, Rashidah was Arabic for "Rightly guided" she had looked that shit up on Google. She was free from the past in all ways and like her name she was headed to a better life.

After her friend got here, she would take the next step in her escape from Detroit and her mother's fate. It seemed like a dream sometimes, that she could be in a city where she wasn't living against the current of life. But she could see it, feel it, in her heart.

Suddenly, Rashidah saw a man walking her way. She placed her hand on the Cobra .38 she kept in her purse. She felt the firmness of the weapon and her nerves eased. She had never fired it at a man but she'd had to pull it once when a lowlife had become violent with her. The sight of it had ended the confrontation.

She had no doubts that she would shoot if she ever had to. After all the shit she'd been through, she'd kill a man without hesitation.

As the man came closer, Rashidah recognized his face and she loosened her grip on the gun.

"About time," she said and opened the passenger door.

"'Sup, pretty?" said the man as he got inside.

"Always late," said Rashidah. "Get yo' ass in the car."

"I ride the pimp," said the man whose name was Quinten, referring to the city bus. "Everybody ain't rolling in a C-Class, bitch. You coulda picked a nigga up."

"I know why you late, said Rashidah smiling slyly. "Busy playing with your new boyfriend."

They laughed. Quinten was notorious for his sexual appetite. Sad thing was; he was damned fine, like all gay men, she thought. When she had first met him, her initial thought had been he could get it for free.

"Yeah, he is something," said Quinten. "Don't know why they get married."

"Because that's how it is in this backwards ass town. You can't do nothing without everybody judging you."

"I know that's right. "So what the hell is so important you had to call me away from my life?"

Rashidah's smile faded slowly. Her face turned serious and her eyes settled into hardness. This was it, she thought; the moment her life would change. She looked at her friend with all the desire and courage in her heart.
"I need you to do something for me...."

The man in the dark hoodie rolled by the little blue Mercedes parked under the streetlight and caught sight of what he'd been looking for. He'd lost her somewhere around Livernois and hadn't seen her take the turn onto Seven Mile. No matter, he thought.

He drove a block past the blue car and turned onto a street. He parked his car near the corner. He made sure the car was pointed away from the blue Mercedes. When he left, he could keep going west, right to the Jeffries.

He reached under his seat and hit a button. He heard a tiny click from the center console. He opened it and took out the .357 Magnum. It was a bit clichéd in today's game but it left no doubt.

He had tried other trendy guns, but in the end, they all had shortcomings that he could not live with. They'd jam or misfire or they were too damned small for his big hands.

On this kind of job, it was the *trey fiddy*, as he called it, or nothing.

He checked the weapon and saw it was fully loaded. He placed it in the pouch of his pullover which was just under the word PISTONS. He got out of the car. He pulled his hood over his head. He'd walk around the corner and come at the car head on so that he was headed back towards his own. He moved away from his car making sure to lock the doors. You couldn't be too careful in this part of town.

Quinten was speechless. He had heard some crazy shit from Rashidah before but never anything like this. His hand was trembling and he had started to breathe faster. He'd averted his eyes from his friend after she finished the story. He had no words. She had lost her mind.

"Well, can you do it?" Rashidah asked him.

"Hell no, I can't," said Quinten. "You are in some deep shit, girl. I may be a lot of things but I ain't no criminal."

"It ain't criminal," said Rashidah. "It's no worse than the weed you sell."

"People get high on weed. Weed don't hurt nobody and weed won't find my ass in jail."

"What you worried about? These people are so scared; they'll just give it up. And when I get it, I'm out this bitch. And you can come with me."

Quinten calmed himself a little. He thought of how good it would be to get out of Detroit. Maybe go to Atlanta. There was a big gay population down there. There, he could be himself, be free. And then he remembered what Rashidah had asked him to do and reality came crashing back to him.

"No," said Quinten. "I'm sorry but I like my face the way it is. I don't want somebody trying to rearrange it for me."

"You are such a fuckin' fag," said Rashidah and there was no playfulness to it. Her face was hard and beautiful and her eyes had narrowed to slits. Quinten knew this side of Rashidah and didn't like it one bit.

"You always talking 'bout how you want to get out," she continued. "Well, here's your chance! But you just another scared ass, running around, living this sick ass life and sucking some married man's dick."

"Better than sucking everybody's dick for a nickel, bitch," his voice became shrill, almost feminine. "You ain't one to talk about nobody's life."

"Get the fuck out of my car," said Rashidah. "You ain't down with me, you can step. I'll call you from New York or Paris or some shit."

"Right," said Quinten as he reached for the door. "Paris wouldn't have your—"

Quinten stopped talking as he saw the man approach Rashidah's window. For as long as they'd lived in Detroit, they should have seen him coming.

He was big and wide and dressed in dark clothes. Quinten only saw his torso as he slid between the window and the street. A second later, the gun appeared. The biggest gun he had ever seen.

Quinten took in air to yell to Rashidah to move, to drive, to do something. For a moment, he thought the man would tap the window and ask them to give up the precious car but then he pointed the gun and stepped back, bracing himself.

Rashidah saw the panic in Quinten's eyes and began to turn her head toward the window.

The shot was like a bomb. The window shattered as Rashidah's pretty face jerked and her head tilted unnaturally as the left side of it exploded in a shower of bone and blood.

The headrest disintegrated into a swirl of flying leather and white stuffing.

Quinten was splattered with her, like someone had swung a wet paintbrush across his face. He felt white heat in his body and he grew rigid. His brain told his hand to open the door but nothing happened. And then he felt it, the warmth from between his legs as his bladder emptied itself.

The man who had just killed his friend lowered his head into the open maw of the shattered window. Quinten turned instinctively and looked at him. He saw the big gun, which was now poking through the window over the still jerking body of his friend. Deep inside a hooded jacket, he saw only the dark outline of a man's face.

"Fuggit," said the hooded man in a whisper.

Quinten found the door handle and pulled it. He toppled out onto the cold ground. Time stood still for an endless second and then death withdrew itself and was gone.

Two seconds later, Quinten's lungs rebelled and he let out a yell that pierced the night.